Tales From the Lake
Volume 1

Paperback Edition

edited by Joe Mynhardt

Crystal Lake Publishing
www.CrystalLakePub.com

Copyright Acknowledgements

"Lady of Lost Lake" originally published in Dark Discoveries #1 (March 2004)

"Witch-Compass" originally published in *Dark Terrors 5*, edited by Stephen Jones and David Sutton, 2000

Table of Contents

A Word from the Editor/Publisher i

Foreword by Rocky Wood iii

Lover, Come Back to Me by Tim Waggoner 1

Don't Look at Me by Elizabeth Massie 15

Devil Dolls—a poem by Blaze McRob 27

Dead Pull by Taylor Grant 34

Alternative Muses by J. Daniel Stone 56

The Reunion by Joan De La Haye 73

Devil's Night by Tim Curran 83

The Fine Art of Wrecking
    by Jennifer Loring 108

Saint Patty's Night at The Crown—
    a poem by Blaze McRob 117

O'Halloran's by John Paul Allen 120

Las Maquinas by William Ritchey 135

Perrollo's Ladder by John Palisano 159

Game On by Charles Day 179

The Lady of Lost Lake by Bev Vincent 191

Junksick by G.N. Braun 203

Witch-Compass by Graham Masterton 211

Biographies 249

A Word from the Editor/Publisher

Welcome, dear reader, to the first of which I'm certain will be many volumes in the *Tales From the Lake* anthologies.

And although this is a non-themed anthology, several of the authors felt motivated to roam towards a lake/water theme, which says a lot of artist Ben Baldwin's talent, as he has once again brought another cover to life.

I must add that reading these stories reminded me a lot of the campfire horror stories I grew up with. I'm certain a lot of you will feel the same way. Perhaps it's just the thought of a lake that brings these memories to the surface.

As many of you remember, this anthology kicked off with the *Tales From the Lake* Horror Writing Competition in 2013. Thanks again to judges and contributors Taylor Grant, John Paul Allen, G.N. Braun, Charles Day and John Palisano for all their time and effort.

From the 128 entries, only 3 stories made it into this collection, as well as earning their respective authors a share of the prize money.

Third place was awarded to William Ritchey with

his story "Las Maquinas." Second place went to J. Daniel Stone, the talented author behind "Alternative Muses." Which leaves Jennifer Loring as the overall winner with her moving story, "The Fine Art of Wrecking."

Congratulations to these three winners, and thank you to all the other participants. Hopefully you'll enter again in this year's competition. That's right, folks. Keep your eyes open for the second *Tales From the Lake* Horror Writing Competition later this year. Each year will be a bit different than the last, but the top three winners will always get a spot in the next *Tales From the Lake* anthology, as well as various other prizes, including money.

Thanks also to Rocky Wood for providing the foreword. I really appreciate it.

But let me stop distracting you from the stories ahead. I hope you'll enjoy reading them as much as I did, and be sure to keep an eye out for the following installments of *Tales From the Lake* . . . Crystal Lake.

Joe Mynhardt
Bloemfontein, South Africa
9 March 2014

Foreword by Rocky Wood

Lakes—in our mind smallish bodies of people-friendly water on which we can paddle or fish, in which we can swim and beside which we can relax. Of course, there are big lakes, such as the North American Great Lakes, which can be dangerous in inclement weather. Lakes can freeze. Some lakes are said to contain monsters such as Ogopogo or Nessie. Wrecks sit at the bottom of some lakes, others have unpredictable currents, or shallows that will snap your neck if you dive unawares into them. But you don't want to know about that. Do you?

On most days lakes tend to sit in our minds as peaceful places on which to float, swim or contemplate. Listening to the call of the loon, the laughter of children, the annoying roar of powerboats or jet skis, the lapping of ever so small waves on a stony beach. Relaxing, natural, soporific, beautiful. Idyllic.

If you came here to read about those lakes—run, don't walk, to the nearest exit. Anyone who's read Stephen King's classic tale, "The Raft" should know that. Tim Waggoner's expert portrayal of a man living in mortal fear of drowning after a near death experience as a boy (weird things do happen at Greywater Lake), opens the collection with pace and guile. Bev Vincent's "Lady of Lost Lake" sure isn't Tennyson's (or even Monty Python's).

Graham Masterton's adept reworking of "The Monkey's Paw" combines atmosphere and grounded reality as the Gabonese witch-compass works its dark magic far from Libreville. That story is a centrepiece of the menu.

As the anthology progresses a veritable fleet of fresh tales fill the pages. I guarantee you will cast a wary eye at your local pets store after reading emerging talent Taylor Grant's take on Purrs, Grrs and Furs; you'll find yourself watching your Xbox screen more closely as Charles Day takes you to the river; GN Braun will transport you to the Apocalypse; and you will learn the hard way about garden gnomes and their allies in Elizabeth Massie's empathetic little tale.

Blaze McRob's poems form a nice punctuation. Poetry is ingrained in the horror genre but rarely gets the exposure it deserves. Certainly these are welcome jewels.

Joe Mynhardt has squeezed terror from the stellar ranks of authors in this book. Read it with caution. Read it in your hammock, your bed, your airline seat, on your mass transit commute. But if you want my advice, I wouldn't be taking it on your next lake vacation.

Rocky Wood
Current President of the HWA
8 March 2014

Lover, Come Back to Me

TIM WAGGONER

"**There's something wrong** with the fish."

Alan sat in the rear of the canoe, paddling. He kept his gaze fixed on Jan's back—specifically on the spot directly between her shoulder blades—and he was concentrating on blocking out the sound of his paddle disturbing the water. Concentrating so hard that at first he didn't hear what she said.

"Alan?"

She drew her own paddle out of the water as she turned to look back over her shoulder at him. He realized then that she'd spoken, and he stopped paddling as he tried to remember what she'd said. It came to him a couple seconds later. Something about fish.

"What's wrong?"

"The *fish*, "Jan said. "Look at them."

Alan had no idea what she was talking about. But then the entire time they'd been out on the lake—at least an hour, if the sunburn on the back of his neck was any indication—he'd only looked at the water in occasional split-second glances. And then only to adjust the canoe's course. But now, with Jan looking at him expectantly, he turned and scanned the water around them. He had to force himself to look slowly, otherwise Jan would give him crap about it later. Even through his sunglasses, the reflected light from the summer sun hit his eyes like hot shards of broken glass. He squinted and forced himself not to look away.

A breeze came through then, and the air felt good on his sore, sweaty neck. He heard a gentle whisper, one that almost sounded like *Welcome back*. He told himself he hadn't heard it, and he refocused his attention on the water.

At first he didn't notice anything out of the ordinary, but then he saw shapes moving through the gray-green water near the canoe—dozens of them. They were close to the surface, maybe only a half-inch below, and they swam in a tight school, packed so close together that they touched side to side and nose to tail.

He took his gaze away from the water and fixed it on Jan's face. Her green eyes—no sunglasses for her— strong cheekbones, angular nose, sharp lips, prominent chin. Despite the sun, she wasn't wearing a hat and her short blond hair clung damply to her head thanks to the humidity. He loved to look at her, and he loved it even more now, when it meant he didn't have to look at the water.

"What's so weird about the fish?" he asked. "We just floated into a school or something." He made himself smile. "If I were a fisherman, I'd think this was my lucky day."

Jan's eyes narrowed. She usually kept a tight rein on her emotions, but he'd been with her long enough to know that a slight narrowing of the eyes indicated serious irritation.

"They're not the same kind of fish for one thing," she said. "There's trout, bluegill, crappie, and catfish in there, along with a few more types."

"And that's not normal," Alan guessed.

"Not in the slightest. But that's not the weirdest thing. Take another look."

Alan was used to her being direct—*bossy*, his family and friends would've said—but there was a note of fear in her voice, which surprised him. She was usually controlled, confident, calm. But now that veneer was starting to crack.

Despite his reluctance to look at the water again, he did so, and this time he removed his sunglasses to get a better look. It took him a moment, but he realized what Jan wanted him to see.

"They're swimming backwards." A pause. "They're not supposed to do that, are they?"

"What the hell do you think?"

He had to admit, it *was* bizarre, seeing the fish crowded so close together and swimming backwards. He wasn't sure, but he thought they might be circling the canoe as well.

He turned to face Jan once more. She was lean and fit, and her T-shirt and shorts hugged her body a bit too tightly for the day's heat. Sweat darkened the fabric over her spine and the base of her back. He figured his clothes were soaked much worse. He probably looked like a drowned rat.

Water roaring in his ears, filling his nose and throat, burning as it flows into his stomach and lungs. He feels so heavy inside, and even though he claws with his hands, flails with his feet, he can't find any purchase in the water. He can't swim, and he sure as hell can't climb out. Everything is gray-green around him, and he sees dim shapes in the water that he thinks might be fish. Even though his eyes sting from the murky water, he won't shut them. He can't endure the thought of being enclosed in darkness as he continues to sink deeper, deeper . . .

Alan's heart pounded against his ribs, but although he desperately needed to breathe, he couldn't force his lungs to work.

Just ride it out, he thought. *Like a wave . . .*

He concentrated on slowing his heart rate, and a few seconds later, his lungs unlocked and he was able to breathe again. He forced himself to do so slowly, to keep Jan from realizing he was trying to manage a panic attack. She believed that a well-adjusted adult—especially a *man*—should be in control of himself at all times. That was why they were here, after all, out in the middle of Greywater Lake when he would rather have been literally anywhere else on Earth.

"I know you nearly drowned there when you were nine, Alan. You would've, too, if your dad hadn't jumped in to save you. I get that you've avoided water ever since, and yeah, your reason for doing so is understandable. But you can't let an experience that only lasted a couple minutes at most keep affecting you for the rest of your life. You're almost thirty, for Christ's sake! It's time you faced your fear and conquered it."

Sometimes Alan thought the only reason Jan was dating him was because she liked having a weak man to "fix." For her, it was the ultimate expression of control. He often wondered what would happen if she ever did manage to transform him into what she considered a *real* man. Would she lose interest and leave him, set off in search of her next project? Maybe.

Even so, he wanted to please her, so he made himself breathe evenly and smiled as he spoke.

"I admit I've never heard of fish swimming like that, but you know I haven't been around water much since . . . Anyway, this could be a normal thing. Rare, maybe, but not unheard of. The kind of thing you read about on the Internet. 'Top Ten Weird Animal Behaviors' or 'Freaky Fish Facts.'"

Jan smiled a little, but she kept sneaking glances at the backward-swimming fish, which Alan was now certain were circling the canoe.

"I think there's more of them now," she said. "A lot more."

He didn't want to look, but he did. Greywater Lake lived up to its name. The water was murky, but from the ripples on the surface, he thought Jan was right. Before the school of fish had stretched a couple feet from the canoe's hull. Now it was double—no, *triple* that. And worse, was their canoe beginning to spin slowly in the same direction the fish were swimming? He thought so.

The canoe creaked, water lapped at its hull, and another breeze blew over them, the air moving gently on his lips, almost like a kiss.

He wore an orange lifejacket given to him by the guy at the canoe rental place. Jan had one, too, but hers rested underneath her seat. As far as she was concerned, she was too good a swimmer to need it. When they'd first rowed away from the dock, he'd had the sense that she'd have preferred he remove his jacket to demonstrate his courage, but no way in hell was *that* happening. He'd come out on this lake once without a jacket—*Thanks a lot, Dad*—and it had almost cost him his life. Bad enough that Jan had bullied him into going out onto the water. But no way in hell would he do so without his lifejacket on.

How far were they from shore? Up to now, he'd done his best to avoid paying attention to their position on the lake, but he made himself look out over the water. The canoe was rotating faster now, and he experienced mild vertigo as he sought the shore. He saw the lodge where they were staying, the small beach, the dock, the canoe rental shack. But it all looked so very far way. Mostly what he saw was a great swath of green from the trees that lined the shore and surrounded the lodge, which from here looked like a child's dollhouse. He'd known Greywater Lake was big, but he hadn't realized it was so *huge*. How far away from the dock were they? A mile? More?

"Let's keep paddling," he suggested. "If we're careful, we should be able to get away from the fish without hurting any of them." Not that he gave a damn about that right now. In fact, he felt a strong urge to start smashing his paddle into the water over and over to take out as many of the finny little bastards as he could. But he held back. Real men didn't lose control like that.

"Okay," she said. "Yeah. Good idea."

Without waiting for Alan, she gripped her paddle with both hands, and slowly dipped it into the water. Alan heard dull thumps as backward-swimming fish struck the paddle, and the sound made him shiver. *The fish should get out of the way,* he thought. *Hell, they should scatter.* But they didn't. They acted as if the paddle weren't there.

He grabbed his own paddle and slipped it into the water. The fish thumped mindlessly into his paddle, just as they did Jan's. The vibrations of the strikes ran up the handle and into his hands, and the sensation caused his stomach to flip. He felt a fresh rush of panic threatening, but he shoved it down and started paddling. Although he would have rather paddled like a motherfucker and get to shore as fast as he could, he matched Jan's slow rhythm. The last thing he wanted to do was capsize the canoe, even if he was wearing a lifejacket. He couldn't stand the thought of bobbing in the water with all those fish swimming backward around him, his legs kicking uselessly, with nothing but more water beneath him. Water that grew colder and darker the deeper it went. And who knows how deep the Greywater was anyway? Fifty feet? A hundred? More? Maybe there *wasn't* a bottom. Maybe the water just continued going down forever...

Stop it! he told himself. *You're not going to avoid a panic attack that way.*

He concentrated on the task of removing his paddle from the water, putting it back in, pushing gently, then repeating the sequence. The physical repetition helped, and while his panic didn't subside, it remained at a manageable level.

It seemed to go well at first. Now that Jan had something specific to do—more to the point, something to *control*—she'd calmed down. But it soon became clear that their efforts were only making the canoe rotate faster.

"Fuck!" Jan shouted. "Fuck-fuck-fuck!"

Another breeze came, stronger this time, and carried with it the sound of a woman's soft laughter.

Alan thought it was another imagining of his, but then Jan said, "What was that?" She stopped paddling and turned to look at him. Her green eyes were wide, and he thought, *That's what an animal looks like when it realizes it's trapped.*

"You heard it too?" he asked.

"I . . . think so. It sounded like someone laughing, right?"

The breeze returned, grew stronger, became a wind.

Thanks for returning him to me.

Jan looked around frantically, as if trying to find the origin of the voice. It seemed to Alan that the words swirled around them, flowing with the air currents. She looked at him then, features contorting with anger.

"Are you doing this? Is it some kind of trick to get back at me for forcing you to go out on the lake? You never would've done it if it weren't for me pushing you, you know."

Her voice had taken on an accusatory tone, and absurdly—given the situation they were in—he felt competing impulses to apologize to her and to defend himself. These impulses canceled each other out, and he said nothing.

The wind grew even stronger and louder, but the sky remained clear and sunny. He wasn't certain, but he thought the fish—still swimming backwards—were moving faster now. Their numbers had continued to increase until now their mass stretched outward from the canoe as far as he could see. He was beginning to feel . . . not right. He'd been holding his paddle in the water for the last few moments, fish continuing to thump into it as they circled. He withdrew the paddle and examined his hands. The skin was smoother, the flesh over the knuckles softer, and while he wasn't the hairiest guy in the world, the backs of his hands were now virtually hairless. And did his hands look smaller? Yes.

Jan was still looking at him, only now with confused disbelief.

"Alan?"

His clothes felt loose on him, so loose that if he stood, his shirt and shorts—and most importantly, his lifejacket—would slip right off of him.

"It's still me," he said. His voice was higher-pitched, no longer that of a man.

Jan shook her head slowly, as if to deny the reality of what she was seeing.

"But you . . . you . . . "

"I'm nine again. On the outside, anyway." He hadn't known this until he spoke the words, but it felt right.

She looked at him without expression while the wind blew stronger and the canoe continued rotating in the increasingly turbulent water. Her blank expression fell away, to be replaced by a mask of outraged fury. She threw her paddle into the bottom of the canoe, stood, and started moving toward the rear where Alan sat. Her movements set the canoe rocking, and Alan dropped his paddle, which fell overboard and was swept away by the surging water, and gripped the sides of the canoe in a vain attempt to steady it. When she reached him, she crouched and then, glaring, smacked him hard across the face. It hurt, but Alan was more shocked than anything.

"Stop it!" she shouted. "Whatever the fuck you're doing, you need to cut it the hell out and make everything normal again. *Do you hear me?*" She screamed these last four words so hard that spittle flew from her mouth and onto his cheeks and lips.

Despite his outward regression, Alan retained his adult mind, and while he was terrified by what was happening, he realized that in a way, it was far worse for Jan. She believed that anything could be controlled if you were smart enough, kept a tight handle on your emotions, and focused the whole force of your will on what you wanted. She was so sure of this belief that she was almost fanatical about it. So to find herself caught in a living nightmare, where she didn't understand the rules and couldn't do a goddamned thing to change them even if she did, had to be beyond maddening to her.

He felt sorry for her, but he almost felt more than a little satisfaction at seeing her freak out. He had, in a very real sense, lived most of his life feeling there was nothing he—or anyone, for that matter—could do to control the world around them. And although he knew it was cruel and petty of him, he was glad that for once Jan knew how he felt.

The wind had become a howling gale by now, and the rate of the canoe's rotation had increased to the point that the world outside the canoe was a blur. Alan felt dizzy and nauseated, and he gripped the sides of the canoe so tight that it felt as if his fingers might break any second. But Jan seemed no longer aware of what was happening outside the canoe. She too gripped the sides to brace herself, but she continued glaring at him, shouting, "Stop it, stop it, stop it!"

Alan felt his stomach drop, as if the canoe was lowering in the water. But he told himself that couldn't be right. Despite the water swirling violently around their craft, only spray struck them, fetid and surprisingly cold. Very little water had gotten into the canoe, so they couldn't be sinking. But then the boat stopped spinning and began moving backward, canted at a slight angle. That's when he realized what was happening. The swirling water had become a vortex, and they were riding the upper edge of it, moving swiftly in large circles around its circumference. A curving wall of water filled with hundreds of swimming gray shapes surrounded them. Alan looked up and could still see the sky, but with every revolution the canoe picked up speed, and the sky seemed to move further away. He knew they were being pulled down into the maelstrom.

Your father took you from me. I reached out to get you back, but I was too late.

Alan remembered the choppy boat ride back to shore when he was nine, coughing up water, his clothes soaked, the outboard motor straining as if the lake was fighting it, his dad cursing the entire way, sounding more scared than angry.

"Make it stop!" Jan shouted. "Make the goddamned voice stop!"

You were such a sweet boy, Alan. Gentle, sensitive, your mind still and quiet as my surface at its most placid. Your soul as deep and intriguing as my darkest depths. I knew at once that we belonged together, so I sent a wave to rock your father's boat. Not much, just enough so that you'd fall into me. I was sorrow-stricken when I lost you. I cried for so long that my tears flooded the shore, and I vowed that when you returned—if you returned—I would be ready. This time, I will not let you go. You will be mine, and we shall be together forever.

It wasn't the words so much as the emotion behind them that soothed Alan, washed away his fears and calmed him. He'd been so wrong to be afraid of the lake all this time, he could see that now. He'd wasted so many years . . . But that was all right. Somehow the lake had given him back those years, so he really hadn't wasted anything, had he?

Still gripping the sides of the canoe, Jan looked toward the bottom of the maelstrom, which they were now very close to. "You think you can take him from me?" she screamed down into the tapering funnel of water. "He's *mine*, and even if he is a weak, pathetic loser, you can't have him!"

She faced Alan once more, let go of the canoe, and with savage swiftness grabbed hold of his throat. She squeezed, and he was surprised at how strong her grip was, but then he remembered that his body was that of a nine-year-old. Of course she felt strong to him. Her wild-eyed gaze bore into him, and she spoke through gritted teeth, softly. Despite the noise around them—a near-deafening roar to rival the largest of waterfalls—he had no trouble making out what she said.

"You won't win, bitch. You won't, you won't, you won't—"

Alan's throat burned and he couldn't draw in

breath. His vision began to blur, and an entirely different sort of roaring sounded in his ears. At first he made no move to defend himself. What did it matter how he died? Either way, he was dead. But then he realized it did make a difference. If he was fated to die this day, then he wanted to do so at the hands of someone—or something—that loved him. Not at the hands of someone who despised him.

"—won't, you won't, you—"

Alan released his grip on the canoe, reached up, placed his hands on the side of Jan's head, and with two swift, sure motions, plunged his thumbs into her eyes.

She shrieked in agony and let go of his throat. She grabbed hold of his wrists and tried to pull his hands away from her face. His body might have been younger, but his will was still that of a grown man. He pushed hard, harder, until he felt a pop, followed by another, and then warm wet spilled onto his hands. A moment later, she stopped screaming.

The canoe had almost tipped sideways by this point, and now that neither of them held onto the boat, they fell out and down toward the darkness at the bottom of the whirlpool. As they fell, Alan let go of Jan's head and his thumbs slid out of her sockets and she fell away from him, limp and lifeless. His lifejacket was too big for his young body, and he slid out of it just as he and Jan plunged into the water. The maelstrom died then, and water rushed in to fill the space the vortex had created. Within moments, the lake had returned to normal, with nothing—not even an overturned canoe bobbing on the surface—to indicate anything had happened.

***

Welcome home, my love.

He did feel at home here in the cool, comforting dark, and for the first time since his childhood, he was at peace.

And thank you for the gift. After all that work, my pets are hungry.

He watched as hundreds of fish converged on Jan's floating body and began tearing off tiny chunks of her flesh.

He smiled and answered in a voice cold as an arctic current.

You're welcome.

Don't Look at Me

ELIZABETH MASSIE

Yeah, yeah, I know. I know I look like shit. But what do you expect? I've sat here in the tangled weeds at a far corner of Concrete City—a wholesale place that sells ornamental lawn decorations, birdbaths, angel and pig statues, and other pieces of so-called concrete art—for more than three years now. Here by the back fence where the property ends against a narrow portion of shoreline of an algae-crusted lake. Here amid the mosquitoes, snakes, spiders' webs, salamanders, and gobs of sticky goose poop. Here with the rest of the concrete outcasts. I disgust you, so don't look at me. Won't hurt my feelings a bit.

I got no legs, just feet peeking out from a ridiculous tunic. Little pudgy hands. No arms. No genitalia. No working eyes, so I can't see. A prissy, pointed hat with the tip chipped off, a hat that starlings find particularly perch-able. If I had a real painted mouth, I could yell at them to get the hell off my head. But my mouth is just a slash in the concrete, which means I can't yell. Or speak. Or even hiss. And so I sit and wait here in the weeds. Wait with the other slightly irregular garden gnomes, elves, and fairies. More than likely no one will buy us. Shoppers prefer the new, perfectly-formed, brightly-colored concrete creatures out front of the warehouse, all lined up in rows for customers to inspect and admire.

Okay, let me clarify a few things for those who don't know. Things that are created in the shape of humans or near-humans have minds and we can think. Statuary. Puppets. Ventriloquist dummies. Dolls of all kinds—fashion dolls, action figures, sex dolls. And yes, garden gnomes like me. That creep you out? Get over it. It's your fault, anyway. You're the ones who made us. You are our gods. You fashion us out of concrete or marble or wood or plastic or stuffed cloth sacks and then you go and get weirded out because there's more to us than you imagined there would be? Or hoped there would be? Grow up. Yeah, we think. And if we have properly painted mouths and eyes, we can also see and speak. You probably suspected that when you were a child. You probably forgot or denied that when you became an adult.

We know what's going on. We know what you're up to.

Rain and snow and sleet here in the far corner of Concrete City doesn't bother me. What bothers me most is the boredom. None of the others out here can see or speak, either. We're all plain, unpainted cast offs, "seconds," banished from the main part of the sales lot but not discarded. On a rare occasion some person will wander back here and pick one of us for a doorstop. We can't see it happening but can hear it. How can we hear if our ears aren't painted? You made us. You tell me.

Yesterday, I heard a little kid back here in the weeds with us. A girl I think, with her fluttering fingers and her high-pitched voice. She talked to herself, prattled on as she moved around in the weeds. She picked me up, put me down. Picked me up, put me down. She left. Then she came back several hours later and picked me up, put me down. She said, "I like you." Then she was gone again in a rustling of the dead grasses. She was alone, I think. I didn't hear any adults with her. Maybe she lives nearby and was just out playing.

I hear a storm on its way. Thunder. A sharp wind rustles the grasses and the water of the lake slaps the shoreline. I smell worm-scented air and I wait for a downpour. It doesn't come, and is hot again in just a few minutes.

Night comes. Then morning. The little girl is here again. This time she picks me up and holds me close to her chest. Her hands are small and soft. "I like you," she whispers into my ear. I wish I could see her. She seems frail but pretty.

And then off we go. I'm tucked under her arm and am carried—*jostle jostle jostle*—away from Concrete City, away from the smell of the lake and the hum of the mosquitoes. If I had a functional mouth I'd call, "Good-bye, suckers!" to the other outcasts in the weeds, but I don't, so I can't.

Five or so minutes later, a door is opened and we enter a cool place. I detect the sharp scents of burned eggs and cigarette smoke. The door is eased shut behind us. The girl tiptoes with me under her arm, up some stairs. Every other step creaks. I realize I'm stolen goods. Kind of exciting, to be honest. I'm not bored now. Little Miss What's-Her-Name has spirited me away without paying. How about that. I wonder if the owner of Concrete City will notice. If he'll even care.

I'm tossed onto a bed, and I bounce once. The little girl drops down beside me, picks me up with now sweaty hands, and says so quietly I can barely hear her, "I'll keep you with my other friends. You'll like them." I don't know if I'll like them, but I don't have much choice, do I? The girl mutters something I can't hear and then I'm swept up and put onto a dusty shelf, squeezed in between some kind of small plastic doll and something made out of wood. I hate to hell I can't see, but I can feel them. No personal space here, obviously.

Someone downstairs screams, "Connie! Get your lazy ass down here, now! I heard you goin' upstairs! Where the hell you been?"

So her name is Connie. And some rude as hell adult is yelling at her. I hear Connie take a sharp breath, hear her shoes slap the floor, hear her thump down the steps.

"Hey, Newbie," says a voice to my right. It's a gruff voice, deep, sounding like sandpaper against a stick.

I can't reply, so I wait.

"Oh, yeah, no real mouth," says the voice. "We'll get Connie to take care of that."

She steals her mother's lipstick when Mom is drunk. Likes to pretend she's an adult, likes to dream about being grown up and out of this shit hole. Lipstick isn't permanent but it should do you for a while. Tastes like wax but beggars can't be choosers."

"As long as the old bitch doesn't catch her with the

lipstick," came a voice from the left. It's another deep voice but smooth, slick. "Remember what happened when Connie was caught with her mom's cigarettes? Damn."

There was a loud, long silence then, as if they were remembering something most unpleasant. *So, I figure, the bitch is Mom. The screamer from downstairs.*

"Well, anyway, Newbie, my name is Bobby," says the voice on the right. "I'm a dummy, but don't ever call me that. Connie got me for her birthday last year. Her dad gave me to her, before he left for good. Bitch threatened to chop me up and throw me in the fireplace once when Connie wet the bed, but they don't have a fireplace. Mom's an idiot."

"Complete idiot," says the voice on the left.

Downstairs, more yelling. "Damn it, Connie! I told you never to look at me like that!" A loud slap. A whimper.

"Bitch," says Bobby.

"Bitch," says the voice on the left.

Bitch, I think.

Another long silence. I start to feel sleepy (yes, we sleep) and then Bobby says, "Hey, Newbie."

What?

"Here's my advice. Just ignore most of what you hear around here. Otherwise, you'll lose your mind."

The plastic doll on the left says, "Yeah. Bobby's right. Just know that we give Connie some joy in her life. Probably the only joy she has."

What's your name, doll? I wonder.

The doll says, "Oh, yeah, I'm Princess Polly. Just shut up about that, okay?"

Okay.

***

Connie comes back to her room much later, breathing hard, sniffling. It wakes me up. I hear her flop down on the bed and mutter into her pillow. Downstairs, a television has cut on and it's some kind of arguing and loud music. Seems Mom can't get enough arguing, either hers or somebody else's.

Bitch.

After a while, Connie's sniffles and mumblings slow and stop. She gets up and pulls Princess Polly from the shelf and sings something so faint I can't pick out the words, but the melody is kinda nice. Then I hear Princess Polly say something to Connie. Connie replies, "Yeah, I still got some lipstick that Mama didn't find."

Princess Polly is put back on the shelf next to me. I hear Connie digging around, in a drawer I think. Then she is back, and she picks me up, spins me around, and sets me down on the bed beside her.

"You got to look nice," she says. "Here."

I feel a waxy substance spread on my lips. Well, on two thirds of my lips. My mouth twitches a bit. I can feel words forming, even though the right corner of my mouth is still dead.

"Thank you," I say, though it comes out more like "Hank you," what with my whole mouth not working and all.

Connie says, matter-of-factly, "Welcome. Now your eyes."

Something wet is streaked around my eye sockets. Connie says, "I messed up. Wait." She rubs the wet off and starts again. Round the sockets with some kind of tiny brush. Then, "Well, I guess it's okay."

I blink. Blurry, painful light bleeds into my eyes. I blink again and Connie comes into view.

I cringe.

She is perhaps eleven, maybe a little younger. She has thin brown hair and a thin sallow face. Bruises the shape of fingers are on her neck and there are scratches on her forehead. Her left eye is blackened.

"I see you," I manage.

"I know," says Connie. "Now I got to put you back. Mama said I better be down to fix supper before five o'clock. I'm going to fry some bologna."

"Okay." I don't know what else to say. I'd like to tell Connie to give her mother a swift kick in the ass for me, but I'm thinking that wouldn't be a good idea.

At least for now.

Connie puts me back on the shelf between Bobby, a one-armed garishly-colored ventriloquist dummy and Princess Polly, some kind of GI Joe doll dressed in Barbie clothes.

"Shut up," says Princess Polly, even before I can poke fun.

I can see Connie's whole room now. What I'd imagined as a pink and lavender fairyland is a tiny, colorless cell with an unmade bed, tattered throw rug, and filthy walls. A picture of puppies hangs at a tilt from a nail. The happiness of this room pretty much matches the happiness of the far, weedy back lot at Concrete City.

Connie sits on her bed and twists her hair around her fingers. She chews her lip. I can see that her fingernails are bitten down to stubs. Then her Mom screams and Connie is up and out of the door.

"Her Mom do all that to her?" I ask Bobby.

"Oh, you bet," says Bobby. "Bitch is crazy, hateful crazy. Blames Connie for everything that goes wrong in her life. Her alcoholism. Connie's dad up and leaving. The fact that she can't hold a job. Smacks Connie around, treats her like a slave."

"Damn."

"She's the ultimate liar, too," says Princess Polly. "A master at it. Got a restraining order against Connie's dad, and the dad's the only good person ever in Connie's life."

"Fuck."

"Yep," says Princess Polly.

"You got a name, Newbie?" asks Bobby.

"Guess not."

"Nobody ever owned you before, then? Where'd you come from?"

"Connie stole me from Concrete City."

"Yeah, Connie," says Princess Polly. "She steals stuff all the time. I think it fills gaps."

"Fills gaps," says Bobby. "So you're a psychiatrist now? Where'd you learn about filling gaps?"

"Hear bits and pieces on one of Mom's talk shows."

"Pfft."

"Shut up."

"Hey, Newbie, I'm going to suggest Connie name you Pointy," says Bobby. "You got that stupid pointy hat."

"I don't care what she names me," I say, and at that moment I really don't. I am thinking about Connie and the lying bitch downstairs and how something has to be done. While we puppets and dummies and dolls and gnomes can talk and see and hear and think, we can't walk. Nope. Even though we have feet and legs, they aren't taking us anywhere. I'd love to jump off the shelf with Bobby and Princess Polly, run downstairs, and stomp the shit out of the bitch.

But we can't.

Still. Something has to be done.

***

Connie comes back upstairs after she fixes supper and her mother screams that the bologna is rancid, there is grease all over the stove, and to quit looking at her. Connie crawls under her bed and I can hear her counting. I think she has stolen some coins from her mother. When she comes back out, I see that yes, there are coins in her hand, some sweaty dimes, quarters. She puts them into a jar and hides the jar in a dresser drawer, under socks and underwear.

"Connie," I say. Stupid lips, only two-thirds working. I say it louder. "Connie!"

Connie looks over at the shelf, her head tipped in curiosity, her stringy hair cupping her cheek. She comes over and leans in. The blackened bruise around her eye is beginning to go green.

"What's the money for?"

"I'm saving it up to run away to my dad."

"You ever run away before?"

Her eyes darken. "Yeah."

"Your mom caught you?"

"Yeah."

"Hey, Connie, give this Newbie a name," says Bobby.

Connie sniffs, rubs what looks to be new, angry scratches up beside her ear. "I can't think of names right now."

"Call him Pointy."

"That's a stupid name."

"It's perfect."

"Shut up, Bobby," I say. Then I try to change the subject. "Connie, your mom's angry a lot, isn't she?"

Connie nods.

"She hurts you."

"Yeah. 'Cause she hates me."

"You want her to stop hating you. You want to make her happy."

"Nothin' makes Mama happy."

"I got an idea," I say.

"Pointy's got an idea," chides Bobby.

"Everybody likes cuddles," I say. Yeah, I'm grasping here, but just give me a minute, okay?

"Mama doesn't like cuddles."

"Sure she does," I say. "She just doesn't know it." Man, does that sound like bullshit. I keep going.

"She doesn't cuddle me," says Connie. "She hates me."

"Maybe she just needs some cuddle practice."

"What's that?"

Bobby and Princess Polly snort derisively.

"When does your mom go to bed?"

Connie shrugs, sniffs, tugs at her hair.

"When, Connie?"

"Whenever. I don't know."

"Does she take naps?"

"Uh-huh."

"Will she take a nap today?"

"Probably."

I bet Bobby and Princess Polly will think the idea is crazy, but I don't give a flying fuck what they think. If Connie agrees, they'll have to go along with it. Since we can't walk, where we go is up to humans.

I say, "Listen close, Connie. When Mama is down for her nap, take Bobby, Princess Polly, and me and put us in her bed with her. Cuddle us up close to her, right up against her so when she wakes up, she will feel the love."

Bobby burst out laughing. "Feel the *love*? You been listening in to talk shows, too, Pointy?"

I don't remember where I heard that phrase but I'm using it. Like I said, I'm grasping. "Yes, she'll feel the love, Connie. That will help her get used to cuddling. Then maybe she'll know how to cuddle you."

Connie's brows furrow. "I don't know. What if putting you in her bed wakes her up?"

"She snore when she's sleeping?"

"Yeah."

"That means she's in deep. She's sleeping hard. It won't wake her."

"I dunno . . ."

"Connie, you picked me out of a weedy patch because you liked me, right? You said so."

"Yeah."

"So trust me."

She purses her lips, looks at her feet.

Then she looks up again and says, "Okay, Pointy."

***

Mama snores like a freight train tearing down a countryside. She's lying in her bed, flat out on her back like a corpse, drool leaking from the corner of her mouth and her eyeballs flicking back and forth behind her lids. Every few seconds, the snoring causes her head to shudder. In one hand is a cigarette, snubbed out, thank goodness. One shoe is on her foot, the other is upside down on the floor.

Connie holds all three of us—Bobby and me each under one arm, Princess Polly in Connie's hand.

"Tuck us up close," I whisper.

Connie moves silently across the floor, but I can feel the fear in her body. *Don't you dare wake up, bitch*, I think. *Stay there in stupor-land.*

Connie leans over the bed, gently places Bobby against the right side of Mama's neck. Then Princess Polly is placed on the left side of Mama's neck. I'm laid down right on top of her throat, so she can see me when she wakes up.

Connie looks at us, uncertain, but then backs away. As she turns to leave, she scoops up a couple dollar bills on Mama's bureau.

Bobby, Princess Polly, and I lie there, alone with Mama. The doll and dummy know what to do; I explained it to them.

"Hey, Bitch," I say.

Mama stirs, snores more loudly.

"Bitch!"

Mama's eyes pop open. She snorts sluggishly and stares, rheumy red eyeball to painted concrete eyeball. It's pretty clear she has no idea what's going on. Maybe she thinks she's having a nightmare. Just as well. "What the fuck? Don't look at me, you ugly piece of shit! Get off me!"

"Now, boys," I say. And cuddled there with Mama, right up close as we can be, we open wide.

Because, you see, not only can our painted mouths speak. They can also bite.

And chew.

And swallow.

Devil Dolls

BLAZE MCROB

Shadows on the wall so eerie, made the little girl
grow teary,
watching shapes of hideous evils casting their disturbing gloom.
As she shuddered, nearly crying, all at once she
heard a prying,
much like someone trying, trying to get in the room.
"T'was some evil thing," she figured, prying to get in
her room.
"More than this, it's bringing doom."

Oh, so clearly she remembered, all was safe when
first she slumbered,
yet 'twas every scary trembler brought its fear into
the room.
Thus it went she longed for freedom, away from all
the bad to come,
in her spread, patchwork of welcome, welcome for
the coming doom.
But the scared and ominous youngster felt the wrath
from evil's womb.
Much noise now within the room.

Blaze McRob

Thus the sunken fears around her, tearing at the edge
of horror
scared her, brought her awful angst that 'round her
head did loom.
So she took to calm the pounding in her chest; she
tried retreating
from the gruesome evil sounds, gaining entry to the
room.
Yes, the gruesome evil sounds, gaining entry to the
room.
This it was and so much doom.

Thus her sweat poured ever faster as her heart became her master.
Who is there, or what, she wondered, wanting now to
enter room.
But the fact was, she was frightened, feelings of her
fears so heightened,
that her heart was oh so tightened, tightened deep
within her room.
So deep inside her frightened mind, she tried to run
from the doom.
Deep angst there, inside the room.

List'ning to the scary prying, as she shuddered,
thinking, crying,
fretting, fearing fears no children ever had to face in
room.
But the horrors were so eerie, and the darkness made
her teary,
and the only thing she wanted was a happy place,
'naught doom.
This she wanted, and her mind repeated of a place,

'naught doom.
Merely this, inside her room.

She returned to blankets hiding, all the fears inside
her chiding,
but this time the sound was grating, closer, closer to
her room.
"I'm scared," said she, "I'm scared about the things
that lurk inside this place,
what could there be the fear to chase, and so much
more 'tis gloom?"
Why could her soul be yet so torn, and drawn to fears
of doom?
'Tis the angst, inside the room.

And no more fear could she handle, her heart aflame
just like a candle.
Inside the room a scream so loud, brought her
mother to the room,
and when the lights were turned on full, Demonic
Dolls did on her pull.
With the force of dolls so awful, so many now inside
the room,
sat upon a floor so shiny, in the middle of the room.
Sat and sat, in room of doom.

Twins on toybox top were sitting, evil faces, twisted
smiling,
blond haired boy with knife so handy welcomed
Mom into the room.
His bright white eyes were rimmed in black, and
stared at her, all set to hack.
Her body not would he let back, for now this room

would be her tomb.
And so the boy advanced to her, and blood tipped
knife t'was spelling doom.
Said the child, "This is your tomb."
She tried to run but was stopped short, for other
dolls came to abort
her effort now turned to failing, dolls swept o'er her
like a broom.
Dolls with her were not agreeing with her plan of
capture fleeing
and now from her was much weeping, as she faced
her final doom.
Many dolls did come to anchor her to floor of daughter's room.
Anchor her in her new tomb.

And so the boy did end her life, no more for her to
feel its strife.
With one move, he finished her, and no more would
she feel the boom
of all hardships she had suffered, and no more pain
need be buffered,
For all the dolls 'round her muttered, "No more will
you feel the gloom,
Your life upon the floor will stay, incumbent not on
the gloom.
Welcome now in to your tomb."

And so more dolls from toybox came, involved for
now, in their new game.
Former playmate now did hover, close to entry of her
room.
Trapped by those now giddy dollies, intent upon

newfound follies,
licking lips ahead of jollies, thinking of the young
girl's doom.
Thinking of what lay ahead, thinking of the young
girl's doom.
Time it was now for her gloom.

Thus the dollies' lips were smiling, inside their minds
so beguiling,
Set upon the girl so fragile, blocking her from leaving
room.
And before her eyes were blinking, the dolls had all
started thinking,
others on the floor were drinking, her mother's blood
inside the room.
All this now, unholy, ghastly, scant and horrible
place of doom.
'Twas the horror in the room.

As they came intent on stopping all the effort from
her leaving,
knowing now their thoughts had changed concerning
changes in the room.
So now they planned on her having, a life in here
everlasting,
as their playmate, keen on staying, lightened mood
inside the room,
Yes their playmate, keen on staying, lightened mood
inside the room.
Change from doom, though still a tomb.

They dragged her next to teddy bears; upon the floor
they had no cares,

though their innards had been torn by knife of evil
boy in room.
Twin girl did jump from off her perch; on top of toybox did
she lurch. Horror—horror and regret from the girl
t'was trapped in gloom.
Damn, oh damn this harsh regret, still within this
horrid room.
Place of gloom, and still a tomb.

Twin girl in white upon the child, did force her face
down mean and wild,
into the blood of her dead mother, the evil girl with
blood did groom.
And twin's white dress, once so flaunted, dripped
with blood, now undaunted.
In this place of horror haunted, much was kept
within this room.
Nothing – nothing more of horror—kept here—kept
here in this room.
Place of gloom, and still a tomb.

"A part of us you now will be, and never more will
you be free.
Demonic Dolls surround you now, and all of us will
share this room.
Become a part of what we are, and never will we
wander far.
And so embrace what now you are, forget about impending doom.
For you will never go too far, forget about impending
doom."
Place of gloom, and still a tomb.

"Heed you now our words of greeting, friend or foe
can be so fleeting.
So stay with us and be our friend, and we will have
fun in this room.
And those against us, who will come, will feel our
wrath much more than some.
And all who rail that we are one, shall feel the
strength within the room.
Together we shall conquer all, and 'round the rest
our hate will bloom."
Place of gloom, and still a tomb.

And so the girl, now is sitting, still is sitting, still is
sitting,
on the shiny floor of horror, deep inside the room of
gloom.
And her eyes have all the knowing of the dolls
around her showing,
and the knowledge still is growing, deep within this
eerie room.
And her mind becomes as eerie as the others in the
room.
No place of gloom, or a tomb.

Dead Pull

TAYLOR GRANT

Every **animal fell** silent the moment Brennan stepped inside the pet store. A modest brass bell above the door clanged dully.

He surveyed his animal kingdom, satisfied with the respect his subjects paid him. It bordered on reverence, which, Brennan felt, was fully his due. The puppies roughhousing playfully only moments before suddenly slinked back to the corners of their cages. The kittens leapt behind their scratching posts and into the hollows of barrels and other playthings. The tropical birds watched him intently, none daring to caw. Even the rodents and the fish had stopped all activity, as if they sensed a storm gathering on the horizon.

The insects didn't seem to notice Brennan, but of course he realized they were too stupid to know any better. He was still working on that.

Fear pervaded the store, strong enough to taste.

Brennan was pleased.

He began his morning routine by flicking on the

store lights, followed by checking the bills and coinage in the register drawer. He was compelled to recount it in the mornings because the two dipsticks on the night shift couldn't count past ten without a goddamn calculator. They shortchanged him more often than not, no matter how many times he'd complained to the owner.

Animals, Brennan had discovered, were far easier to teach and control than people. Unfortunately, he couldn't get away with conditioning people as easily as animals. Control was what Brennan desired; lack of it had blazed a trail of disaster throughout his life: alcoholism, failed career ambitions, a monumentally disastrous marriage, and a body that increasingly tipped the wrong side of the scale.

Brennan was startled when the phone rang, shattering the silence of the store. He glanced at the kitschy wall clock that was made to look like an owl, its eyes clicking side to side as the pendulum swung.

It was exactly 7:59am.

He pondered whether or not to answer the phone. After all, the store wasn't officially open for business for a full sixty seconds.

On the tenth ring, he gave an annoyed huff and answered it. "Purrs, Grrs and Furs, the happy pet store," delivered deadpan with the word 'store' warped to rhyme with 'fur'.

A husky voice on the other end of the line said, "It's me, Brennan. I meant to leave ya a note, but I forgot."

It was Guthrie, the storeowner.

Brennan did his best to sound perky, never an easy task. "Morning. What's up?"

"I meant to tell ya last week. I approved a work

internship for Ed Mackey's kid, Billy. He's gonna shadow ya today. He'll be working with us through the summer for school credit – Monday through Friday."

Brennan felt his face flush and his fingers tightened around the phone like a boa constrictor. "Listen, I don't—"

Guthrie cut him off, "I know ya like to work alone, Brenn. But Mackey's an important customer. I met his kid and he's sharp. Wants to be a freakin' zoologist, specializin' in fish or some such, ain't that a kicker?"

Christ, that's all I need, Brennan thought, *some little smart ass rambling on all day about the finer points of goldfish reproduction*. Between gritted teeth, he replied, "I guess I don't have much choice."

Guthrie cleared his throat. "Hell, me neither. Mackey spends more money on them exotic fish that you earn in a whole year. What would ya do in my position?"

Brennan didn't have anything to say that wouldn't get him fired.

"It's all settled then," Guthrie said. "Stay on your best behavior now. I know how territorial you can get."

The moment Brennan heard the dial tone he flung the phone across the counter. It hit the tile floor with a jarring *clang*. One of the tropical birds in the back gave a startled squawk.

"Shut up, goddamnit!" Brennan shouted at the bird.

The store went deathly quiet.

A moment later Billy Mackey knocked on the front door.

***

The boy spun through the store like an ambitious

cyclone. He stocked more shelves in the first hour than Brennan normally did in two days. By hour three he'd completely reorganized the amphibian section and was tackling a cat food display in earnest.

Brennan's sufferance ended abruptly. He grasped the boy's shoulder firmly and said, "Listen up, Rookie. It's time for the dead pull."

Mackey gave Brennan a confused look. "Dead pull?"

"Sure. Loads of fun."

Mackey put the finishing touches to the cat food display, and then raced through the aisles to catch up with Brennan. The store was claustrophobic, overflowing with every conceivable—and some inconceivable—pet need.

Brennan noted that the animals seemed to take a great interest in the teenaged boy. Several puppies and cats came out of hiding for the first time since Brennan had stepped into the store. The youngest Yorkshire Terrier gave a yip or two and tried to catch Mackey's attention, his tail wagging wildly as his paws scratched against the thick plastic of his cage. Brennan made a mental note to teach the little furry bastard a lesson about scratching at his cage.

When they moved past the bird section, the largest Congo African Grey gave a mighty squawk and two small lovebirds cooed. Brennan ground his teeth, saying nothing, his face deepening to a fierce red. He suddenly realized he would have to constantly keep his anger in check with Mackey around. The little cocksucker's prying eyes would be on him five days a week.

But not for long if I can help it.

As they entered the aquatics section, Brennan flicked on the special aquarium lights, illuminating an array of native and exotic fish. Dashes of brilliant color darted through the water.

Mackey was immediately drawn to a particular freshwater tank.

With an intensity that belied his age, he said, "Has anyone checked the PH and ammonia in this tank?"

Brennan busied himself with two tangled fishnets, refusing to justify the boy's question.

Mackey studied a school of luminous Neon Tetras. "These Tetras are developing some 'Ich'. You see those white spots?"

Brennan's temper rose. "I know what Ich is, Rookie."

Mackey immediately caught Brennan's tone and realized that he'd overstepped his bounds. He pulled in his head like a scared turtle. "Right . . . right, of course."

Brennan tossed him a small net and pointed to three plastic buckets on the floor; one marked "Freshwater," the other "Saltwater" and the last "Feeder." All were filled with chemically treated water.

"Don't mix the nets," he growled. "It taints the water and spreads disease."

Brennan knew the kid was fully aware of this. Hell, his family was a bunch of fish freaks. But it felt good to reinforce his authority. It also pleased him to watch Mackey biting his tongue, wanting to shout: *I know all of this*! Apparently, the little shit was smart enough to keep his mouth shut.

Brennan reiterated, "Take special care to keep the feeder nets separate. They're the worst carriers of bacteria. You got that?"

"Got it."

"Good." Brennan pointed at a wooden clipboard hanging on the wall. "Right here's the dead pull list. It has to be filled out every morning."

"You mean . . . as in pull out the dead ones?"

"You catch on quick, Rookie."

Mackey shifted on his feet, apprehensive. "Are there usually a lot of dead ones?"

"Welcome to the glamour of pet retail, Pal."

Mackey's face deflated as if it had sprung a leak, which gave Brennan great satisfaction.

"First, you pull all the dead ones from the tanks," Brennan said. "Then, you put 'em in those plastic baggies over there. Make sure to write the name, quantity and stock number on the dead pull list. Think you can handle that?"

"Sure. Of course," Mackey said. He seemed to be trying extra hard to keep things friendly.

Brennan remained austere. "When you're done, you can do the same thing with the reptiles and small animals."

Brennan had just finished ringing up his first customer for the day when he glanced over and saw Mackey pulling a dead, bloated rat from its cage. It was stiff as a frozen pack of meat and he knew from experience that it probably smelled even worse than it looked. He chuckled at Mackey's disgusted expression as he tried and failed to stuff the rat's long, unaccommodating tail into the small plastic baggie. The boy appeared more disheartened with each and every dead pull.

Just wait till you see what's next, Kiddo.

A few moments later, Mackey called out with

genuine concern, "Some of these kittens back here are pretty sick."

"Don't sweat the 'free adoptions'," Brennan yelled back, while inserting a fresh roll of tape into the register. "They're donated."

Mackey was clearly upset by what he'd seen. "But they're . . ."

"I said *forget it*. We don't pay for mongrel cats, so who gives a shit. Now come on, you've got more important work to do."

Brennan hated many things, but the basement was near the top of his lengthy list. It was poorly lit, cramped, and suffused with the stink of death. The grease-stained walls were lined with bags of rotted pet food, broken merchandise, forgotten overstock—and God knows what else. It hadn't been cleaned in years, and his boss Guthrie—who was easily the most unkempt person Brennan knew—never seemed to push the issue.

Thank God for small favors.

Brennan sure as shit wasn't going to take it on himself. Eight bucks an hour didn't cover giving a crap. Hell, eight bucks an hour didn't cover much of anything. Besides, if the health department ever busted the store, Guthrie's fat ass would take the heat. That's why he made the big bucks.

Brennan unclipped a set of keys from his belt loop with a jangle and unlocked the basement door. It was stained black with patches of mold.

Mackey choked on a waft of putrid dust. "Man . . . it's nasty down there."

Brennan suppressed a grin as he ambled down the stairs.

He knew to breathe through his mouth. Mackey wasn't so fortunate. The rancid air caused the boy to stumble; a bagful of dead animals slipped from his grasp and dropped to the floor a few steps below. Tiny, wide-eyed goldfish sliced moisture trails into its dusty surface.

Embarrassed, the boy scrambled down the steps to pick them up. Brennan stopped him with a firm hand and said, "Screw the feeders, Rookie. We inventory those in bulk anyway."

"But they'll rot down here."

Brennan waved his hand with aplomb. "Nah. They'll get eaten by morning."

Mackey cocked his head awkwardly. "Eaten?"

"Sure. Didn't you notice all the shredded bags of pet food down here?"

Mackey swallowed audibly. "Rats?"

Brennan felt a quiet glee warm his heart watching Mackey's face grow pale. "Rats, snakes, lizards . . . you name it. Every once in a while one escapes from their cage. The damn things are impossible to catch once they end up down here. And let me tell you . . . some of those bastards have gotten pretty big."

Mackey glanced nervously at the darkened corners of the basement.

Brennan continued, "But hey, you're good with animals, right? Ain't nothin' you can't handle."

Mackey put on a brave face. "No . . . it's fine."

But they both knew it wasn't fine at all.

They reached an old wooden door at the farthest end of the basement; *Freezer Room* was stenciled across it, and again Brennan had to unlock it. As they stepped inside the musty space, the smell had become just a nose hair short of unbearable. A single light bulb flickered overhead, revealing an antiquated freezer against the back wall with an ominous strobe effect.

Brennan flipped through the keys on his impressive key ring until he found the right one, and opened the lock on the freezer door. Purposefully, he waited before opening it.

"The dead pulls go in here."

Mackey took a wary step toward the humming, rusted appliance; he looked as stiff as the tiny corpses dangling from his hands. The intensity of the smell caused him to gag a bit, though he tried to conceal it.

"You can thank the boss for the lovely aroma," Brennan said. He's too damn cheap to replace this old bitch of a freezer. Hell, it barely stays above room temperature inside there.

Brennan stepped back from the droning apparatus and moved toward the doorway of the room. "Arrange them nice and neat in there, Rookie. Our vendor collects the dead pulls on Fridays and he's a real pain in my ass if they're not organized."

Mackey offered a pitiful nod. Brennan could see the boy's enthusiasm draining like dirty water from a bathtub.

"When you're done organizing the dead pulls," Brennan said, sweep up this room." "Then you can start on the basement. There's a broom and dustpan buried . . . I don't know, somewhere in here, and there's a box of garbage bags in that cabinet just above your head."

Mackey gazed at the walls, Brennan thought, like a first-time convict exploring the walls of his new prison cell.

Brennan smiled, but it came off more like a grimace. "Have fun, Kiddo." *You think the smell is bad now . . .*

Brennan had made it halfway up the basement stairs when he heard Mackey open the freezer door with a slow creak. The boy immediately started to dry retch.

A satisfied chuckle rose in Brennan's throat.

Mornings were always the slowest, and by 11:00am only two customers had come into the pet store: a neurotic regular who bought his cat food one freaking can at a time and an exceedingly tattooed woman wanting a leather collar with spikes. Whether it was for her dog or her own couture wasn't clear.

Brennan hadn't heard a peep from Mackey since he'd left him retching in the freezer room. He probably should have warned the kid about the door's nasty habit of swinging shut. And it might have been a good idea to make sure the doorknob wasn't locked either. But, hey . . . these things happen.

When another hour and a half passed without a sound, Brennan decided it was time to check on the brat's progress. As he stepped down into the basement, he scanned the shadows for any sign of Mackey. From the look of things, nothing had been touched.

"Hey Rookie . . . you down here?"

The room seemed to hold its breath.

Intrigued, Brennan moved toward the freezer room. Much to his delight, he noticed that the door was shut tight, locked from the outside.

"You in there, Rook?" he called out, fumbling with his keys in the gloom.

A mewling sound emanated from beyond the door,

causing a field of goose bumps to spring up on Brennan's arms.

That can't be good.

As he opened the freezer room door, he half-expected to see Mackey curled in a ball, drooling and staring into the darkness like some asylum escapee.

He wasn't far off.

Mackey sat on the floor right next to the freezer, slumped forward, his body stiff and unmoving. The rusted metal door of the freezer gaped open; inside a meager bulb glowed dismally. Brennan presumed that Mackey had left the freezer door open to help illuminate the tenebrous room. Inside the icebox, a menagerie of faces offered dead stares from behind plastic veils. On the bottom shelf was a baggie filled with what looked like a frozen rodent orgy. Brennan looked into the dead, clouded-over eyes of a Siamese cat, its face congealed into a perverse grin.

He quickly averted his gaze.

Mackey's chin was touching his chest. It reminded Brennan of a picture he'd once seen in a magazine: a man gunned down by a firing squad, slumped against a blood-splattered wall.

With false concern, he said, "Hey Rook, you okay?"

The kid's body jerked at that, startling Brennan. His nostril's flared from the fusion of smells that pervaded the room. Glancing down, he noticed that the crotch of the boy's jeans was dark with urine.

A corpulent rat with filthy white fur and ugly, pinkish eyes scuttled over Mackey's legs. It gave Brennan a quick once over before stuffing its gluttonous form through a gnawed hole in the wall.

Mackey's face was wan and streaked with tears as

he stared at Brennan. The knuckles on his hands were swollen, torn open and bleeding—most likely from a futile session of pounding on the door.

His eyes bored into Brennan and he choked, "I wanna . . . go home."

Brennan almost felt sorry for him.

Almost.

***

The next day was business as usual. Billy Mackey had been successfully traumatized, and Brennan thought it unlikely that he would ever set foot in the store again.

It had been a calculated risk, of course. The little shit could have blamed him for the incident and he might have lost his job. At the same time, he knew that the risk of working with Mackey for any length of time was far greater. It wouldn't have ended well.

These types of situations never worked out well for Brennan.

Fortunately, his gambit had paid off. He'd known it would work the moment he saw Mackey trying to conceal his urine-soaked pants. The boy's profound embarrassment would keep him from telling anyone about it. Brennan was convinced of it.

That thought gave him a profound sense of control. And the control he wielded over his life seemed to begin and end with the pet store. Working there enabled him to dictate the day-to-day operations, as well as the lives of the store's denizens. The animals answered to him. Depended on him. And, more importantly, they feared him.

Those that couldn't be controlled were killed.

Brennan preferred control to killing, but he wasn't

averse to dispatching uncooperative subjects. Nor was he averse to convincing the huddled masses when necessary – just to keep them in line. He'd found that teaching by example was a powerful tool; particularly with the higher intelligence animals like cats and dogs.

Fish, of course, were the easiest to lord over. They were the most vulnerable and inherently fearful.

That is, until *it* showed up.

The special delivery package arrived exactly one week after the basement incident. It was marked 'live animals', and had come courtesy of the Mackey family. An attached card offered a well-written thank you from Billy's father to Guthrie, and an acknowledgement of Brennan's exemplary tutelage.

The card went on to explain that Billy had received a rare opportunity to work at the local zoo and would no longer be able to continue his internship at the pet store. But thanks for giving him the opportunity and won't you please accept this rare exotic fish as a token of our appreciation?

Brennan had read the card with delight, relishing the subtext. The 'opportunity' at the zoo may have been real enough, but he also knew it was the Mackeys' elaborate way of saving face.

However, over the next few days, the 'gift' would become the bane of Brennan's existence. And he was determined to kill it. Unfortunately, the fish had arrived on one of Guthrie's scheduled work days (planned with great precision by the Mackeys no doubt), and Brennan wouldn't be able to dispose of the fish without raising suspicion.

Better not to do anything drastic for a week or two.

In the meantime, Brennan was forced to create a

home for the unidentified fish in the large, center aquarium. *A place of honor*, were the hopelessly fawning words Guthrie used.

The description attached to the fish's shipping crate was infuriatingly cryptic. There were no instructions or identifying information other than the fish was a rare, freshwater species that thrived best alone.

Brennan wasn't surprised. It was just like the Mackeys to show off their ability to acquire extremely exotic species, daring all and sundry to identify it. *Smug, self-important bastards*. They loved to make everyone aware of their access to all things elite.

Brennan had yet to identify the shimmering black fish a week later. Oddly, none of his usual aquatic resources could find a match. Aesthetically, he found the fish to be rather unremarkable. Its physical characteristics were an amalgamation of any number of exotic species.

But there was something about its eyes. There was a cognizance he'd never seen in a fish before. Its huge, iridescent eyes seemed to peer into his soul, and disapprove of what it saw.

Brennan was reminded of the looks his father had given him during some of his more terrifying drunken benders. He felt that same kind of hatred radiating from the fish.

He'd end those hateful looks by killing it, as he'd killed his father on his thirteenth birthday. Killing, he'd found, was often the simplest solution to a difficult situation. It had always come easily to Brennan. The hardest part was getting away with it.

His ex-wife had been a real challenge.

Taylor Grant

Yes, he'd enjoy getting rid of Little Mackey (the moniker he'd given the hateful fish), but he'd have to be extremely careful. And he obsessed about the best method for the next few days. The easiest answer was to simply add salt to the tank. The problem was that it would take a fair amount to kill the fish and he didn't want to risk anyone noticing the crusty residue.

Another option was starvation, but there was no way to keep the morons on the night shift from feeding it; especially that goddamned tree-hugger, Jenkins, who doted over fish nearly as much as Billy Mackey.

Brennan also considered using the poisoned pellets he'd developed specifically for aquatic life, but he had a feeling the damned fish wouldn't eat them. And he couldn't take the chance that the pellets might be discovered at the bottom of the tank. Jenkins, in particular, would happily rat him out.

If worse came to worst, he knew he could always go with the final option: snatch the little pecker from its tank and watch it suffocate.

He'd entertained the last idea on several occasions, but the risk of damaging the delicate fish deterred him. Not that anyone would inspect the fish for foul play, but he liked to keep his dirty work clean. He had immense pride in his ability to avoid detection. Besides, after the early joys of brute force, he'd found he wasn't nearly as satisfied nowadays as when he created more ingenious killing methods. He took this as a sign of maturation.

In any case, his decision became imperative the day he noticed a power shift happening in the aquatics section. Brennan's fish subjects stopped responding in the way to which he was accustomed.

Normally, they were reactive, hanging on his every move. His threatening gestures caused them to cower from his mighty hand and retreat to the bottom of their aquariums. Conversely, if he were playing the role of benevolent God, they would race toward the surface of the water in anticipation of their daily sustenance—thankful for the grace of the Brennan-God.

Now, they stared at him with accusatory eyes.

He thought: *It's influencing them somehow . . .*

The idea was preposterous, he knew. And yet there was no denying the abrupt change in his subjects, the condemnatory looks. Brennan had felt the same way under the chastising gaze of his father; a look that said: *you're a pathetic waste of flesh.*

"Quit staring at me!" Brennan yelled at the thousand eyes.

This seemed to increase the intensity of their gazes.

Angrily, he hurled a fish net at the center aquarium, hitting Little Mackey's tank with a dull, wet *clunk*. The raven-colored fish didn't budge. It simply floated dead center in the tank.

Defiant.

Eyes burning with hate.

Brennan looked away. He refused to have a stare down with a goddamn fish.

He'd kill it and that would be the end of it.

***

The next day, Brennan arrived at the store ready for the final showdown.

Little Mackey's bulbous eyes followed him with suspicion as Brennan approached its tank and angrily yanked off the lid.

"Time to die."

He angled a long, plastic spout directly over the fish and poured in a deadly mixture of food-based oil and grease he'd mixed the night before. Little Mackey darted out of the way with blinding speed and narrowly avoided the sludge.

Brennan grinned. He knew the diminutive fish was merely delaying the inevitable; there was no escape in such a confined space.

He criss-crossed the oil across the surface of the water and used a net to force it down. He watched the swirling trails of oil with great anticipation. Little Mackey continued to dodge and weave, but eventually the toxic blanket of oil coated it with a viscous sheen.

Soon the oil would clog the fragile gills of the fish, preventing it from extracting oxygen from the water. Ironically, this made Brennan breathe easier.

The ebony-colored fish would die of—what looked like—natural causes. If any suspicions arose about the murky water, he'd simply blame it on a bad filter and replace it, giving the tank a good cleaning while he was at it.

Best of all, it would show Little Mackey's buddies what happens when they give disapproving looks to their Brennan-God.

Two hours later, Little Mackey was still glaring at him.

Brennan was close to panic. Every moment he spent with the fish meant more of his control was slipping away.

When the longest shift he could remember finally ended, he raced all the way home, spurred to desperate energy by the memory of the other reptiles, birds, and small animals that populated the pet store.

All of them had stared at him accusingly, too.

***

Brennan spent some quality time with his good buddy *Jack Daniels* that night. He was determined to wash away all thoughts of the pet store jury. Between gulps, he cursed Billy Mackey's name and his Godforsaken fish.

Around midnight, during a rather intense rant, Brennan slurred his words and pronounced Mackey as "Mackerel." The irony dropped him to the floor in a fit of hysterical laughter.

But as his alcohol-induced gaiety slowly faded away, despair crept back in like an ocean fog, obscuring everything with its cold invasiveness. A distorted face peered through the mist, floating through Brennan's drunken haze.

The eyes were unmistakable.

Get out of my head!

But the mental specter of Billy Mackey sitting in that darkened basement, with those accusing eyes, remained.

Brennan heaved an old wicker chair at the wall out of frustration, losing his balance and collapsing onto the floor.

Why can't I put him behind me? What is it about that kid?

Distorted images of the boy were projected onto the screen of Brennan's mind: a slideshow of bloodied knuckles; pants wetting, and cries of terror in the darkness.

Brennan's thoughts transported him back in time, to his harrowing experiences as a child in the basement of his house. To the terror of those countless, merciless beatings he'd received from his father in the yawning darkness. The gut wrenching feeling of betrayal – it all came crashing back.

He'd seen that look of betrayal on Mackey's face that day.

At that moment, for the first time since as far back as he could remember, Brennan felt tears welling up.

He threw back another swig of liquid forgetfulness and noticed a familiar black fish—wriggling inside his bottle of *Jack Daniels*. It dove straight down toward his throat.

He flung the bottle away in horror. It shattered against the far wall, spraying the room with alcohol and shards of glass. He spun around in a frenzy and looked for any signs of the little terror. He wanted to see it flopping on the carpet, gasping its final breath. But after a futile search, he finally collapsed onto the floor, woozy from the exertion.

It was a drunken hallucination, he thought.

Or worse: a conscience that he didn't want.

On that final disturbing thought—he passed out cold.

***

Brennan was grateful for his brain-splitting hangover the next morning; it helped distract him from the fear of facing the pet store again. He gave the performance of a lifetime, acting as if nothing had changed when he strolled through the front door, maintaining the pretense that the animals remained his royal subjects.

As he moved through the narrow aisles of the store, he felt the eyes of the entire pet populace upon him. It unnerved him, but he refused to give them the satisfaction of a reaction. Instead, he focused on the day's steady stream of customers and did his best to avoid eye contact with the animals.

The reckoning was coming, of course. But he wanted it on *his* terms; and he knew that he would have the greatest advantage after store hours. Today was Sunday and the only day of the week the store closed early. He wouldn't have to deal with the usual idiots working the night shift.

Perfect.

When evening arrived, there was the usual feeding and cleaning to be done, as well as a dead pull that he'd already postponed from the day before. By the time he locked up the store, he'd finally mustered up the courage to face his bestial tribunal.

Time seemed to suspend as Brennan mopped the tile floor in the aquatics area, preparing for the face-off. He gradually—methodically—worked his way toward Little Mackey's tank. Now, more than ever, he felt its pervasive malice, like a pall of darkness over the room.

Brennan drew closer and closer with each wet swish of his mop, until he was finally standing next to the tank. He bent down to look at the hideous little thing; his face mere inches from the glass. The fish struck at him like an enraged snake, smacking against the glass with a resounding *thunk*. Brennan stumbled back, knocking over his bucket of dirty mop water.

The entire store rose up in a macabre cacophony: birds cawed, cats shrieked, puppies howled, and lizards hissed.

Brennan's mind began to scream, too. *Were they laughing at him? What the hell was happening here?*

As he took in the nightmarish spectacle, he realized

that he'd crossed the point of no return. If he didn't make a stand now, he would no longer be seen as their king—but as the royal fool. He forced himself to meet the stare of the little black fish, fury buzzed in his ears like a swarm of enraged bees. His breath was forced and ragged as he rose to his feet.

The fish glared back.

Mocking him!

A mental dam inside Brennan's mind broke.

He smashed through the store like a river of rage, ignoring the screeches, barks and squawks that taunted him at every turn. He was searching for anything to kill the fish with, all pretense at finesse evaporated. It didn't matter what it was, as long it could tear, rend, smash—

Kill!

He yanked open cupboards and drawers, his thickset body tensed with rage, face twisted and feral. He came across a serrated knife he'd used only the day before to chop up vegetables for the reptiles.

Now he'd use it to chop up Little Mackey.

Just like sushi, a crazed voice said in his mind.

The pet store had become sheer pandemonium; every animal seemed to shriek for blood from behind their cages. Barking, squawking, hissing, shrieking—Brennan's ears rang and his aching head whirled.

He raced toward the aquatics area. In his mind's eye, he could see the little black monstrosity impaled on his knife, wriggling in agonized death throes. He charged toward Little Mackey's tank.

The black fish glanced down at the wet, slippery floor with a knowing look.

Brennan saw it coming then, but he didn't have

time to stop. He felt a moment of lost equilibrium and then he was lighter than air. His momentum carried him all the way across the room.

Upon impact, his face smashed straight through one of the aquariums. A thick shard of glass impaled his throat, turning the contents of the fish tank into a crimson waterfall.

Brennan hung there, flopping back and forth. Not unlike a fish out of water, gasping for air.

He'd missed Little Mackey's aquarium by half an arm's length.

The shimmering fish swam over from the neighboring tank to watch Brennan become the store's latest dead pull.

Brennan forced his gaze toward the hateful fish with his dying breath. What he saw there made him want to scream—though he physically could not.

Staring back at him was a grotesque little fish with Billy Mackey's eyes—filled with cold satisfaction.

Alternative Muses

DANIEL J. STONE

I dream of needles curved into claws, epidural baths and ice crystals incinerating my guts. Legs open, wishbone pale and ready to snap . . . but who would get the bigger half? Me riding Peter in one of our predictable drug-blazed sexcapades, my tits hanging like strange fruit and his big hands cupping them as if to pluck. His bottle blonde hair coarse as matted fur, mine a finer velvet dyed darker than black. The heat of him violating my warm wet core, and he drops his seed in a vicious sticky tangle, smearing thick between my thighs as he pulls out and runs away.

Then the shark hook plunged, unzipping the wrinkled flesh between my legs, the result of it scattering darkly and beaded red on the apex tip, rising toxic fragrance like carrion. My screaming became the agony of ecstasy; I wanted no part of that gestating glob of meat inside me, no part of birthing innocence and raising it corrupt. I only wanted Peter's mouth on my pussy, fat lips on lips. I wanted him to drown in the menstrual blood he stole, wanted him to excavate that life sucking liability he left behind like a dark treasure. Men have it so easy: spill their love in a few liquid pumps and then move on. It's the woman who has to deal with the consequences.

Why do we dream of such abandon? Why do we long for sudden death when we're all on borrowed time? Though I deserved no redemption—pain transcending pleasure—the idea of my body bursting at the heat of passionate contact with sharp metal vexed me. Why let this thing take over my body, deplete me, erase me? Mammalian procreation is as supernatural as the story books tell it: a creature growing within, thus which lives off your blood.

And then I remembered the invitation.

Human Suspension.
Celebrate the darkness and the wanton beat of your heart.
No drug can take you higher.

Filthy excuse for a club in the Meatpacking District, sideswiped by a lowly alleyway where the rats fucked on display and the sounds of the Hudson stretched like skin waiting to tear. A few raucous stops on the L train from Brooklyn—loud Puerto Ricans cracked out of their minds, book-worm hipsters trying to hide their vulnerability—and we arrived, living in-real-time the dissonances, disconnections and debaucheries wrought within the city's last subculture of self-mutilation. The human body is the final canvas after all, our ultimate escape. We've used up all of our other artistic resources—pen to paper, pencil to sketchbook, acrylic and oils, dance and music.

But art is a bottom dweller: it always finds a way to survive.

The patrons careening outside were all young and vicious, a crowd I knew all too well because they were all like me: the darklings, the funzies, the furiously bored and the lost. Kids out of work, kids who had too much time on their hands to paint their faces white with arsenic, kids who dyed their hair like a Mardis Gras stew; kids with too many emotions to control and too many family members telling them how ugly and stupid they are. If there was a chance for any of them to feel normal, it was within a place where metal fixed into flesh suspends you high above any reality, a place no drug could ever bring you to.

Peter and I only wanted to scope out the joint. On the ride over I explained to him the Superman and Suicide pose, how one can look like they're flying or hanging on a noose, depending on the area in which your body receives the hooks. *Receive*, not pierce, because suspension is a holy benediction. Peter put his arm around my shoulders hesitantly (he just didn't want to hear about that stuff), and then his hand touched my stomach, which was protruding softly through my PANTERA T-shirt. It was his reminder to me that I was knocked up, that I had to resist the temptation of serious fun, and that he wanted nothing to do with the suspension club. Peter said it was a primitive practice only very few understood, and added that I was a modern poser trying to show off.

"You can't be serious," he said.

"I'm *dead* serious."

"Don't talk like that, Mom."

"Take this damn thing out of me. I don't want it," I hollered.

He pulled me back into the subway, my heels

clicking fast, his shoes scraping the bad black top, and we headed back to Brooklyn. He wasn't wrecked enough so that I could control him, wasn't that same Peter I'd met last year, that lost soul who wanted nothing more than to drift like ash across the scariest seas, to live life like there was no tomorrow. Had he forgotten he was the one who showed me invitation? Haunting words splattered like a crushed blood orange, concealed in plastic like something dangerous, or ancient. I dangled it between my middle and pointer finger while smoking a hand rolled cigarette. I was skilled in this fashion, could manipulate any of my limbs to catch a drag off the joint while snorting a bump of coke sprawled on a mirror, or lap up a tab of weak acid to melt over my tongue.

The tobacco was Peter's, cheap as the parchment rolling paper. We lived cheap, ate less than modest but didn't consider ourselves dirt poor. We hardly worked. Peter sold whatever he didn't snort and I tricked a few times a month at a sad titty bar in Williamsburg. A lot of guys called me Lydia or Marilyn (fuck if I know if they ever found out my real name) but I liked to refer to myself as a young Dita Von Tees: powdery skin, velvet hair like a crow's wing, ruby red lipstick and the finest wardrobe of lace and fishnet you can buy at Ricky's.

Now the crappy attempt I'd made to roll a homemade cigarette left me in a battle against gravity, trying to not let it fall apart. Peter was best at rolling cigarettes . . . the best junkie, the best lover, the best purveyor of pain. He was the best at everything that is deemed terrible. So naturally that attracted me to him. We met at a metal dive bar and upon first kiss he sliced my finger with his pocket knife because he said he wanted to make sure my blood was red, said that I must like pain given all the gauges and studs of surgical steel running through my bottom lip, my nose and both ears.

We've not been able to take our tongues out of one another's mouths since. He was the answer to my fucked up prayers; I'd been craving a man who can keep up with my love for pain before pleasure, ridicule before compliment and self-mutilation to the forefront. What fun it is to dangle your problems like the carrot to the hungry horse, to only swallow it like the best pill in the world, or cut it away at the command of your own hand.

Peter was a travelling gypsy: thin scruffy face, lanky bones, big brown eyes and long matted hair twisted out of control. His clothes revolved around one pair of ripped jeans, filthy Converses on his feet and one leather vest that hung off his shoulders like an old skin. He'd come to New York for the drinks and the sights, so what better in-the-flesh sight than myself, a girl born and raised in the city that never sleeps, the kingdom of horror and glum. Don't you think? While everyone else fools themselves thinking New York is the capital of fashion and glamour, I remain busy looking for its deepest, darkest, baddest places. I yearn for the smell of gun powder, the clicking fingers of corner gangsters and the taste of blood like sucking on a green penny. Have you ever looked beyond Fifth Avenue, ever gone into the deepest parts of the subways, the whorled expanses of tunnels and dipped your head over the side? Afraid of what you might see? A dark mirror reflecting the miniscule reflection of your pathetic life? Afraid of the abyss looking back at you?

"Hey, Trigger. You really liked that place?"

That's my name, like the finger's final destination before the bullet plows through someone's head. He said it so sweet, of course, a way that made him irresistible. By then he was strung out on three caps of poppers, a film cleaner that blossomed within the 70s drug scene but died big time to ecstasy and GHB in the 90s. His hair was sticky with bad gel and his pupils were dilated to make his eyes fully black. We'd argued just minutes before, about how I was corrupting his thoughts, polluting his willpower and depleting his self-esteem. The truth was that he'd already corrupted me by giving me this living, growing disease.

In my eyes I hadn't corrupted him *enough*. If he wanted he could run away at any second. Never settling down lived within the blood of the Gypsies; they'd been doing it since the fall of the Roman Empire. Thus, Peter didn't quite follow everything I did. He rejected conventional cigarettes, drinking liquor from the bottle (he liked everything to be orderly) and challenged the radical views of our ever-shrinking world. But don't be fooled to think he's such a good boy, because like anyone in this fucking world (and they're a liar if they say they aren't) he was very constricted... imprisoned by his own vices.

Peter was what you'd call an old school junkie, the kind who worshipped the psychedelic swirl of lava lamps, strung out over the godly presence of black light posters stapled to every corner of our Brooklyn studio. Aliens smoking fat joints, The Madonna's nipples tipped with blood before a carnivorous infant (the

Holy Mother, not the singer) and neon Rage zombies tumbling out of a 3D poster. He could babble for hours about the eerie similarities and radical differences between Pollock, Dali and Bacon, or Burroughs, Kerouac and Corse.

I didn't care for any writers or painters. I focused my attention on testing the limits of my own flesh, marking myself up with piercings like fine beadwork and tattoos as if I was a living canvas: The Illustrated Woman. Our stark differences made our relationship all the more interesting. We abused one another, we abused together, we loved to hate each other's vices, but still made time to celebrate life as if tomorrow the world would end. Peter's famous excuse was that we as a human species are all doomed to be placed into a wall, six feet under or sent to the incinerator to be turned into a pile of useless ash. Running from this near future or into it? The ice caps are gone, the carbon dioxide levels in the air are at its highest. Extinction is near. So why not live it up? Why not fall headlong into your own destiny?

That's half the reason he did not believe in rubbers and more of the reason why I kept drinking when I noticed my menstrual blood stopped, when I saw my belly begin to swell as if I'd swallowed a football in my sleep. I skipped the doctor—couldn't afford that shit— and managed to get my hands on a home pregnancy test via five finger discount. That night my brain was swirling on craft beer and salvia smoke; I peed madly, missed half the bowl, but managed to get enough on the stick. I waited in angst, and fuck my life, it was true: pregnant.

The thought of my and Peter's DNA being passed

down to a miraculous little son of a bitch at first was enlightening. We could start a new breed of people, the type that are not born prude and uninspired, the kind that celebrate art, creative substance abuse and passionate literature. We could make a billion children that would do something to help save this fucked up world. And then I was struck with an image, of a selfish infant begging for my tit milk. I thought about it a billion times. It freaked me the fuck out.

"We could just drink until you puke out your uterus, or hang you upside down and beat you with a stick," Peter joked. "Piñata style."

"Where's the fun in that? Might as well shove your hand up my cunt and rip out my damn womb."

"Or we could actually, you know, pretend to be normal. Young parents are everywhere in the boroughs."

"But don't you see all those advertisements in the train stations against people like us? All those crying baby faces, all those confused, unhappy parents. *Honestly, Mom, chances are he won't stay with you. I'm twice as likely not to graduate high school because you had me as a teen.*"

"Since when do we listen to the advertisements meant for the simpletons?"

"Just making you aware."

"That creature inside you is special. It's made of what we're made of."

. . . he won't stay with you...

Six weeks and still growing, even with my terrible diet of beer, smokes, stale crackers with peanut butter; me growing weaker as the days languished on, just as I'd predicted. I guess no matter what a woman does, the fetus will find a way to survive, find a way to adapt to its toxic environment. Peter tried to make me feel better, tried to convince me that us becoming a family was special. I somehow knew he was lying. I'd already dreamed of him leaving me, dreamed of the utmost gruesome abortion: my own body rejecting the fetus; a claw raking me clean from the inside out.

"Trig, baby, I'm just as scared as you. But curious at the same time. Don't you wanna know at least what it *looks* like?"

"I'm not curious," smoke looping around me. "I'm still deciding what to do with it."

"Keep it, baby. Keep it."

Peter's deep eyes locked into mine—all pupil—and so I couldn't see the shady grey irises that I fell in love with. But I was so hormonal Peter no longer had any power over me. He could not fuck me with his mind games, could not make me think any differently. I stood around playing with my hair before the mirror, attacking myself at the weight I was gaining; my heels didn't fit right anymore, my fishnet stockings tore thanks to the new water weight.

My face blew up like my stretch-marked belly and the piercings all of a sudden were painful, choking. I was forced to take out the black jewel in my navel because the skin was beginning to thin around it like parchment. I hated myself. I wanted a change, wanted to rip my soul clear out of my skin and throw it down a drain . . . at least that would save it. No one should tell me what I can and cannot do with my body. It's my world, my universe, and my temple. This thing inside is not part of me. I reject it like an intestine does feces.

***

I'd rather experience a thousand half-loves well worth leaving than to take your madness home and watch you dance inside my uterus . . . where no one sees you but me.

4 a.m. and Peter asleep; me pacing the studio like a fucking lunatic, the call of the club chewing me up inside. That or the fetus? I contemplated that wire hangar staring back at me, a home-made weapon fit for abortion. It would indeed be bloody. So I ran out the door, mouse quiet, and headed for the Meatpacking District. The L train is full of latent lunacies at night, solitary bastards, muttering crack heads and an overwhelming sense of hostility. The lights barely work and the conductors are all but human. I wondered if real people drove the trains anymore.

Grimy night, and the insomniac bodies were caked in the greasy odors of food trucks. I walked the triptych streets and paid attention not to my grumbling stomach, or my aching pussy. I wanted metal, no doubt. I wanted that ultimate sodomy. Nothing in the world could have satiated me more; not Peter's touch, not conversations with a highly trained psychiatrist, not even a fucking drink. The call of human suspension was too strong.

I came up to the club on its side. Smoky and cryptic, marked up with hundreds of band insignias like charcoal art. Freakishly young faces were smeared in what seemed to be blood but could have easily been lipstick. I didn't get close enough to find out. You would think at this harsh hour, where dawn is about to break over the sharp city skyline, that the dark little clubs and bars would be emptying. They should have been raided by police or shut down by the city government for illegal drug recreation and underage drinking.

Not here.

Bodies folded into one another, zombie-slouched and slow; hands crawled like white spiders across the bar tops, across flesh wet and pleasing. Leather covered limbs locked into one another as chaps clasped tight against pale spongy asses. I smelled sweat and sex and death laced into one sinister stench; pain and curiosity and glum raced to get to the finish line. This was a tiny island where the breeding of folly and brutality was the best idea. It seemed whatever decency people were taught as growing babes, as half-educated school kids, was left at the door before entering.

And then she arose on stage left.

Dark princess, hair like jellied tentacles, limbs as flimsy rubber bands and eyes precious as jade stone. She saw me; I saw her. We made love through the dark electric air without an iota of physical touch. Angel. Devil. Sorceress. But then the selfish growing bastard inside me kicked, breaking our telepathic fuck session. The pain shot down to my legs, numbing them, then to my head where fireworks dripped before my eyes. I stumbled; a fat juicy metal head caught me and balanced me back into reality.

The show began.

"WHO WANTS BLOOD?" she screamed.

Her arms spread wide and her head lolled, gyrated. The music was a loud soundtrack of screaming guitars and raging dark techno. I watched her feet leave the stage, watched her soar high above the surprised faces.

Her tits hung flaccid, nipples like the stems of old mushrooms. She was in no pain other than the ecstasy of transformation in her self-mutation. Suicide Pose. She was a solo vignette. She gave poetic reason to hang from hooks, gave purpose to it. I thought how freeing it must feel, how beautiful it is to choose your own destiny . . . even if it's for just a little while.

I wanted that ephemeral freedom as well.

***

"Where the fuck were you?" Peter's early morning voice stroke-like.

"At the club," my voice tainted with satisfaction.

"You're knocked up, did you forget?"

"Don't remind me."

Spilling sun yellow warm as egg yolk, and Peter sitting Indian style with a pipe to his lips that smelled of berry tobacco. He wasn't mad at me of course, that wasn't in his nature. I could possibly do no wrong in his eyes. But I will say that for every passing day with this growing child inside me, Peter was starting to become more and more obsessed with the idea that he had to take on some kind of responsibility. But if I asked him to go to a reputable job, like working the kiosk at the mall and make some real money, he'd laugh and continue smoking his strange and colorful Gypsy leaves.

"I thought we had a deal to never go to that club. I let you look at it from the outside . . . but that was it."

"I had to find out."

I was before that damn mirror again, undressing slowly, the spot between my angel wings tender. *Suicide Pose*. As soon as my shirt hit the floor and my hair snapped against the middle of my back, right up against the spot where she hooked me, I saw Peter's eyes widen in the mirror's reflection. No blood, just a set of welts. Peter knew exactly what it was, and he jumped to his feet and began the strangest tirade in the world. He pulled at his hair and raked his scruff with the nails he didn't have. Not angry, not concerned, just appalled.

"You used to be so into this," I snapped.

"Before I knew I was going to be a father, I'd willingly try any poison you put in front of my face."

"And you're such a rational being now? I told you, I'm not keeping this thing. I'm going to drop it off in a dump—"

His hand gripped my mouth hard enough for my teeth to sink into cheekflesh like the fish hook did to my back. Spit and blood and lipstick were all I could taste. In all the years I'd known him he'd never showed any signs of physical abuse. Everything changed at that moment. He was now the Peter I'd already dreamed of, full of confusion and ready to run. I half hoped he'd punch me in the stomach, self-abort this thing. But he didn't.

Peter's grip on me was nervous but strengthening and his face froze in fright as if he had no idea what he was doing. We were both in an awkward position. And so that's when I felt the bitch inside me take over. I cocked my elbow toward his face and clocked his nose. The cartilage crushed warmly; the bone cracked horribly. He shrieked and began to run, but I was on the immediate offensive and pulled him to the floor by his hair, using all of my baby weight to pull him down by his dirty cardigan and climbed on top of him punching and spitting.

All of a sudden it was over.

He gave up.

A shimmering squeal of blood was his face.

"Goddamn it, Trigger, I'm bleeding!" he cried.

"Don't ever touch me like that again," I said. "I'm in a *delicate* condition."

"Why . . . why are you doing this? Trying to get me to HATE YOU! Trying to tear us apart?"

"It's in your pathetic nature to do such . . . Gypsy scum!"

"I love you, Trigger . . . LOVE YOU! Why did you do that to yourself?"

"I'm my own person, Peter. Fucking forget that?"

And just like that he was on his feet. Didn't grab anything, not his pipe, his records, his books or even his clothes. He didn't even look at me or the apartment we shared. Out the door he went. Out of my life he was forever.

Alone.

With this thing—his thing—still well and alive inside me.

***

I dreamed of clawed hooks and sexual abandon. Faces covered in leather masks and eyeliner so dark I could only see black. Here the monsters would come alive, but not the kind you have come to expect. I watched myself as if I were outside my own flesh, free from the imprisonment of bone and conscience. Swollen belly stretch-marked and ugly; my hair tethered and my skin vulnerable. Earthquake beats blared from the DJ booth as terrible looking bodies thrashed, moshed and convulsed.

Alone, so alone. Peter definitely gone, no more

tears left but the ones that were to come from agony. She was above me again, Dark Princess, raging beauty queen, and I was hers to control. The ultimate succession into human suspension. Like I'd already learned: the body is the final canvas. *There is no difference between love and pain. They are the same hopeless obsession.* The hooks dived, my legs opened and my back arched. Blood misted my face; pussy juice slicked my inner thigh as my water suddenly broke.

***

The next night I had to get to the club.

4 A.M. is a time that never lets me down; it knows why I have nightmares, and why I want to suspend myself above them. L train lunacies berated me once again, but this time I noticed the people as if under a different light. They were all rather sad, gaunt and bleary. Their faces were to be pitied and their hands kept shaking, their legs jittering for another quick fix. No matter how much the deranged governments of New York City have cleaned up the boroughs, they can't rid us of our flavor.

The Meatpacking District was scarily alive. Darkness laced with sizzling urban neon. Regret stitched up in the night like a black silk blanket. The High Line Park gloomed above me with trespassers and graffiti maestros. I was envious of their creative freedom, their passion, and their drive. They had to do what they were doing, had to create. There was just no other acceptable life than that.

I was inside fast, my memories of Peter fleeting and the ache within me about to be cast off. Stage left, stage right, it didn't matter. I passed the first check point with ease, as if they already knew the click of my heels, the way my protruding stomach curved through my lace cardigan. She found me, or I found her, and we didn't exchange any words, any warnings.

It was time.

Face up, legs open, and this time I'd be flying like Superman, but upside down. There were many hands, many faces, but no towels to wipe up the blood. A skilled piercer draws no blood to begin with. The first hook rushed through the clamped flesh of my vulva. The pain was sharp, hot, shivering all the way up to my womb like electricity. The next few hooks dived into the muscles between my breast and armpits, my upper thighs and finally my nipples and navel. I was a canvas of red, black and blue. I was suddenly able to fly.

All for the price of loving myself in losing Peter's fetus.

They began the hoist. Each tug on the rope was a war of my body against the universe, against gravity's pull, against the linear alignment of stars. My skin clutched hard to my bones, unwilling to let go; my muscles turned to liquid and my nervous system exploded. I was creating my own story high above the human landscape below me. I was the new reigning queen of body modification vignettes. The Dark Princess was me.

And then I saw Peter. He was crying, appalled and angry. His hair was frayed and his mouth was bleeding from biting his bottom lip. But I turned away from him. Physical pain is just a sensation, fleeting. It passes, even as your skin separates from your body, even as you fly high above the shimmering candyscape of strobe lights and swirling smoke. I knew so much about pain then. It hurt the most to see him sad, but I could not and would not know the pain of childbirth. I'll remain in this anti-hero pose forever, like meat hanging and waiting to dry, or until the hooks rip into my uterine cavity and carve it hollow.

The Reunion

JOAN DE LA HAYE

The wind howled over the small lake causing white horses to form on the surface. Frank had inherited the old house from his grandmother and turned it into a boutique hotel. The old lady was probably spinning in her grave at the idea of the local riff-raff sleeping in her bed, but the house was the perfect setting for honeymooners or couples on romantic getaways. The only problem was that when the cold weather rolled in, his love-struck guests rolled out.

He'd sunk all of his inheritance from his grandmother and his parents into fixing the house up so he could turn it into his dream—a five star boutique hotel. Unfortunately, the monthly expenses to keep it running exceeded the income from the hotel guests. His cooking wasn't good enough to make the restaurant a draw card for the Johannesburg culinary types or for the less picky Pretoria bunch.

The Magaliesburg was known for its B & B's and little hide-away restaurants. Most of them were close to the main access roads, but Frank's place was hidden and only accessible by dirt roads. Someone kept stealing the signs he put up on the main road, so his guests kept getting lost on their way to him and then decided to stay at one of the places they could find more easily. In short, the competition was stiff and Frank was broke. But he kept hoping that with just the right marketing strategy those honeymooners would start streaming in, even if the weather was cold and the roads crap.

As it was, his wife had just left him. Tracy hated the hospitality business and her feelings towards Frank were decidedly cold. He was now running the place on his own. The only help he had was Bettie, the maid he'd inherited with the house. She was eighty, and managed to make him feel like he was a naughty school boy who needed a smack every time he asked her to do something. He'd known Bettie his entire life. She'd practically raised him. It was Bettie who'd taught him to tie his shoelaces, not his mother. He'd learnt to speak Zulu before he'd learnt English. Bettie's grandson, Mpho, had been like his brother. Mpho had died of AIDS several years ago, and Frank still missed him. They should have been running the hotel together. Bettie would have liked that, his grandmother and parents on the other hand may not have felt the same way.

As he went through the house, closing the windows to guard against the unseasonal storm that was heading his way, a small, bashed up old Mini Cooper bounced along the drive towards the hotel. A young couple, who made no effort to keep their hands off each other, fell out of it in a giggling heap. They'd obviously had a few drinks. How they made it down the dirt road without crashing or how they'd managed not to get pulled over by the Johannesburg Metro cops was a mystery to him. He made his way to the front entrance to greet them, like any good hotelier should. After all, hospitality was the name of the game.

He stepped outside the front door and noticed the sky had turned that grey yellow colour that always seemed to precede a hailstorm. Winters in South Africa were supposed to be dry. Storms happened in summer, but lately the weather had been unpredictable and the storms were the worst he'd seen in twenty years. It looked like the latest one was going to be one for the record books. One of the wooden deck chairs that he'd forgotten to fold up and put in the storeroom rolled across the front lawn. The chair impersonated tumbleweed with remarkable aplomb. Its journey to the water was stopped by the canoe he'd pulled out of the water and turned over to resemble an elongated turtle. The house wasn't really equipped to withstand a bad storm, but that wasn't something he would put in the brochure. In anticipation, he'd stocked up on candles for the inevitable power failure. He needed a generator, but couldn't afford one, so paraffin lamps and candles were the best he could do, and that combination probably wasn't a good idea. He reminded himself that the house had been standing for a hundred years and would probably, with a little maintenance and some cash, be standing for a hundred more.

The couple clung to each other as they stumbled up the long gravel pathway towards the front door. A blast of wind tried to separate them, but only managed to make them crumble to the ground in a hysterical mass of laughter. A flash of lightning cracked the sky. The thunder clap was only a few seconds behind. The lightning strike was close by, a few kilometres away and getting closer judging by the rumble. The man got back up on unsteady legs. He looked to be in his late teens, early twenties. He'd probably only been shaving for a year or two. The girl was even younger—fresh out of high school and still wet behind the ears. He didn't envy either of them the hangover they were going to have in the morning, but he couldn't help but envy their youth and the happiness they shared in their drunken stupor. Had he ever been that young and that in love? He couldn't remember.

Something shimmered at the periphery of his vision. The hair at the back of his neck and on his arms bristled. He put it down to the electricity in the air created by the incoming storm, but a feeling in his gut made him look over his shoulder. In that instant he wished he could rewind those seconds and ignore his gut. Four men stood behind him. Their pale skin and blood shot eyes turned his stomach. Not to mention the assortment of knives, axes, and bloody machetes they carried. Fear and confusion tore at his brain. He blinked, hoping that they were simply a horrific mirage. When he opened his eyes the men were gone and he was still alive. He let go of the breath he'd been holding and thanked a god he'd never been sure he believed in, but saying a little prayer seemed appropriate. He chalked the ghostly vision up to his overactive imagination. There'd been a few grisly murders in the area over the last couple of years and no matter how much security he put up, sooner or later someone was bound to show up and try and take what was his.

The young man, who on closer inspection was little more than a boy, stood behind him holding up the girl. He had one of those ridiculous patches of beard on his chin and the girl had bleached her hair that silvery white blond that seemed to be the fashion with young girls. They both wore happy grins, which made him feel old. Frank wondered how they'd gotten up the pathway so quickly. Just a couple seconds prior, they'd been falling about laughing at their car. It should have taken them longer to make their way up the pathway. He'd only turned away for a split second, he was sure of it. He shrugged his confusion off and chalked that one up to being over tired.

Men's laughter came from inside the parlour. Those men *were* inside his house. They hadn't been a figment of his imagination. He tried to calm himself down. Panic would only get him killed. He'd last seen Bettie upstairs pretending to dust some of the bedroom furniture but he knew, from previous experience, that she'd probably dosed off on one of the beds. Bettie was a tough old bird who wouldn't have let anybody, who wasn't a paying guest, inside without a fight. He hoped she was still asleep and blissfully unaware that they had unwanted guests. His other, newly arrived, guests looked at him expectantly.

"Hey, bro," the boy-man slurred. "Can we have a room? We just got married."

"Look, now's not a good time," Frank said. He couldn't let the kids inside. He needed them to get help. Although he wasn't sure they were capable of doing much of anything in their condition.

"Sounds like there's a party going on," the boy ignored him and pushed past Frank, stumbling inside with his young bride hanging on his arm.

"Shit," Frank swore under his breath. He didn't want to die. He hadn't changed his will yet. Tracy would inherit the house and that would really piss him off. She'd probably sell the place off for a fortune and spend it on her new toy-boy. He took a deep breath, pulled his shoulders back and tried to control his bowls as he stepped inside the house to face his deadly guests. Perhaps he was wrong about his visitors. Perhaps they were simply there to have a good time. Perhaps their idea of a good time didn't include killing anybody. A man could hope.

The four men stood at the bar his great grandfather had built in the 1920s. Their weapons had been carelessly discarded on the polished mahogany surface and they'd each poured themselves a generous glass of Johnny Walker Red.

"I can still remember how that little boy squealed just before I stabbed him again and again. He only stopped squealing after the fifth time I stuck him like a pig," one of the men said, fingering a knife lying on the counter next to him. His hair looked like he'd put one of his fingers in an electrical socket and the bulge in his pants caused by his recollection was disturbing to say the least. Frank wanted to run away screaming, but he and his two young guests were transfixed.

"The boy probably sounded like you did when they fried your brain, Sparky. I always did enjoy a good electrocution, especially when a paedophile like you gets fried. They should never have gotten rid of the death penalty," the man with a face like an exploded melon said. "If I'd been on death row I would have lived longer and had a better last meal."

"I might have been fried, Pretty Boy, but at least I didn't get a beat down like a bitch in the prison yard."

"Fuck you! Those guys were a bunch of cowards and I took a few of them with me."

"Who are you calling a coward? I gave you that face," said the man with a missing eye.

"And I took your eye for your trouble. So I guess we're even, One-Eyed Jack."

"Not by a long shot. It took me a week to die from an infection thanks to your dirty finger nails. Do you know how crap it is to die in a prison hospital? My nurse was a horny inmate with a cock like a bull who thought it would be funny to rape me while I was in a coma. My arse still hurts. You and I will never be even."

"Do we have to go through this every year? For twenty years I've been listening to you idiots moan about the same shit. Can't we just kill a few people and enjoy our weekend without all the other crap?" asked a man with rope burn marks around his neck and blood shot eyes. There was something familiar about him. Frank was sure he'd seen his face before. A memory scratched at the edge of his brain.

"Speaking of victims," One-Eyed Jack said. "Slim pickings this year. You really picked a crap spot. I told you we should have gone to Knysna. There are tourists there all year round."

"You can choose any spot you like when it's your turn, but I had the pleasure of raping the slut who used to own this place upstairs in her bed. She was my first. I made her boyfriend watch before I slit his throat. She came to say goodbye at my execution with my kid on her hip. She smiled and made my son wave goodbye when they made me do the hangman's jig. This house has a special place in my heart," the man with the rope burn said as he looked around the room and nodded. "Good memories here."

Frank's grandmother had never spoken of what had happened to her when she was a girl, but he'd seen old newspaper clippings in the attic. That was why the man's face was familiar. He'd seen his face in those old clippings and it was his father's face. What had happened all those years ago was something nobody in the family ever talked about. No-one spoke about the fact that his grandmother never married or that his father had been born nine months after the rape. She'd kept her son when most women would have given him up for adoption. Sometimes he wondered if it wouldn't have been better for his father if she'd done that, though. Knowing that he'd been the product of rape and the offspring of a notorious serial killer had haunted his father all his life.

"And here's the fruit of my loins. He's a disappointing sight, isn't he?" the ghost of his serial killer grandfather said. "Must take after his mother's side of the family. Doesn't look a thing like me."

"Lucky for him," said One-Eyed Jack. "I thought this was supposed to be *our* reunion, not a family one."

"It's not a family reunion, just some unfinished business."

"What unfinished business?" Sparky asked.

"That's between the kid and me," his grandfather said as he put his empty whisky glass down and walked towards Frank with a panga in his hand. A bolt of lightning struck one of the trees outside the parlour window. The windows rattled from the blast. An orange glow emanated from the flames as they licked the dry tree branches. Frank hoped the rain would put out the blaze, he didn't foresee any fire fighting in his immediate future. As his grandfather walked towards him his future looked short and bloody. The girl screamed as One-eyed Jack pulled her towards him. The boy tried to punch Sparky's leering face, but his fist passed right through what should have been solid matter.

"Hey," Pretty Boy said. "Where's mine?"

"Up-stairs, asleep on the old slut's bed," Frank's grandfather said. "She's waiting just for you and she probably hasn't seen any action in the last twenty years."

Pretty Boy's laughter as he ran up the stairs to find Bettie stirred Frank's watery bowls.

"Just don't piss yourself," his grandfather said over the sound of Bettie's and the girl's screams. "Me and the boys get together every year and remember the good old days when we were alive and killing our way across this country. We have fun together, just like we used to," he said as he put his arm around Frank's shoulder. Frank got a whiff of old blood as his grandfather waved the panga under his nose. "Your grandmother was a slut and I should have killed her the night I put my seed in her belly. I should have come back when I found out she was having my bastard, but the cops stopped me before I could. I let your father live because he, at least, was a man. That little wife of his knew what would happen if she didn't respect him. He knew how to give her a good slap if she stepped out of line. But you, my boy, are a disappointment. Look at yourself. You're a disgrace."

Blood sprayed the curtains as One-Eyed Jack and Sparky sliced and diced the young couple. Bettie's screams came to an abrupt end followed by the sound of Pretty Boy's gurgled laughter. Frank watched as his grandfather brought the panga down on his neck. His own, short lived screams were accompanied by the sound of the rain and thunder.

"Don't worry, Son. That wife of yours won't live here for long. The boys and I'll pay her a visit next year on our way down to Knysna." His grandfather stared down at him as his blood pumped out of his severed artery. He drifted off to the sound of laughter, glasses clinking, and rolling thunder.

Devil's Night

TIM CURRAN

About three weeks after the gates of Hell opened and civilization went to its knees, pissing and shitting itself like a rheumy-eyed, loose-bowelled geriatric, Mick shared the secret. The very thing that would keep them alive and whole while the demons—or whatever in the Christ they were—laid waste to city after city, plucking humans from boarded houses and barricaded buildings like sweetmeats from tins.

"It's real simple," he told Bones Rickman, who had once tried to kill him in prison with a homemade knife. "Sacrifice. That's what it's all about. *Sacrifice.*"

"Sacrifice?"

"Sure, like in the old movies and stories. You know, like to the Devil and that shit. You give them sacrifice and they leave you alone. Then you're like a fucking high priest or something."

Bones wasn't buying it, not completely, but Mick knew he'd come around. Ever since they'd escaped from Brickhaven—or been set free, depending on your point-of-view—he'd been listening to what Mick said like he was some kind of sage and not a three-time loser who'd been sitting on a twenty-year stretch for narcotics trafficking. Mick had told him some real crazy shit and he accepted it, because, hey, it had worked out so far . . . but this? Sacrifice? Like an offering to the Devil?

Well, that was enough to give you the fucking creeps.

"I don't know," Bones said. "I've done some things in my life I'm not proud of, but I don't know about that shit. Christ, my old lady was a Catholic and all. Don't seem right."

"You'll get used to it."

Mick was still having sweaty godawful nightmares about the night that thing came to Brickhaven . . . the way all the cons and guards alike had screamed like they were being peeled with a dull knife. It went on for hours. Bones and he had been spared. He figured there were others that had been spared, too, but they had run off when the power grid went down and the cells were no longer locked. Regardless, when Bones and Mick discovered by first light that their respective cells were open, they slipped free.

Brickhaven had become a morgue . . . though maybe *crematorium* was more applicable because every last man behind those high gray walls had been reduced to a charred, blackened corpse. In the thin morning light, they were still smoldering. They looked like chicken wings burnt black that somebody had gnawed on and tossed aside. And that wasn't too far from the truth because something with really big teeth had bitten into most of them like it just wanted a taste.

Mick and Bones had been on the run ever since.

But whatever was out there wasn't done with them yet. It was hunting them, getting a little closer every day.

"Sacrifice," Mick said again, remembering the prison and those bodies, how they had split open from the heat like natural-casing wieners on a really hot fire . . . their bones hanging out. "It's the only way."

"I don't know. Like I said, my old lady was Catholic and all. Hell, I was an altar boy until they canned me for robbing the collection plates."

Mick had been a Catholic, too, but he didn't tell Bones about that. He didn't want to get into any of that shit about how he'd been a real good kid, bright-eyed and innocent, until Father Tomlinson had gotten hold of him. He had purged most of that from his mind. Sometimes, though, when he closed his eyes at night, he could see Father Tommy's toad-face and bulging eyes, feel his spongy, moist hand take hold of his own. The drool shining on his lips when he said, *"C'mon, Michael, walk to the rectory with me. I want to show you something. Something secret."*

"You want to go through that shit last night again?" Mick said to Bones. "You want to hide like a rat while that fucking thing hunts you down? You want that?"

Bones shook his head. It had been bad, real bad, and he had the white hairs to prove it. "So what do we gotta do?"

Mick smiled. That was his boy. He loved how he could work old Bones like warm clay in well-oiled fingers when he poured it on. That's one of the things that had kept him alive in Brickhaven. Mick hadn't been a particularly big, pumped-up animal like some of them, or a natural born killer that the others naturally left alone so they didn't get cut or bitten. No, but what he did have was smarts. Twisted, lopsided smarts for sure, but smarts all the same. He'd been like that ever since he was a kid, real sharp. Like a fucking tack. Those smarts bought him straight A's in school at Our Lady of Mercy. It wasn't until Father Tommy got a hold of him that those smarts were perverted into something else: an absolute cunning that was not shackled by anything so trifling as ethics or morality.

The Father had fixed that for him. Set him free.

"I wanna hear what we gotta do before I do it," Bones said.

So Mick told him.

***

The night the world ended was like any other at Brickhaven state pen. All the cons were standing inside their cells for the mandatory eight o'clock headcount before lights out. It took about thirty minutes. When it was done, the cells would be locked down for the night.

Mick's cellie, a hardcore strong-arm thief everyone called Wichita, was saying, "You coming with us or what? We're going tonight."

"I might sit this one out."

Wichita didn't like that. "I'm in the same cell as you, fuckhead. You stay behind, you'll rat me out."

"Never happen."

"Fuck it won't. Once they start sweating you, once they leave you down in the hole in the dark day after day . . . you'll rat. Seen tougher guys than you roll over." He got real quiet when the hack passed by, twirling his stick. "Listen, I want you to come with me. It has to be tonight. I got people leaning on my ass because they want something I promised 'em, only I ain't got it."

"I hear you."

"Tonight or not at all. If I wait, I'll be a dead man by the end of the week."

"Let me think," Mick told him.

"Well, think fast, motherfucker."

Mick knew how it worked; Wichita had talked about it enough. It was all arranged. Wichita, a Latin gangster named Loco, and a biker named Deadeye were going out. They had some medication that would make them vomit blood. It would buy them a quick trip to the infirmary where they had knives hidden. They'd take a guard hostage, get outside the walls where a car would be waiting for them a mile out in the woods. Then a helicopter at an abandoned airfield. A fishing boat to Mexico. They had it all clocked out. Twenty-four hours from start to finish. By the time the hogs knew what was up, they'd be in Mexico.

That was the plan and Mick wanted no part of it.

Then, around midnight, the prison started shaking. Hurricane-strength winds came out of nowhere and cons were shaken right out of their racks. The guards were running around, the lights flickering on and off. The cons were all screaming and shouting and it was absolute chaos. Mick and Wichita had a window at the back of their cell—barred, three-pane unbreakable Plexiglas, heavy iron screen over it—that looked down into the yard. Only they couldn't see the yard because it was a vortex of wind and debris and blowing grit. A dust storm had engulfed Brickhaven. It was howling and rumbling, but even through all that Mick heard something else . . . a screeching, squeaking sort of sound like a million bats crying out.

It got louder.

And louder.

Then the air got hot. Real hot.

The screaming of the cons became a banshee wail as whatever had come with the storm went cell block to cell block, murdering men, tearing them apart and incinerating what was left. The stink of burning flesh and hair filled the prison in a gagging, rolling smoke. Mick knew the smell. He knew it well. His first time in-stir, he'd been in the cell next door to a black drug dealer named Ray Ray Kong who had stiffed some Italians on a drug deal and was treated to a down-home barbecue: they threw gasoline through the bars of his cell, drenching him, then tossed a match in there. By the time the guards showed, he was burnt real bad and would die three days later in the infirmary.

Regardless, that was a smell you never forgot.

That night at Brickhaven, Mick smelled it . . . only a thousand times worse. The stink of human meat roasting on a spit. A sickening stench that put men to their knees. And cell block by cell block, that nameless thing that rode the hollows of the dust storm like plague on a dry wind came and harvested lives, reaping its human wheat by the hundreds and thousands.

Then it came down E Block.

Mick's block.

By then the lights were out and the heat was almost unbearable, like being downwind from the mouth of a smelting oven. A hot, boiling stink like burning sulfur and battery acid that was strong enough to ream your nose out came blowing down the corridor along with churning dust, human ash, and that howling wind. It was an absolute shitstorm of debris that put Mick and Wichita down on their knees.

The cons shrieked their minds away as it took them.

Mick heard that thing squeaking and squealing as it came, throwing a dirty yellow light that swam with grit and dust. He could barely see anything, but as he smelled the stink of the thing getting stronger and his lungs filled with a desert-dry heat, he thought he saw two cons across the way burst into flame like matchheads as some immense and undulant shadow reached through the bars for them.

Wichita saw it, too, because he turned back and looked at Mick in the yellow glow and his face looked like that of a seventy-year old man . . . furrowed and discolored, eyes glazed, the color sucked from his skin. Then the heat, that building black heat of funeral pyres filled the cell and Mick thought, *it's coming for you now and you're going to die in a way more horrible than anything you can imagine and you're going to scream, God how you're going to scream! Your hair will light up and your skin will blister and bubble. Your flesh will go to hot greasy tallow right before you flare-up and burn down to a blackened, flaking mummy . . . unless you do something.*

Unless you do something right now.

RIGHT . . . NOW.

He hadn't been thinking clearly, of course, but his instincts honed in one hardtime lock-up after another were sharp enough. When trouble started, when something threatened you, you lashed out. So, the hair on the back of his arms curling and crisping, he dug out his homemade knife and rammed the sharp end right into the side of Wichita's throat until the blood gushed out and went to steam in the air.

"TAKE HIM!" he shouted. "TAKE HIM! TAKE MY OFFERING AND LET ME LIVE OH DEAR SWEET CHRIST LET ME LIVE—"

And the thing had.

It took Wichita. In fact, when it was all over with and Mick was curled-up underneath the bunks that were bolted to the wall, wet with his own piss, scorched and sobbing and wild-eyed, he saw there was nothing left of old Wichie but a lot of gray ashes, some crusted-black rib bones, and a melted state-issue shoe with a knob of anklebone jutting from it. When he'd gotten up the nerve to crawl out from under the bunk, pieces of his cellmate had crunched under his step like charcoal.

But he was alive.

And so was another con judging by his whimpering.

***

A couple hours before sunset, Mick and Bones crept down 43rd Street until they got near the Church of the Holy Ascension down by the cab stand. It was creepy, all right. All those cars parked at the curb, nothing but skeletons in them. There were bones everywhere, too, most of them burned and well-gnawed by rats. All the trees and telephone poles looked like black sticks. There was a cab in the middle of the street. Its tires were melted, paint blistered down to the metal, the oxidized skeleton of its driver hanging out the window.

There was no doubt that the fire demon—or, as Mick began to call it, the *fire-eater*—had been through here with a vengeance. Yet, he knew for a fact that some had survived. Maybe not the ones that had lived here, but others. *Squatters.* Those that moved from neighborhood to neighborhood, trying to keep one step ahead of the beast.

Mick was amazed that they had avoided last night's purge.

All through the night there was the sound of screams, some distant and some not distant enough. Parts of the city were still burning and he could smell it on the breeze.

"So what now?" Bones said.

"Now we get us a lamb," Mick told him. "Then we make us an offering."

It still wasn't registering 100% with Bones, but that was okay. As long as he did what he was told, that's all that really mattered. Squatting down behind the blasted shell of a bus, Mick told him how it would work and Bones kept nodding the way he always nodded. How much was sinking in was anyone's guess.

"Got it?"

He nodded again. "Sure. Simple."

"Then go to it."

There was a group of kids living in the church. Mick had had his eye on them for awhile. No adults around, just the kids. Right then they were out in the churchyard off to the side. Regardless of the well-cooked carcass of the world around them, they were doing what kids did: hanging around, playing games, throwing balls around, the little ones picking leaves out of the grass. *Herd animals.* That's what Mick thought. Like on a nature documentary on TV, they looked like gazelles grazing on the veldt, not a care in the world. Good. He watched Bones sneak across the street like a lion moving in for the kill. He sidled along a few parked cars, crept up on the sidewalk . . . and charged.

The kids started screaming right away.

Mick got into position.

The kids had no cohesion in their group. They didn't stand together; they just ran in every which direction. One of them—the one Mick wanted—cut off to the side and sprinted down the alley with Bones on her tail. Perfect. Bones had separated her from the pack just like he was supposed to.

As she came bolting down the alley, Mick stepped out and reached for her. She froze, started to go back and saw Bones coming. She turned towards Mick, deciding he was the lesser of the two evils and that just showed how terribly naïve she was. She stood there, indecisively, breathing hard, her twelve-year old body tense and wiry, morphing into a fighting stance.

Well, I'll be fucking damned, Mick thought.

He stepped cautiously towards her because you just never knew with some of these kids. They'd been through a lot now and some of them could be pretty damn vicious. Especially when they were cornered like animals. Some of the meanest things in God's world came in very small packages. That was something he knew from doing time.

"Don't be scared," he said to her. "I ain't gonna hurt you. I just want to . . . want to—"

I want to show you something. Something secret.

"—want to ask you something, honey. That's all. Just relax, okay?"

But the kid wasn't relaxed. She stood there, breathing hard like she was trying to puff herself up like an adder getting ready to strike. Her greasy dark hair was hanging in her face, a bubble of snot expanding at her left nostril every time she exhaled. Mick didn't get too close because he was getting a bad feeling from her. He expected her to break down, crying and whimpering, but that wasn't happening.

Bones was coming up behind her, real slow, stalking in her direction.

Mick held his hands out so she could see how harmless he was . . . and that's when she pulled the knife. She let out a scream and came right at him like she not only planned on cutting him, but maybe skinning him when she was done.

She slashed out with the knife and the blade cut Mick across the back of the hand. He cried out and she made to slash again, but Bones took hold of her. He locked one arm around her throat and seized the wrist of her knife hand in the other, putting an immense amount of strength behind it as he twisted. There was a creaking sound like a green twig will make when you try to snap it and the girl cried out, dropping the knife.

The cut wasn't bad, but it pissed Mick off. "All right, you little cunt," he said. "All right."

He came at her and she tried to kick him. He grabbed her leg and punched her in the stomach. She went limp in Bones' arms and he let her fall to the ground. Mick jumped on top of her. He took hold of her head and smacked it against the concrete, realizing he was getting a hard-on. If Bones hadn't been there, he just might have—

"Okay, enough," Bones said.

"Yeah. Fucking little twat."

Mick grabbed her by the hair and dragged her down the alley like she was his cave-bride and, again, if Bones hadn't been there, that's exactly what she would have been.

***

Just up the block from the apartment they had taken over, they duct-taped the girl to a tree. By the time they were done, that little girl wasn't going anywhere. What disturbed Mick to no end was how oblivious she seemed to all of it. Bones held her to the tree and he taped her. The entire time, she did not speak, she did not fight; she just watched him wrap the tape around her until she was thoroughly cocooned.

"There," he said. "You ain't going nowhere."

She just stared at him. Fuck was with this kid? No fear? No apprehension? He knew he hadn't smacked her head off the concrete that hard, just enough to take the fight out of her. Yet . . . she was completely emotionless like some kind of mannequin.

"What do you think of that?" he asked her.

She just stared.

"You got a voice, you little bitch?"

She stared.

He was tempted to slap her across the mouth, but he knew that would just get Bones worked up. He was already having trouble with the whole thing and that might put him over the edge. So Mick played it cool, and just after sunset the fire-eater came.

The thing was, he *felt* it coming long before he saw the pyrotechnics. Both he and Bones started getting nervous. Some kind of low-level anxiety began to build in them and they started snapping at each other, getting on each other's nerves. For Mick, it was kind of like some cool electricity feeding up his spinal ganglia. It made the hairs at the back of his neck stand on end and his skin tingle with gooseflesh. His throat began to feel constricted as if the air had gone bad and he couldn't draw a single decent breath. His scalp began to feel tight and sweaty.

Then the wind came with a moaning, spooky sort of sound like it was blowing through a buried pipe. It became a wild howling tempest of flying dust and sand, dirt and debris, all of it spinning and spinning in the mother of all shitstorms. Mick went out into it because he knew he had to. Bones refused. He was scared white. He sat there gripping the arms of his chair, barely breathing, his eyes bulging from his sweaty face like ping pong balls. A sour, almost infected sort of smell came from him that reminded Mick of sick rooms.

Thoroughly pussified, that's what.

Outside, Mick had all he could do just to breathe and stay on his feet. He gripped a STOP sign not more than thirty feet from the girl and hung on for dear life, his ears filled with the shrill screeching/squeaking sound of the fire-eater. He felt the rising heat and saw the night lighting up with that weird yellow radiance that he had seen the first time at Brickhaven. It came right out of the storm, pulsating from its marrow and limning the world with a dirty amber sort of glow and throwing out spokes of lightning that crackled like static electricity. Of course, Mick couldn't see much of that because the wind was throwing a fine pulverized grit right into his face and he had to shade his eyes with his hand so he wasn't blinded.

But he did see the fire-eater, oh yes. It came snaking out of the storm like a river of ghost-fire, twisting and turning, pushing out a swirling vortex of steam before it. Right away, trees in the distance were catching on fire, glass shattering, rooftops blazing up like straw-dry haymows. The consuming heat was driving stragglers from their hiding places and they stumbled out into the streets, screaming and insane, right into the path of the fire-eater who gladly accepted them as offerings. They were sucked right into its hell-mouth like flaming hors d'oeuvres and Mick had seen enough of that monstrous, living oven by that point to know they would be spit out the other side, looking like melted, carbonized plastic.

The heat singeing his eyebrows and making his eyes feel like they were boiling in their sockets, he stared into the cremating black heart of the fire-eater and cried out: "HERE! HERE SHE IS! TAKE HER AS AN OFFERING! TAKE HER BODY AND SOUL AND LET ME LIVE OH PLEASE LET ME LIVE!"

That was about it for ceremony.

Mick ran shrieking to the apartment up the block, falling into the doorway and just avoiding the awful, searing suction of the fire-eater. He saw it take the girl. She started screaming about the time her hair caught on fire. Which was about the same time something like the coiling, fire-blackened tongue of a burning witch reached out for her. She didn't get drawn into the hell-mouth like the others. Not in one piece anyway. The duct-tape held her fast in a bubbling, gooey plastic embrace to the tree and she superheated, melting like a marshmallow dropped into a fire pit . . . sizzling and popping, splitting open and flaking apart into a whirlwind of human ash.

After she was vacuumed into the thing, Mick caught a glimpse of it . . . just for a second. In the revolving tornadic storm-kiln, he saw a smoldering black shape spreading wings like those of a gargoyle above the rooftops of the city. It stood there in the pulsating glow and funneling smoke for just a second, standing on what looked like a thousand branching legs. It let out a screeching, creaking cry like a million rusty hinges, then it dissolved into the firestorm and was no more.

Half out of his mind and wet with his own piss, Mick crawled up the stairs on his hands and knees. By the time he got through the door, he was hysterical and raving. The only thing he said that made any sense to Bones was, "That girl . . . *hoo-boy* . . . she's one crispy critter."

***

That night, the grass was green and the living was free, as Mick's old man used to say. They were safe and the fire-eater was happy, its belly full. It was good to stretch out and not worry about what might be coming in the night. Bones was having trouble with his conscience of all things, but Mick knew he'd get over it. Mick had been like that himself his first time in the joint. He saw things there that turned his stomach and left the indelible impression on him that human beings were nothing but animals scratching in the dirt.

As he told Bones after he had a bath to cool his scalded skin, "Quit thinking of them as people. Think of our offerings as . . . *cattle*. If you don't slaughter the cattle then you ain't got no meat and if we don't offer a few tender morsels to our pal then we won't be alive long. Simple."

This was real world logic in his way of thinking and completely applicable to the matter at hand. Bones just nodded, which was about all he was good for outside of the deadhead strong-arm stuff.

He didn't want to know about anything that happened down there, so Mick told him in gruesome detail what it had been like. Poor Bones. Tough criminal, hardcase con . . . he threw up. He ran over to the sink and ejected his stomach contents while Mick laughed at him. It went on for five, ten minutes, the constant gagging and spewing. It wasn't so much like he was getting rid of what was in his stomach as purging something far worse deep inside.

None of it bothered Mick.

Hell, he was alive and he knew exactly what to do to stay that way. Maybe it was ugly business—Jesus, was it ever—but once you purged your conscience and trifling things like morality and ethics, it was really only a matter of survival of the fittest, pure Darwinism. And Mick knew all about that. It was a basic tenet of nature and he had practiced it most of his life.

So while Bones moaned and groaned, Mick embraced the fact that he was still alive. He ate canned beans and spaghetti, topped it off with some Vienna wieners and cream cakes. He enjoyed every mouthful. Relishing them, delighting in the simple sensation of swallowing and filling his belly.

Life was good.

***

As he drifted off that night, the memory he fought so hard to suppress came to him, and he was at Our Lady of Mercy. Father Tommy kept him after class to wash the blackboard because it was his turn. Father Tommy, as he was known, always made the boys stay after to do it because he said it was "dirty drudgery unfit for ladies". At the time, of course, Mick hadn't realized the significance of that. It wasn't until later that it all began to make sense to him. That day he was chosen he *knew* he was going to be the one to stay after because Father Tommy kept staring at him with a peculiar twinkle in his eye.

When he finished up with the blackboard, he asked if there was anything else he could do and old Father Tommy smiled. His lips were pink and glistening like the entrails of a hog, his teeth very sharp behind his narrow grin. "Oh yes, my boy. There's something you can do. Most certainly there is." He stood up and put one flabby hand on Mick's shoulder, still grinning. Later, that's all Mick would remember . . . the feel of that hand like a blob of warm dough and Father Tommy's grin of teeth like the jaws of a shark coming out of the depths.

"C'mon, Michael, walk to the rectory with me, my boy. I want to show you something. Something secret."

And at the sound of his voice, something had tightened in Mick like a screw. He heard his own voice in his head. It seemed to be calling to him out of the darkness, sad and alone, *Oh no, Father Tommy, I'd rather not do that. I'd rather not go there and see your secret. I don't want to know about it.*

But, of course, he'd gone.

In the rectory, the Father had been breathing very hard, practically panting, and it had little to do with the exertion of the walk itself. His Adam's Apple kept bobbing up and down as if there was something distasteful in his throat he could not swallow down.

There were tears in his eyes. When Mick asked him what it was he wanted to show him, Father Tommy could not seem to speak. He made a strangled, gurgling sort of sound like his mouth was full of something and indeed it was: saliva. Drool coursed over his shiny pink lips. An unbroken strand of it hung from his chin, dripping down to his Roman collar and finding the gold watch chain of his crow-black coat. Mick remembered being amazed by that string of spit. It looked like spider-silk.

When the violation began, there was pain but there was something far worse than that. The pain was only an insult to his nerve endings, but the real damage, the real tragedy and trauma occurred deep inside of him. Something at his core was drawn into itself, it closed up like an exotic hothouse orchid in a January draft and he knew it would never open again, never bloom in the sunlight.

"Not so bad," Father Tommy had said, his hot breath against the back of Mick's neck smelling oddly like warm, rising yeast. "Not such a bad thing at all."

When it was over and Father Tommy was praying with his pants around his ankles, insisting that Mick pray with him, he knew the priest had taken something necessary from him much as, perhaps, it was once taken from him.

***

Over the next three weeks, they did four more. The fire-eater seemed perfectly happy with one a week and the fourth was sort of a bonus. *Like dessert,* Mick told Bones who, by that point, was barely even speaking anymore, the guilt of what he was doing to stay alive and *unpicked* (as Mick liked to put it) taking a horrendous toll upon him both physically and mentally and perhaps even spiritually.

It was never a good thing making offerings to the fire-eater, but sometimes it was worse than others. The fourth one—dessert—had been particularly bad for Bones because for some crazy, masochistic reason he had decided he wanted to see it happen. Mick told him he wouldn't like it. In fact, he promised him it would make him feel sick and black inside, but Bones insisted. Maybe his self-loathing could not be complete without a little voyeurism.

The sacrifice was a woman with a particularly large, unpleasant wart on her chin like some cauldron-stirring witch from a storybook. They pulled her out from under a porch where she had been singing psalms. She was filthy. Lice were hopping in her hair. She screamed and fought . . . then she just broke down into laughter. In fact, she wouldn't stop laughing until Mick cuffed her a few times.

They tied her to a fire hydrant and duct-taped her mouth shut.

Just after dark, the fire-eater came for her. It was the same as always: the dust storm, the wind, the pulsing glow, and that squeaking, shrilling sound of hundreds of bats or locusts. The woman wasn't laughing by then. Even with the tape over her mouth, they heard her scream.

When her hair lit on fire, Bones screamed himself.

By then, the phantasmal form of the fire-eater was crawling out of the storm, worming itself free like a corpse-worm from an eye socket. As usual, with the heat and flickering light and whipping wind, Mick saw very little of it. But what he did see was electroplated onto his mind: *eyes*. Two huge sinister red eyes that looked to be about the size of tractor tires.

The woman was burning by then.

She was jumping and contorting, fighting against the ropes that held her which, of course, were also burning. The duct-tape at her mouth seemed to melt right into her face like a blood blister and steam rolled off her in stinking white plumes.

It wasn't until later that Mick realized that what he saw was probably her blood boiling away.

For two days after that, Bones would not even speak. Mick had warned him that it wasn't a good thing to see, that the images had a way of replaying every time you shut your eyes... but Bones had insisted and the reality of it had devastated him just as the memories picked at his bones like buzzards. He was used up, drained like a fucking battery.

"We can't do that again," he said when he finally managed to speak.

Mick just smiled at the absurdity of such a statement.

***

Because they *had* to do it again.

They snatched another kid and this one—a boy— barely even fought. They caught him off by himself, kicking a can along the curb just off 43rd. When he saw them coming, he did not run. He just waited there for them to take him and take him they did. The blank indifference in his eyes was more than a little shocking. He had no weapons on him and when Bones led him away with one sweaty, trembling fist gripping the boy's wrist, the kid said, "You're the ones, aren't you? The ones that sacrifice people? I heard about you. I heard all about you."

Bones made a choking sound in his throat.

Mick sneered at the kid as he used to sneer at men in prison who frightened him. "And what if we are? Kid like you, you were asking to get snatched. Hell, you didn't even run. It was like you wanted this."

The kid just looked at him with empty eyes. "I'm not afraid," he said. "Not like *you*."

Mick laughed with a high, wheezing sort of sound like air bleeding from a leaky balloon. "Oh, trust me, you'll be afraid. You'll be *really* afraid."

"I'm more afraid to live than to die."

And whatever Mick was going to say to him died right there on his lips. He recognized a certain wisdom in those words, but he wasn't about to admit the same. No way in hell he was going to glom philosophy from a fucking kid. He wasn't afraid. Hell, no . . . he was *mighty,* he was *invincible* . . . but he sure as hell wasn't afraid. Nothing scared him, nothing.

I want to show you something. Something secret.

There was no true way to know when the fire-eater might show, but Mick often got a funny feeling in his gut the morning before. Just as he did when they grabbed the boy. It was a clear, warm day, but inside him he was feeling a definite storm warning. He began to feel the tension and Bones was feeling it, too. By sundown, they were getting under each other's skin once again. Bones kept staring at him with accusing eyes and Mick just gave it back to him with looks of utter contempt.

Then, as darkness shrouded the streets, Mick heard a voice in his head say, *it's coming. It's on its way so you better get ready.*

When he went downstairs and out to the street

where the kid was duct-taped to a STOP sign, Bones insisted on tagging along. Mick didn't like it, but there was no way he could stop him. No way at all.

It came in the usual way and Mick's guts flipped over on themselves as the world turned inside out and was laid raw. The darkness seemed to churn upon itself in a vortexual cyclone of ever-increasing wrath and heat and energy. Then the dust storm came, blowing out of the guts of the vortex with hurricane winds peppered with bone grit, human ash, and flying debris. The squeaking/creaking sound was next and then through squinted eyes, Mick saw something like an animate, walking tornado, a Biblical pillar of fire and smoke striding out of the unearthly hell-storm itself.

In his mind, it was a particulated blizzard of millions, *billions* of specks of dark matter forming into a single diabolic shape . . . a rushing, smoldering shadow, a night-winged form reaching out with red-hot talons to seize and incinerate the offering.

About the time that Mick was ready to cry out for it to take its offering, Bones snapped. He went running right at the thing . . . though, with the wind blowing out of it hot and jetting, it was more like a slow forward jog as he leaned into it.

"TAKE ME! TAKE ME! TAKE ME!" he shouted with volume, but the deafening noise of the thing reduced his voice to a plaintive, broken cry. "I'M THE ONE YOU WANT!"

There wasn't a damn thing Mick could do.

He just clung to the railing of the steps as the fire-eater came for Bones. An immense paralyzing fear overtook him as he watched it take Bones *and* the kid.

He didn't see what happened to the kid really, but Bones . . . he was pulled off his feet and seconds before he would have made contact with the thing, the incredible cremating heat of it split him open and everything inside him was sucked into the fire-eater in a burning, smoking tangle. The STOP sign the kid had been duct-taped to was bent nearly to the ground and was guttering with flame like a birthday candle.

That's when Mick himself screamed.

It had taken its offerings, but it wanted more. Bones and the kid were just appetizers to whet its hunger. What it *really* wanted was Mick, because he was swollen black with sin like a juicy plum and the beast hungered for him.

He saw it coming for him: a crooked, cyclopean shape that towered over the buildings, a living inferno, a hissing and crackling fire demon bearing down on him like an engine of lunatic hatred. It had two red fireballs for eyes, blue chain lightning forking from its mouth, and curling charred talons hot as branding irons.

His bladder letting go, Mick ran.

He knew he wouldn't be safe in the apartment building. In fact, he didn't think he'd be safe anywhere from that burning horror. So he ran blindly, all the while feeling the almost magnetic pull of the fire-eater. It would have him. He knew it would have him. It would be satisfied with nothing less.

Then he saw the place where they had snatched the girl that day: the Church of the Holy Ascension. Of course! Of course! It was a demon and demons couldn't come into holy places and maybe that was why the kids had been living there in the first place.

He raced up the steps and pulled the huge double doors open. It took everything he had to get them closed again in that howling wind of bone ash. But he did. He raced down the aisle, past the pulpit and altar. There was a little door back there and he knew it must lead to the rectory if it was like the churches he had known as a child.

He went through it, his breath barely coming.

He heard the doors blow off the church and a whirlwind of heat enter the holy place, pews exploding into flaming kindling, the pages of prayer books falling earthward like burning leaves. The church was not stopping it; it had no fear of the place. The entire building was shaking, the walls cracking open and ancient wood splitting with reports loud as pistol shots. The beams overhead groaned. The stained glass windows blew out in eruptions of fire.

Mick saw the knob of the rectory door turn bright red until it melted to the floor. The old panels split lengthwise. He went down on his hands and knees, praying feverishly for divine intervention much as he had prayed that day with Father Tommy. He felt the heat at his back. He felt the hairs on his head singe. He smelled smoke and charred meat, the sulfury stink of burnt matches as the thing came up behind him.

In a voice very like Father Tommy's, it said, "I want to show you something. Something secret."

Mick did not dare turn around. He could not look it in the face. The cremated stink of it was enough, more than enough. He crouched there, his back blistering from the heat, tendrils of steam rising from his hair. Droplets of sour-smelling sweat ran down his face, smelling as dark as the sin that infected his soul.

Two hands grabbed his shoulders, the fingers scalding him through his shirt. Hysterically, he continued to pray, only crying out as a burning lance entered him from behind, driving up high and deep inside of him with immeasurable agony. The good thing was, it didn't last long. Because as it burned into him like a red-hot poker, his hair blazed up and his skin blistered, his eyes steaming in their sockets and splashing down his face in rivers of molten lava.

But by then, his brain was a bubbling gray pudding and he didn't feel anything save the screaming descent into the void.

The Fine Art of Wrecking

JENNIFER LORING

A **fog** **rolled** in off the Atlantic, smothering the beach in a downright frigid shroud. Sometimes, if you thought too hard about it, it felt like God's judgment, pitiless and absolute. But this wasn't a job for thinkers or moralizers. This is what you did when God left you no choice. When God was just a half-remembered rumor.

There were no churches in Attewater.

Jack smelled a storm coming behind the fog. The ship from Florida was due anytime now, but further down shore by the port and lighthouse. He crouched on the treacherous rocks and held up the lantern that a captain might easily mistake, in this miasma, for a beacon. It could become a very sunny day after all, if this wreck proved better than the last.

Recent rains made the beach slippery, and one new to the job or simply careless could easily break a bone or several; nothing Jack hadn't seen a thousand times. Christopher, on the other hand, was just a kid, measuring each step as if it would be his last.

"Don't you get worried?" Christopher asked.

"About what?"

"You know . . . the stories."

Most wreckers, by the time they reached Christopher's age, already knew the sacrifice expected of them, if not the hour of its arrival. But that was his family's business to tell him, and none of Jack's. "Just stories, is all. I've spent most of my life out here. Look like it ever happened to me?" Jack spat a gob of tobacco on the mossy stones. "What'd you take this job for if you're so scared?"

"I ain't." Christopher pouted and white-knuckled his crowbar. It was the only tool a good wrecker ever needed.

"Remember, soon as you see the crew—"

"Yeah, I remember."

"Good. Look at it this way, kid. You're supporting your family, right? Doing what your poppa did for you until he died."

"I guess so." Christopher's gaze never strayed from the misty horizon, where the water and the sky melted into a sheet of solid gray slate. "But so are those men."

"Those men got what we need. We don't take it, we all die."

Christopher said nothing, but his eyes spoke volumes. Kid like this didn't belong out here. Didn't have the stones for the messier inevitabilities of the job.

Jack had never been difficult to convince. He'd been a young husband with few skills and no money. Love alone wasn't going to buy Lizzie pearls, or keep little Sarah's belly full. A man had to do whatever it took to provide for his family, and Lizzie was none the worse for knowing his vocation. Hell, if Sarah had been a boy, he'd have taught her the fine art of wrecking, too. Still might. She didn't have her momma's fine features, and with her hair in a cap, she looked well enough like a boy. Wouldn't hurt her any to help out the family. Jack did the same for his momma and siblings, just like his three older brothers and Poppa.

God bless his poppa, swept out to sea when a storm blew up during a wreck. It was his time, and the ocean claimed him at last. He had already begun to change by then. The last time Jack shook his hand, the webbing between Poppa's fingers had expanded, grown translucent. No wrecker's body ever drifted back to shore, and so at each funeral the people of Attewater paid homage to a floral wreath embracing a painted portrait of that day's nautical hero. A fine and brave man Poppa was, taught Jack everything he knew. But the sea, a hungry and merciless lover, replenished what men took from Her with their dead bones. A white garden beneath the waves, where fish frolicked amongst rib cages and skulls. Every family on the coast owed their lives to Her, no matter how many of their men She devoured, and they continued to accept this Faustian bargain as long as She kept making them rich.

The hull of a ship broke through the haze. Jack held the lantern as high as he could, his other hand gripping the crowbar.

"Get ready, Christopher."

The boy nodded as the ship drifted toward the shallows. "She's running aground!" the captain shouted, too late. Rocks champed into the wood, splintering planks and tearing a hole into the vessel. Jack and Christopher ducked behind a large outcropping of rock, and Jack put out the light. The crew jumped from the deck onto the beach to inspect the damage.

"I saw the damned light with my own eyes," said the captain, and kicked the battered hull. "Someone's screwin' with us."

"I think it's a bad sign, Captain."

"Now," Jack whispered. He and Christopher leapt from their hiding place onto the beach. His crowbar connected with a crewman's head; blood flowered onto the man's blue knit cap, and he crumpled like a wad of used paper. "Get the other two!" he shouted. "I'll get the captain!"

Christopher vanished into the haze. Jack turned his attention to the captain, who had begun to climb the rocks in an escape attempt. He grabbed the man's leather boot and yanked him back down as the captain's hands scrambled to find purchase on the slick rocks. His free foot desperately tried to connect with Jack's head. Jack slammed the crowbar into his spine. He jerked and howled in pain, reaching a hand up toward the heavens for mercy he would not find. Jack struck the base of his skull and let him slide down to the beach, where he twitched and gasped and finally was still.

Christopher beat one of the men until blood sputtered up out of his mouth. The man collapsed onto his back and began to choke on it. The other crawled toward the water, seeking a kinder death, perhaps, than the one promised on shore. He would find no such thing, for the vast and unknowable sea did not deal in compassion. Christopher crippled him with two blows, one strike to the back of each knee, and left him to drown in the foam-tipped shallows.

"Good work, kid. You got it in you after all. Now let's check this wreck out and see what we take home today." Jack led the way up the rope ladder on the side of the ship to the deck. Wind-driven mist battered their faces like pellets of ice, and the sails flapped with a ferocious intensity.

"Better hurry," Jack said. "Weather's really starting to turn. Get down into the hold and let's see what they were carrying."

Christopher moved to the center of the ship and bashed the lock with his crowbar until the door to the hold swung open. Jack gazed into the pitch darkness at the bottom of the steps. He'd left his lantern on the beach.

"Christopher, you see a light anywhere?"

"I think there's one over here." He grabbed at something hanging from the wall that to Jack's eyes resembled a lantern. "Hope there's oil in it." He turned it on, and a pale yellow glow illuminated the stairs.

"Perfect. Go on. I see crates down there."

Christopher hurried down the stairs with Jack close behind. He had a good feeling about the wreck. After all these years, he could practically smell gold the same way he could smell a change in the weather. When they had pried the crates apart and Jack peered inside, the glimmer of jewels danced in the lamplight.

"Lucky first day for you, kid. Grab everything you can. Put it in your pockets, in your hat, in your boots. Hell, in your ass, for all I care. Wherever you can. Your momma's gonna be proud of you tonight."

Christopher smiled for the first time that day as he crammed necklaces and earrings into every available space his clothing allowed. Pearls, gemstones, and beautiful shimmering gold bulged from Jack's pockets. It was the best wreck he'd had in months. He could finally buy Lizzie that dress she'd had her eye on and take her to the society ball clothed like the good woman she was. Wrecking wasn't honest work by any means, but it was profitable, and he didn't know a man worth a damn who wouldn't kill for the sake of his family.

"Come on, let's get back up there. We have to get the bodies into the water."

Storm clouds cast an ominous shadow over the beach. Jack and Christopher rolled the sailors to the edge of the water and kicked them in, their offering to the sea for Her delivery of treasure. The wreck looked like a perfect accident now, a victim of the impending gale. Others would come for the ship itself and hack it up for firewood. It was simply the way of life out here, where too many hard winters and illnesses that devastated entire families had hardened them into creatures of opportunity.

The skies finally burst open. Rain hammered the beach, sluicing away the sand and the blood left behind by men destined to become part of the ocean's perpetually growing garden.

"Get some rest," Jack called to Christopher as they climbed up the rocks and started back on the muddy road leading to town. "I'll need you at your best again soon."

Christopher nodded and, pulling his cap down, ran toward his house with a heavy jangling step, strands of pearls flapping at his sides.

***

A wan and fog-drenched sunset bled over the horizon

and into the water. Jack and Christopher stood a mile further up shore than they had a couple of weeks earlier, as Jack held aloft the lantern that guaranteed them a vessel of one sort or another. He knew better than to expect a repeat of the last wreck, but a ship with even a quarter of that cargo would please him just as well.

The weather had been fairly calm since the storm that eroded part of the beach, but Jack again felt that strange sense of cosmic contempt, though he was not one given to ruminations of a philosophical nature. He already knew the universe cared nothing for him or any other man. It carried on with or without them. Sometimes you saw blood on your hands, on your clothes. You heard the voices of the dead in your dreams. It would drive you crazy if you let it. The trick, of course, was to take on a soldier's mindset. To view them not as human at all, but as mortal enemies. Maybe he couldn't wreck forever, but guilt had nothing to do with it.

Today the waves broke with unsettling force against the shore, spraying flecks of foam into the bitter air. The sea churned as if boiled by a hellish heat, whipped by winds verging on Nor'easter violence. Where the swells struck land, they left a crimson stain. A trick of the dying sunlight, or reminders that no matter how inclement the conditions Her servants endured, the sea thirsted. Further out, where the seabed dropped off and riptides swallowed at least one swimmer every summer—always a tourist; the locals knew better than to tempt fate—sparkling blue stars glowed in the water. It usually happened after a ship had passed and stirred up Gods knew what in the depths. Disturbing Her garden, maybe. Or perhaps She sent Her shiny and slippery progenies to keep watch over those with whom She shared Her abundance, their gelid and unblinking eyes fixed upon the shore.

Jack rubbed the mist out of his eyes. He saw no ship, not even the ghost of one on the horizon. Yet two sailors waded through the water and marched onto the shore, their clothes tattered and sullied with blood. Kelp coiled around their bodies like serpents, and fat, flesh-colored worms writhed atop their smooth skulls. The spasmodically palpitating gills at their necks gasped for water. The lantern slipped from Jack's hand, shattered, and sputtered out. So soon.

Christopher, behind him, scrabbled up the rocks like a rat and screamed, "I told ya, Jack, I told ya!" until he reached the safety of the road. Jack turned to follow, but the sailors locked their dead-fish arms around his and dragged him backwards toward the sea. Jack's flailing legs did nothing to deter them as the beach receded. He bucked, he twisted, and still the men held fast. It was merely instinct to fight them; in truth, there was nothing to fight. He and all the others were promised to Her generations before his birth.

His arms grew numb from the pressure. The crowbar thunked onto the sand as glacial marine air burrowed into his marrow. Christopher could run, but he'd be pronounced mad by morning. He'd never return to the ocean, even if his family had to starve. And they, along with the entire village, would do just that. She'd send no more ships or fish for them to eat; She'd turn the weather so that the tourists stopped coming, what few hadn't already once they saw that no churches existed in Attewater, once they heard the dark shapes chanting on the beach to their Mother and Father. She would have Her sacrifice, Her soldier, Her wrecker, for all that She had given of Herself. And if he would not go willingly, then his family would give him to Her.

The frothy water soaked into his boots, his pants, through his coat and into his shirt. The men passed through it as if it possessed no more substance than the fog and hauled him onward. Jack thrust his head back to keep his nose above water. He wished he'd brought Sarah out here, even once. He had no sons to carry on the tradition, and what would Lizzie do without him? Would she tell Sarah of her father's work, would she tell the little girl, "It's up to you now", and send her into the fog? She was so young yet. She didn't know. She didn't understand that he would live forever in a great city beneath the sea, where Mother bided her time and nurtured an army.

He managed to suck in one more breath before pain crushed his lungs into uselessness. As he sank, seaweed or the suckered appendages of abysmal things tugged him down, and the phantom sailors faded away into the ineffable nothingness. He drew in a mouthful of water, pulled the sides of his throat together, and forced the water through the gill slits that had opened on his neck. Jack wondered if Poppa awaited him somewhere in the gloom of the vindictive sea. And he wondered if Poppa would be proud.

Saint Patty's Night at The Crown

BLAZE MCROB

St. Patty's night t'was at the Crown,
And no ones' face did have a frown.

Green beer into pitchers flowin',
Luscious women charms a showin'.

Revelry was high and mighty,
Passions rose and sex was flighty.

And in the basement was a place,
Where men and women could embrace.

Twas' many rooms with each a bed,
A perfect place to lay one's head.

Into the night the scent did rise,
As lovers uttered their sweet cries.

Midst' the glory of orgasms,
A little man had fits and spasms.

Blaze McRob

He lived behind the wall so near,
In tunnel dark he had no fear.

For he could come and he could go,
His presence not would have to show.

A leprechaun so small was he,
Indeed his size was hard to see.

But now the joy these people feel,
He knew for fact he had to steal.

And so he slipped out through a door,
With axe in hand he crept on floor.

In each and ev'ry room he came,
And took them into his new game.

His axe he reared above his head,
Before the men their brains did shred.

The bodies he would shove aside,
Then on their ladies jump astride.

As soon as he had had his fun,
His axe would fall and she was done.

In ev'ry room the scene replayed,
Their guts and organs all were splayed.

He took his axe and went upstairs,
Relieved the patrons of their cares.

Saint Patty's Night at The Crown

Before that fateful night was done,
Where had been many now was none.

Past cut up bodies he did go,
Back to the tunnel with a glow.

His lack of stature mattered not,
He had to do what was his lot.

So now he went back to his nest,
Prepared to get some needed rest.

A warning now to one and all,
St. Patty's Day is not a ball.

In to the Crown you should not go,
The fear of Leprechaun to show.

For ev'ry year he will arrive,
And many will not leave alive.

O'Halloran's

JOHN PAUL ALLEN

Fuckin' rain, **Tom** Johnson thought, entering the lobby of Northeast Memorial. He stomped his feet on the extra mat, placed to prevent the less careful from slipping. The registration desk clock read 7:58pm. *Two minutes.*

"Let me in," Tom said, waving the damp clinic admission form at the woman behind the glass. She half smiled and pushed the button. In sync with the buzz, he opened the door then followed the map on the pamphlet. Three turns and he reached the room. Without knocking he entered, moved across the floor, and took her hand. "Babe, let's talk."

"Perfect timing," Helen said. A white sheet draped her legs. Her socked feet dangled, as the stirrups were folded down. "Second thoughts? Too late. At least this gives you something to write about. It's all material, right?"

"It's eight o'clock now," Tom said. He glanced in the mirror over the sink and noticed a bruise below his hairline. The moment wasn't right for explaining. "They couldn't have done it already."

"Surprise, someone canceled."

"Hey, I tried . . . " Tom said.

"Please, no pitch," Helen said. "It's over. We killed our baby. We killed our daughter."

It was silent. Conversations were few since Helen had told him the news. She thought it was time for a wedding and kids. He disagreed. A legal commitment wasn't the problem. Tom compared an added mouth to jamming a stick in bicycle spokes. He told her things worked so well for them because they stuck to their plan. "We moved in together, got degrees, found teaching jobs, and we're building financial security," he'd said. "Now I can concentrate on my writing."

For Tom, until the pregnancy their life was ideal. Helen was the best partner he'd ever had and when needed she gave him space. She understood at times his craft took precedence. During their final year at Vanderbilt, a small publisher released four of his stories as eBooks and he now sought a taker for a novella. More shorts and a novel would follow. The goal was to build a readership. "Three or four books puts gas in our car. Twenty pays for graduate school," he'd told her. Late night feedings, dirty diapers and constant crying ruined everything. He also believed she'd missed a pill on purpose. The way she acted around women with small children gave her away, and until minutes before returning to the hospital he believed the abortion was fair.

"Ms. Shaver, how are you doing?" The silence broke as the doctor entered the room. Tom noticed no name tag and thought it intentional. "I'm afraid you'll have to leave, Mr. Johnson. She'll be in recovery at least another forty-five minutes. After that you can take her home."

"Leave?" Tom asked, "but I'm . . . "

"It says here you're a friend," the doctor said, reading the form. "There's fresh coffee in the cafeteria."

Tom checked the time again. "It's 8:15. I'll be back in an hour." He touched Helen's hand, hoping she'd speak. She didn't. "I'm gonna get some."

"Of course," Helen said, avoiding eye contact. "I wanted to call her Katelynn, after my sister."

"Maybe the cancelation was a sign of what was meant to be," Tom said. "You know I want a family . . . someday." He released her hand and walked out of the room. As the door shut his defensive mode kicked in. *I'm not the bad guy,* he thought walking toward the cafeteria. *It wasn't my fault someone canceled. Hell, I told her I wasn't ready, but she got knocked up anyway.* By the time he reached the vending machine his guilt subsided and the desire for coffee morphed to something stronger.

Tom looked at his phone and decided finding a nearby bar was a good move. He could down a couple of drinks and hurry back without Helen knowing. It would give him time to think about what he'd say to help them move on. He stopped at the security station to ask if there was any place near the hospital, but found it empty. *There's got to be a bar around here,* he thought. *No one drinks more than doctors and nurses.*

Tom headed out the door to the parking garage. There were six levels, and his Eclipse waited on the top floor. Though lower level spaces were available he knew the top one never filled and he didn't like parking next to other cars. The inconvenience led to fewer scratches. Reaching the elevator he found it out of order, so he took the stairs. It was when he got within eyesight of his vehicle and reached into his jacket pocket for his key that he heard the voice.

"Hey bro, there's a water hole a few blocks from here," he said.

Tom approached the garage custodian and read 'Hector', stenciled over his uniform pocket just above the hospital logo. "Excuse me?" he said.

"O'Halloran's," Hector said. He continued talking as he moved to the front of Tom's car to pick up trash, "good place to regroup the soul . . . just a few blocks off the main drag." Tossing the litter into the container he lifted a spray bottle from a shelf on his cart and released the contents into the air.

"Jesus, you could tell me to move first," Tom said, waving at the mist as he backed up, "and what do you know about me?"

"Sorry bro, I'm just here to clean up the mess. You'd think by now this would get easier," Hector said. "I'm here to get you to reflect." He pointed at the pamphlet Tom still held and continued toward the down ramp.

Reflect, Tom thought, turning toward his car. As he unlocked the door, the rain started again. He inserted the key, turned it, and groaned when the engine wouldn't crank. "Shit." He put the keys back in his pocket and decided to walk. As soon as he got off the hospital property, the clouds opened up and he was quickly getting soaked. Looking back toward the hospital, he thought maybe coffee made more sense. Then he noticed the flashing letters coming from the side street. As he got closer he read: O'Halloran's.

"Thank you, Jesus," Tom said. He could tell that the place had been there for some time, and looking at the pamphlet he still held wondered how many others Hector had sent this way. *I'm sure the abortion dad isn't that uncommon.*

Entering, Tom studied the room. Twelve tables filled the floor—all occupied with pairs, most made up of two men, but two of the tables had a man and a woman. He found it interesting that the place was packed, because the parking spaces outside were empty. A small stage was set in the corner for a Saturday night band, and on the right side of the room were two pinball machines and a pool table—all unused. To his left was the bar with fifteen stools across its front. He weaved between tables and found an empty seat there.

"The usual?" the man behind the bar said, glancing at Tom's reflection in the mirror over the bar as he grabbed from the top shelf. In one motion he scooped the ice, poured the drink and smiled. While waiting he turned to check out the mystery bruise on his head and noted it gone.

"I keep running into mind readers," Tom said. "This is my first time—" Before he could finish, the bartender set a Jack on the rocks on a napkin in front of him. "Whoa, how did you know?"

"Hector sends all of you my way," said the bartender, taking a sip of Tom's drink then setting it back down. "You always want something strong, no red tape, just whiskey."

"Hold it, you're the doctor," Tom said, noticing the bartender wearing a lab coat. "What the hell are you doing—I just left you."

"If I had a buck for every time I heard that," the bartender said, holding out his hand, "I wouldn't be pouring drinks. OK, maybe I would be. As the saying goes, we all play our part. Josh O'Halloran's the name.

"What the hell's going on? You are the guy who booted me out of the room twenty minutes ago. You're still wearing a fucking lab coat. I didn't know doctors moonlighted. I guess those who do your type of work don't bring in the big bucks," Tom said.

"You think I do it for the money?" O'Halloran asked.

"Sorry, Doc, but you were kind of rude to me as well. So tell me, did everything go ok—no complications? What's Hector's connection to this place? How'd you get here so fast?"

"That's four questions, Tom. Which one do you want answered first," O'Halloran said, picking up the untouched glass. "Let me guess . . . did everything go ok?"

"This is nuts," Tom said, pushing away from the bar. "I think the stuff that guy sprayed me with did something to me. I'll have his ass when I get back." On the way to the door he glanced down at one of the tables and stopped. On the table, between two men, sat an appetizer basket. Within it Tom noticed tiny hands and feet as a gloved hand reached with medical shears and snipped an umbilical cord. "What is that?"

"That's the house special," O'Halloran said. Tom turned to find the bartender seated at the table behind him. "I call it Choice with Fries. Your mind controls the entrée. Have a seat and finish your drink. Maybe you'll get some of those questions answered." Tom took the empty chair and drank the Jack with one gulp before looking up at O'Halloran again.

"You can't be him . . . the doctor," Tom said.

"Don't get bogged by questions, Tom. You'll be shooting out the door without any answers and you'll just have to come back."

"Who are you and where am I?" Tom asked. "Is this place really here?"

"Where will answer who, and we are definitely here," O'Halloran said. "Sorry for the word play, but there's no easy way to explain. What was it that Helen said to you at the hospital?"

"We killed our baby."

"No, the other thing. She was repeating you . . . kind of a motto, a Facebook type thing to justify your writing."

"It's all material," Tom said. "What's that got to do with anything?"

"Come on Tom, you need to work this out. I can't give it to you," O'Halloran said. "What does it mean, when you say it?"

"What the fuck are you talking about?" Tom asked. "Why am I here?"

"Bingo," the other customers shouted. Looking around the room, Tom saw faces staring back at him, and in unison they all turned back to their conversations. That's when he noticed one person at each table wore a white lab coat.

"They all made it to the why question. Each answer is different. Why is it all material?"

"Why . . . well it wasn't because I killed a baby," Tom said. "It's not a kid until . . ."

"Until you believe it's a life," O'Halloran said. "You don't . . . or didn't, and those catch phrases are pretty clever, though someone you care about disagreed. I'm not here to debate you, Tom. I just point things out, because the aftermath won't be easy. That's the why—to get you through this . . . through everything. How often do you put your life into your stories?"

"It's a catch phrase—a tool," Tom said. "It justifies no limits to subject matter, because I'm inspired by life."

"So nothing's off limits?" O'Halloran asked.

"Not if it works for a story. The goal isn't to hurt anyone. It's to make them think. You're making more out of this than you should," Tom said, wanting to change the subject. "So Helen will be ok, right? She'll be able to handle this."

"Like your mother handled it?" O'Halloran asked. "She had your eyes."

"I only know what my mom told me," Tom said. "She was young and couldn't raise me alone. As for my dad, he had a tough life and ended it before I was walking. I know what it's like not wanting a kid. You don't happen to have a picture of him, do you?"

"He had his own issues, and if Helen was as strong as your mother . . . Your partner might be different."

"Helen usually sees things the same way I do," Tom said. "The pregnancy warped her thinking. It's a hormone thing, but now that she's fixed she'll normal out."

"If she doesn't see it your way?"

"Give her time. All that matters tonight is that this crisis is over," Tom said. "We scheduled it at eight and she got it done on time. Actually I had doubts and wanted to discuss them with her, but I was too late. The doctor did the procedure right on time. How often does that happen?"

"Eight o'clock, maybe you need to check the time," O'Halloran said, looking at the clock on the wall.

"Seven-thirty. I left around 8:10," Tom took his cell out of his jacket pocket. Pushing the power button he saw the reading 7:31. "Hold it, this can't be right."

"Stranger things have happened around here, Tom," O'Halloran said. "You just dropped her off at the entrance and went to park your car. You'll hurry back to her, escort her to the clinic, get her situated and step out for some fresh air."

"This is all wrong," Tom said, standing then moving toward the door. "You're clock . . . my phone . . . their both screwed up. I'm getting out of here."

"Wait, we haven't figured out that why question yet," O'Halloran said. "Hurry back, you're going to find all this interesting."

"You're nuts," Tom said, opening the door. "This whole thing is crazy."

"Possibly, Tom. But imagine the material."

Once outside, the rain pelted Tom's face, forcing him to turn back toward the bar. "What the fuck?" he said looking at the dilapidated building. The windows were covered with boards and there was a locked chain on the door. *What the hell's going on here?* he thought. *What did that guy spray in my face?*

Turning outward again, Tom pulled his jacket over his head knowing it wouldn't keep him dry for long. *I just have to deal with it, until I come down from this trip.* He chose a direction and began walking. Wet or dry, it shouldn't have taken him more than ten minutes to get back to the hospital. *That is unless I'm a fucking idiot*, he thought, realizing he wasn't sure which way he should be heading. Moving in the direction he believed would lead him to Northeast, he found himself moving deeper into a world of side streets. He thought he could hear traffic from the main road to his left, so he turned a corner into that direction and noticed something down the street.

"That's impossible," Tom said, running toward the sign: O'Halloran's. He reached for the door handle and entered. Once inside he was surprised to see a similar setting, with a much different cliental—same stage, pool table, pinball machines and tables fashioned as it was in the first O'Halloran's he'd visited. The difference was the coupling at the tables. No lab coats were worn and there were no appetizer baskets holding baby bits. He also noticed that the combinations included two men or a man and a woman, but there was no pairing of two females. Each seemed to nurse a drink, and it was obvious to him that one at each table seemed uncomfortable.

"Shut the door, or you'll be mopping it up," said a voice from across the room. Tom spotted a woman seated at the end of the bar. *Christ, she could pass for Helen's sister*. He thought of making his way to the empty stool next to her. Seated, he swiveled to view the room's activities.

"Gee, no one's shy here," Tom said, watching a woman at the table nearest where he sat giving her date a hand job.

"Nothing like free entertainment to get you in the mood," the woman said. "You are in the mood, aren't you, sweetie?"

"So where's O'Halloran?" Tom asked, ignoring the question.

"Right here, babe, but you can call me Kate," she

said. "I usually don't get asked for by name. My reputation must be spreading."

"What is this, a chain?" Tom asked. "I was talking about the guy."

"You mean grandpa," she said. "Truth is, you never know who or what you're gonna get when you walk in here. Sometimes he's wetting your whistle and sometimes I am, if you know what I mean. So what do you say we wet ours together? You're buying of course."

"You work fast," Tom said, "but I'd guess you don't need to pay for your drinks." Studying her he noticed a name tag he was sure wasn't there a minute ago. "Katelynn, nice name."

"My mom liked it, but didn't get a chance to use it much," Kate said, noticing how Tom was staring at her low cut T-shirt. "I'm guessing your attention is directed elsewhere."

"Can't blame a guy for looking," Tom said. "It's not like you're trying to hide anything."

"Totally understandable, sweetie," Kate left her seat and walked to the inner side of the bar where she fixed him a Jack and mixed herself something he didn't recognize. "Why don't we carry these to my table in the back and continue this conversation. If you're lucky I might let you do more than look."

"I should probably feel guilty," Tom said, taking both glasses and following her, "but I've got a feeling none of this is really happening. I'm guessing you're a product of Hector."

Kate led Tom into an area he hadn't noticed at the other bar. Away from the main area, they entered a smaller room with a solo booth. The imitation leather seat curved around both sides of the table and as he slid in he watched her walk over to a juke box in the corner. Without putting any money into it, she punched a combination of letters and numbers until Phil Collins began singing In the Air Tonight. Ignoring him, she gyrated to the music, moving her hands over her body. As if she felt him harden she bent to allow her ass to become the focal point, then turned and laughed as she faced him.

"Didn't mean to ignore you," Kate said, sliding into the booth next to Tom, "but that song makes me move, if you know what I mean."

"No complaints, I'm still waiting to see where this is going," Tom said. "I'm not sure if I'm hallucinating or what. I've always heard a person doesn't know when he's dreaming."

"That's interesting," Kate said, scooting closer to Tom. "Let me send this trip into overdrive while you enjoy your Jack. Hope I got it right."

"Hard to mess it up. You and your grandfather seem to know a lot about what I like, and you both look like people I've met. Your version of Helen is a bit tainted, nothing personal."

"Grandpa's been here quite a while," Kate said. "He had multiple conflicts including abandonment. Him being the guilty party of course. Hector was his first victim. He had practice before you. Enough of that serious stuff, looks like you're ready for another drink. I think you'd like mine. Would you like a blow job?"

"Whatever this is, I gotta fight it," Tom said, feeling Kate's hand move beneath his shorts. "I need to get back to the hospital." Before he could get up she moved on top of him and he gave up and watched her work him.

"I bet Mom was never this good," Kate said, then smiled.

"Jesus Christ." Tom shoved Kate off of him. "Your eyes—they're the same as in that photo."

"You love it when she looks up at you like that. Least you did before the interruption. That's what you called me."

"Who the hell are you?" Tom moved against the back of the booth.

"You also called me the mistake," Kate said aiming her mouth for Tom's crotch again, "but that doesn't matter now. Let's do some daddy-daughter bonding."

"Get the hell off me," Tom said, pushing her onto the floor. "This is sick."

"Sick?" Kate asked, standing back up. "As sick as some dude yanking your daughter out seven months early?"

"It was a fetus."

"I was your daughter. I will admit not completely formed, but you never gave me a chance," Kate said. "You sure didn't take after your father."

"My father walked out on her," Tom said. "The asshole left a child with a kid."

"The asshole didn't ask her to give you up," Kate said, "and I doubt she would have if he did. The positive is that you only had one opportunity. He did it twice."

"What the fuck are you talking about? Why in the hell am I here?"

"If I had lived I sure hope I would have taken after Mom," Kate said. "At least I wouldn't have ended up like this, a low-life skank who'd fuck her father. How many times before you figure it out, Daddy?"

"I'm sorry, but even if I believed all this, there's nothing I can do to change it. Right now Helen is in the middle of recovery. You will never exist."

"What if you could," Kate said. "What if by knowing the outcome you could change things? Isn't that what it's about, finding the material then controlling it?"

Tom pushed past her and ran out of the room, through the bar and out the door. The rain had stopped and once again when he turned around he found himself standing outside an abandoned building. He took out his phone to check the time. "What the fuck, it's only 7:45," he said. "I still have time."

Tom began running toward the lights, turning down a side street and then a second until he saw the hospital ahead. *Got to get the pass from the car*, he thought heading for the stairs. Climbing the first three levels easily, he met Hector with his cart on the fourth segment.

"Whoa bro, the stairs can be slippery when it's raining," Hector said. "You need to take it slow while ascending."

"Get out of my way, Hector, I got to get to my car and to the clinic in ten minutes," Tom said. "Don't know what you sprayed me with, but I'm going to have your fucking ass for it."

"Sprayed you?" Hector asked, gesturing that there were no bottles attached to his cart. "That won't happen for another hour."

"What are you talking about?" Tom asked, watching Hector as he began rummaging in the trash bag of his cart.

"It's hard to explain," Hector said, pulling out an

empty beer bottle, "let's just say I'm giving you a chance to reflect. Maybe you'll make it this time, little brother."

Hector aimed at Tom's head, hitting him with the bottle and knocking him to the ground. Without another word he continued his rounds. Tom laid for a moment on the concrete, sat up and blinked a couple of times. He stood and shook his head. *What the hell just happened*? he thought. Taking his phone out he checked the time again. *It's 7:53. I've got to get the pass from the car and back down to Helen in seven minutes.*

Tom rushed up the final two flights of stairs, reached his car and found the pass between the front seats. Before locking the car he looked in the rearview mirror and saw the lump left by the bottle. He departed the car and headed back down the stairs. Reaching the open lot between the parking garage and the hospital the clouds opened up.

Fuckin' rain, Tom thought, entering the lobby of Northeast Memorial. He stomped his feet on the extra mat, placed to prevent the less careful from slipping. The registration desk clock read 7:58pm. *Two minutes.*

"Let me in," Tom said, waving the damp clinic admission form at the woman behind the glass. She half smiled and pushed the button. In sync with the buzz, he opened the door then followed the map on the pamphlet. Three turns and he reached the room. Without knocking he entered, moved across the floor, and took her hand. "Babe, let's talk."

Las Maquinas

WILLIAM RITCHEY

The pounding on the cabin door and windows continued through the night. Las Maquinas, the name given to them by the Mexicans, had the numbers to overwhelm us any time they wanted, but that wasn't their M.O. Since they became organized, their tactic was to isolate small groups— "Criers" they called us—to terrorize, torture, and eventually kill. Carmen, Daggett, and I knew the risks we took coming here and the fate that awaited us if we were taken. We tracked the cell's base of operations to this remote area deep in the forest of southwestern New Mexico. Now we were the hunted ones.

"Come out and play," the voice called to the cabin in a drab monotone. Something struck the door with a loud thud that shook the wall. Footsteps—some slow, some running—circled on the deck around the cabin.

"They're getting ready to rush us," Daggett said. Faint sunlight crept into the room so I could see Daggett beside the door for the first time in hours. He was on the ready with a Louisville Slugger poised above his shoulder as if waiting for a fastball. I stood by the rear door with a fireplace poker. Carmen was squatted in a corner where she'd been most of the night staring at the floor, rocking with her knees pulled to her chest.

***

The letter was delivered late on a Friday afternoon. The lone manila envelope, amidst all the white, first drew my attention. I opened it intending only a cursory scan. Daggett and Carmen had already left for the Front Page Lounge where we always met on Fridays, and I didn't intend to be far behind. I tore off the end of the envelope and found a photograph with two sheets of paper underneath. A young man was in the photo wearing an Atlanta Braves cap outside Turner Baseball Field. A marquis was behind him with the day's opponent, the Los Angeles Dodgers, and the date of 19 April, 2011. The photo had been taken eighteen months earlier.

Underneath the picture was a typed list of nine names. I skimmed them, recognizing two. Beneath the list was an article cut from a newspaper that described several grisly murders in rural Arizona and New Mexico. The items were curious, but I had friends waiting and a powerful thirst.

"What kept you, buddy?" Daggett said. He and Carmen were sitting at the bar. Jeremy Daggett and I met studying journalism in college and had been fast friends since. We graduated in the same class and were hired the same day by the Atlanta Journal and Constitution.

"Not much. I stopped to open an odd looking letter."

"Flattery from one of your adoring fans?"

"No. I don't get many—any—of those. This was really bizarre. It had a picture of a young guy at the Ted. He couldn't muster a smile for the camera, but it was unremarkable, otherwise. There was also a list of names; J.C. van der Goes and Chauncey Camp were on it."

"Two of the richest men in America," Carmen said. "van der Goes made his fortune in real estate. Camp made billions as owner of an IBM clone company in the '80s. These days, they're recluses. I read that Camp's terminally ill."

Carmen Richardson joined the AJC a year after we did and quickly became one of us. Her straight-laced character complimented ours, perfectly. Daggett and I had religious beliefs but never practiced them. I'd been to church three times since college, all three for weddings. Carmen held her faith close, attending every Sunday.

"Camp lives here in Atlanta," I said. "The weirdest thing in the envelope was a newspaper clipping about thirteen murders in Arizona and New Mexico. Authorities were investigating them as unrelated, but the reporter believed they were linked."

***

Monday morning, I threw my backpack onto the visitor's chair and lifted the envelope off the top of the pile before I sat down to my computer. I started down the list, searching for information about each name. The other seven people—four men and three women— were also wealthy. They all had two things in common: they were all multi-millionaires whose deaths were imminent.

"Let me see the picture," Daggett said. "Maybe I'll recognize him." He held the picture up, wrinkling his brow. "Nope. He's no one I've ever seen. The dude's a blank slate, though. That face has the charisma of an L.L. Bean mannequin. Let me have the envelope, and I'll find out who sent it." Daggett went to his cubicle to trace postmark.

Carmen took the picture from Daggett and stared at it for a moment, then got a quizzical look. "Maybe it's—no way," she said. "Geoff, do a search on Chauncey Camp."

"Why? We know all about Camp," I said, still typing his name.

"See if there are pictures of him," she said, looking over my shoulder.

"They've got pictures of him out the wazoo. This dude had a camera in his face every time he peed."

"Are any from the '60s or '70s?" she asked.

"You're talking bell bottoms and leisure suits. Yeah, here's a couple of him before he left IBM. This is a good one," I said, pointing at a posed picture of a young man with glasses sitting in front of an ancient desktop computer. Do you want to tell me why we're looking at them?"

She held the photo from the envelope next to the picture on the monitor. "They could be the same guy," she said.

"The ballpark picture must be his son," I said, then scrolled down to his personal information, beneath the photo. "Daughters—Erin and Meghan . . . no sons. I don't get it. Who is he?"

"The picture looks exactly like him. It's not a son or a relative; it's him!" Carmen exclaimed.

"Have you been into the wine this morning? That's crazy. There's no way it's the same guy."

"It would explain why someone sent it to a newspaper. Can you think of another reason why someone went to the trouble of sending these things?"

"Okay, let's say for a minute it is him. What do the names on the list have to do with a seventy-five year old who looks thirty-five? They're all sick, but there are plenty of wealthy sick people. There has to be more to it than that. Maybe it's where they were treated?"

"That must be it. Did they all go to the same doctor?" Carmen asked.

I remembered one of the articles mentioned a clinic one of them visited. "Check it out. It says a Japanese man, Hideki Yamamoto, looked into an experimental treatment with a Canadian company—Therapeutic Epigenetics Corporation."

"TEC. I've heard of them," Carmen said. "They're a biotech that genetically engineers medicines to treat everything from cancer to hepatitis. They're renowned among the biotechs for the funds they pour back into research."

"You don't suppose—" I searched on Chauncey Camp and Therapeutic Epigenetics Corporation. Camp had visited TEC. "I'll be damned. Let's see if the others went there." I searched each name with "TEC", returning several links each.

"It's not remarkable that nine wealthy people looked into experimental treatment, but their involvement with TEC must be why they're on the list. I wonder if they all did as well as Camp; he didn't look terminally ill in the ballpark picture."

Daggett joined us. "I may have something on where

the letter came from," he said. "The other American on the list, J.C. van der Goes, lives near Santa Barbara, the city on the envelope's postmark. It could be coincidence, but that's the facility that processes letters sent from Summerland, the town where he lives."

***

A woman answered after several rings. "Hello, this is Geoff Reynolds with the Atlanta Journal. I'd like to speak to Mr. van der Goes."

"This is Lucille van der Goes. Hello, Mr. Reynolds. You're calling about the envelope I sent."

"Well, yes . . . that's right. Its contents were very interesting. I looked into the names and linked them to Therapeutic Epigenetics Corporation. Is that the connection you hoped I'd make? And the picture you sent—it looks like Atlanta businessman, Chauncey Camp."

"Mr. Reynolds, you must first understand . . . if they know we're aware of what's going on, they'll kill us," she said. Her voice had lowered to a whisper.

"They who? TEC?"

"We had a series of murders in Santa Barbara similar to those you wrote about Atlanta—the Atlanta Cabbage Town killer, I think you called him. Your police don't believe—as you do—that they're related. You'll find a rash of murders near the homes of everyone on that list."

"What does TEC have to do with it?" I asked.

"TEC has everything to do with it. My husband's behavior was extremely odd when he came home from their treatment. I thought it understandable, with the drastic changes to his health and appearance. He was eighty-three and terribly sick when he left. He came home six weeks later in excellent health and fifty years younger."

"That's fantastic! I've never heard of anything like that. Why hasn't something that remarkable been publicized? How does it work?"

"The doctors used stem cells from J.C.'s blood to replace every cell in his body. They changed his blood stem cells into the kind that can become any cell in the body. They circulated them in his blood for six weeks."

"You said he came home acting oddly. Odd how?"

"He came home emotionless . . . distant. He'd stare at the wall for hours. When I told him about one of our dearest friends dying, you'd think I told him lunch is ready. Even his walk changed. He used to have a swagger—the walk of a self-made billionaire. After treatment it was slower, almost mechanical." Her tone turned solemn. "We'll both die horrible deaths if they think we've discussed this. The New Mexico article I sent didn't describe the horrible things they do to the victims."

"You have my word I'll link anything I print to my research on the Cabbage Town killer." No one would want to kill this elderly woman, but I respected her request.

"I didn't realize how changed he was until we witnessed a traffic accident. Then I knew he was—," she paused for a second, "—evil.

"Two cars collided, head-on, right in front of us. We pulled onto the shoulder and got out. Others ran from their cars to help. J.C. walked calmly to the wreckage of the closer car and peeked in. The driver was already dead. He sauntered across the road and looked into the mangled wreck at the other driver. Her wails for help drowned out everything else. She was pinned in the wreckage with terrible injuries. Small flames flickered from the engine. While everyone else was trying to pry open the door to free her, when he thought no one was looking, J.C. gawked in at the hysterical woman with a puzzled expression that turned to something like a smile.

"The scene became horrible. It's the worst experience of my life. The car burst into flames, chasing everyone back. The young girl saw the flames rise up and cried out in shrieks for help. I will hear those terrified screams . . . they'll haunt me the rest of my life. The flames engulfed the car and the screams grew faint. I took my hands from my face and saw J.C. looking in at her as close as the heat would allow, smiling, mesmerized by her. On our drive home, he was more animated and invigorated than he'd been since he left for treatment.

"After that, he started taking long walks. Soon, bodies started turning up. I noted the days he walked, and within a day or two, a body would be found."

"Did the TEC people explain why he acted that way?"

"I went to their offices in Quebec and saw a manager—McGowan was his name. He said their treatment couldn't cause J.C.'s behavior. He said none of a thousand other patients had complained. They shuffled me out like I was crazy.

"I contacted other patients by searching the Internet for wealthy people who'd visited TEC. I found fifty-eight who received the treatment. Nine of them, the nine on the list I sent you, came home like J.C."

"Did anyone know what happened to those nine?"

"No. They contacted TEC and were given the same lies. One day J.C. left for a walk and never came back. The only clues I found were credit card charges at gas stations on I-10. I think he forgot he gave me access to that account before he left for treatment. The first charge was in California at the Arizona state line; the other was near Tucson. His trail stopped there. I checked newspapers in eastern Arizona and western New Mexico daily for any mention of him. That's how I found the article about the murders in Arizona and New Mexico.

"I sent you the envelope after I read your articles about the murders there. Those articles have put you in danger. Jim Elliott, the reporter in New Mexico, has disappeared. Chauncey Camp's wife is a missing person, too. Goodbye, Mr. Reynolds."

Two days later, I read Lucille van der Goes had gone missing.

***

"You won't believe what Lucille van der Goes thinks is going on." Carmen and Daggett had listened to the conversation. I told them the whole, fantastic story filling in the gaps they hadn't heard.

"There are other things you should know," I said. "She says they're killing anyone who knows about them. Chauncey Camp's wife and the New Mexico reporter have disappeared."

Daggett and Carmen didn't speak. "You know if either of you wanted to walk away, I'd understand. There may be some truth to her warning."

"That's just like you," Daggett said. "We do all the hard work, and you want to take credit for the best story ever. That lame threat's not chasing me off," he said with wide smile. His smile quickly faded as he stared vacantly across the room.

"I'm in, too. If they're going to kill everyone who knows about them, it's too late for us, anyway," Carmen said with conviction, but there was a hint of a waver in her voice.

"Then it's settled. Let's take a road trip to New Mexico," I said. I took Camp's picture from my desk. His expressionless face now seemed threatening. Looking at the face of a thirty year old, and knowing he was in his eighties, was mind-boggling. The once emotionless stare, now seemed to have an evil agenda, peering right at me. The cold expressionless face belonged to the Cabbage Town killer.

***

From the airport, we drove straight to the newspaper office of the Silver City Sun. The office was set in a row of two story, brick buildings with facades facing the two lane main street. Jennifer Milam, the editor and branch chief, sat at a desk just inside the door, smiling at something on computer when we entered.

"Hello. We're from the Atlanta Journal. I'm Geoff Reynolds. This is Carmen Richardson and Jeremy Daggett." She sat upright in her chair with her hands in her lap.

They hadn't heard from Jim Elliott since he left. Police investigated his disappearance as suspicious but found no clues. She offered to show us Elliott's desk and his filing cabinet where he kept the information he'd collected. His cluttered desk sat in the rear of the office, opposite his filing cabinet. Daggett searched the cabinet; I searched the desk.

"Have there been any more murders since Mr.

Elliott disappeared?" Carmen asked, as she and Jennifer watched us going through the papers.

"The last was in April. Since then, there have been three, including Jim."

"Since his disappearance, has anyone looked into his story?" Carmen asked. "I'd think that would be reason to check it out."

Jennifer stiffened. "Jim urged me to stay away from the story, especially if anything happened to him. I'm taking his advice."

A thick folder was in the desk's center drawer labeled Las Maquinas. It was filled with handwritten notes and diagrams about the thirteen unsolved murders in the area. He'd circled details in red ink that were similarities he'd found in each one. They all showed signs of prolonged torture before death. The killings stopped in April.

Another folder was labeled Missing Persons. The first was on April 13. The rate of disappearances grew steadily from one or two a week to fifteen or twenty. Elliott called authorities about missing persons as far away as Colorado.

The rural Mexicans called them, Las Maquinas—the machines—because of the methodical tactics used to abduct victims and their cruel lack of emotion. Interviews told of friends and relatives who were stolen in the night and their tortured bodies found days later.

The folder had a map with a red X a couple of miles into Arizona. We rented a cabin deep in the Gila National Forest from a realtor's office a few doors down from the Star.

***

William Richey

After an hour long drive into the forest, we arrived at the cabin. It was perched on the crest of a hill with a yard cleared all around for a hundred feet. The yard ended at a tree line, thinned so that patches of the valley below could be seen. We carried our bags up wooden stairs to the cabin's front door, enjoying the peaceful setting.

"Look at this deck," Carmen said. "I've got to check it out." While I tried the keys to unlock the front door, Carmen walked around the cabin's exterior on the wrap-around deck. Through the front door was a great room with a fireplace of stone bricks that rose up to the wooden beams on the ceiling. The bedrooms were to the left and a kitchen to the right.

Carmen and I had just finished the dishes and were carrying a couple of chairs to the door to watch the sun set over the forest. Daggett sat on a couch facing the fireplace, hunched over a coffee table in the living room, poring over a map.

The solitude was broken by a loud blast and the clinking of glass fragments raining onto the cabin floor. A strange object lay on a rug in the center of the kitchen area. Its unnatural gray color slowed my recognizing it as a human foot. Carmen screamed.

"What the hell!" Daggett shouted. "Christ! It's a foot." I ran to the window but saw no one in the open yard. Among the trees, in the fading sunlight, I could just make out the dark shadowlike shapes.

A voice called from the yard on the other side of the house. "We're going to kill you slowly." Daggett and I ran to the window on that side. A young man stood motionless, holding a machete by his side, staring. His face was covered in a dark crimson, making the whites of his eyes, in the fading light of dusk, stand out. At his feet was a half stuffed burlap sack. "You've come to investigate Jim Elliott's accusations," the man said while reaching into the bag. "Would you like to meet him?"

He pulled a round object from the bag and threw it towards us. The object flew at the window. We ducked to the sides before it hit the upper trim with a bang and bounced onto the porch. We crept cautiously back to the window. The round object on the deck, to my horror, was a man's head, lying facing me, with its mouth hanging open. I recognized it was Jim Elliott from the pictures on his desk. The crimson faced man was already pulling another object from the bag. He threw it toward the window, and this time it crashed through glass.

"Have you met Lucille van der Goes?" he asked. Her white hair was matted in dried blood turned black that covered most of the head.

"You'll be joining them in the bag soon," the dreary voice said. Daggett ran to a closet next to the rear door where recreational equipment was stored. He returned with a baseball bat and stood watch by the front door. I grabbed a poker by the fireplace and hurried to the rear door. Another loud thump echoed from impact against the outside wall. Footsteps of the man with the burlap bag were now audible on the porch. "We're coming for you, Criers," he said. Through the broken window, I could see four others approaching the cabin. They were close enough that I could see two were women. They were in their twenties or early thirties with faces painted dark red.

"I can see three walking to the cabin," Daggett

yelled, looking through the broken window. "Come and get it, freaks," he shouted. Loud thuds of pounding came from the front door.

***

After sunset, I turned on the outside floodlights illuminating the areas around the house. They made no effort to come inside; they were prolonging the torment. Daggett retrieved an archery set from the closet where he found the bat. He shot an arrow at one of them standing in the yard. The shot missed but was close. The man scurried off for cover. The rest of them pulled back to the tree line.

The silence was broken from bangs of objects striking all the outside walls of the cabin. Dark sections appeared in the brightly lit yard, growing until all the floodlights were broken. The yard was now black looking through the windows from within the lighted cabin. We quickly turned the inside lights off. Pounding on the doors and windows continued through the night.

At daybreak, their silhouettes were positioned along the tree line on all our sides. "Come out and play," a flat voice called.

"They're getting ready to rush us," Daggett said. He lifted the Louisville Slugger to his shoulder.

The sound of shattering glass drew my attention to the windows in the kitchen area. A dark gray object shaped like a soda can bounced then spun on the floor, spewing a white cloud. That was followed, seconds later, by another, then another. I dropped to the floor hoping the gas would rise.

***

My eyes opened to steel bars. As the fog from the gas

lifted, I could see a wall outside the bars and a door hanging slightly askew in its right corner. I turned to a rustling behind me. Daggett was stirring, face down on the dirt floor. Carmen was lying in the rear of the cell, still unconscious. In the back corner, a hole had been dug in the dirt floor that stunk of human excrement. Its inner edges were grooved from the fingers that dug it out.

The walls and ceiling were made of mildly curved, unfinished planks whose only purpose was confinement, since they did nothing to keep the weather out.

"Where are we?" Daggett asked.

"I don't know. The last thing I remember, I was lying on the cabin floor. This is bad. We've got to get out of here," I said trying to be calm. Daggett walked along the bars, pushing and pulling each one. They were attached securely to the floor and ceiling with a heavy metal frame. He then inched his way along the walls testing each board for a weak spot. I could see keys hanging on a hook outside the bars on the wall next to the door. They were ten feet away.

Carmen stirred awake. Daggett and I moved next to her, to calm her as she realized our situation. "Where am I?" she asked. I held her hand, and Daggett had his arm around her. "Oh, dear God, we were being attacked in the cabin. Have we been captured?" Neither of us wanted to answer.

"We're going to find a way out of here, Carmen, I promise," I said.

"These walls are flimsy, I'm sure I can find a weak spot," Daggett added. Carmen had just sat up when the voices of two men carried from a distance; they were growing louder. Daggett peeked through a crack in the boards in their direction. "I see them," he whispered. They spoke in lifeless tones that were too distant to understand. I looked toward the approaching men and could see small shacks behind them in the distance.

The door creaked open and the two men walked into the room coldly staring with impassive expressions. "We'll take the big Crier tonight," the larger one said, pointing at Daggett. I recognized him; he was Chauncey Camp. "We'll take the smaller male tomorrow morning and the female tomorrow night."

"Why are you keeping us here?" I asked. "We weren't doing you any harm." I stared into Camp's eyes; they held the emotion of marbles, reminding me of the eyes on cadavers I'd seen in the morgue.

"Mr. Reynolds, we're aware of why you've come to New Mexico. You do mean us harm. If you had been allowed to continue, you would've released details about us and our activities to the authorities. Eliminating you serves two purposes. It quells your threat to us and will provide an invigorating treat for our group."

"What the hell went wrong with you?" Daggett shouted. "They saved you—gave you young, healthy bodies. What turned you into vicious killers? Chauncey Camp, you've been a philanthropist for twenty years. What could change you so drastically?"

The two men looked at each other for a moment. Camp's companion said, "The truth can only distress them further."

Camp turned to Daggett. "We're the next step in man's evolution. Through mishap, we're changed into perfect humans. We aren't handicapped by emotion that muddies your decision making. If you Criers are allowed to continue on your current path, you'll destroy the earth and everything on it, someday."

"You can't believe emotions are bad," Carmen said. "They do sometimes cause harm—things like greed, jealousy, crimes of passion. But, it's also human emotion that has inspired all of man's beautiful creations. What happened at TEC that removed your humanity?" Carmen asked.

"Two TEC doctors we harvested from Canada explained it before they died. TEC discovered, quite by accident, a regeneration therapy that could replace aged or diseased cells with young healthy ones. The numbers they could treat were limited, so they targeted terminally ill patients who were very wealthy, charging exorbitant sums we gladly paid. During the six week treatment, many of us died from our illnesses before the regeneration was complete. The treatment's pluripotent stem cells and oxygenating nanoparticles survived, continuing to replace diseased cells after the heart stopped. The cells replaced diseased organs until, sometimes after days, the heart would begin beating. Those of us who experienced the dark period of enlightenment, returned with clear, emotionless thoughts."

Carmen and Daggett stood wide-eyed. Carmen spoke first. "I understand now." Her face distorted into a grimace. "You all died during the treatment. The cells replaced your diseased bodies back to a living state, but you died. Your souls or spirit or whatever you want to call that spark that makes us human, it left you and didn't return. The philanthropist, Chauncey Camp, took his rightful place in Heaven. What was left behind is a soulless abomination."

Their detached expressions were unchanged. "You'll never know how truly superior we are. Plans are already underway to deliver maximum casualties on criers throughout the world. Groups of us are banded on every continent. We number nearly three hundred and growing."

"What do you mean you're growing?" I asked.

"Our bodies are perfectly healthy and function in every way. We're producing offspring as quickly as possible. Eleven second generation members of us exist and sixteen more are on the way. A second generation child, three years of age, lives with us here in this camp. His ability to act, unabated by emotion, is far superior to those of us in the first generation." With that, Camp and the other man left.

Carmen's expression screamed in fearful silence while they were leaving. Once they were out of earshot, she said in a forceful whisper, two octaves above her usual pitch, "Did you hear his explanation? All of them have died. Some were dead for days before they were revived. They're reanimated corpses like Frankenstein."

"What would happen if they ever actually did take control?" I said. "Their purpose was to keep us from destroying the earth, but they thrive on torture and murder. The atrocities they'd enact would be unimaginable."

"That's all interesting stuff, but they'll be coming to take me away soon. We need to find a way out of here," Daggett said.

***

The keys dangling on the hook were our best hope. For hours, we tried to find a way to reach them. As sunlight faded, our efforts became frantic. Daggett paced along the walls, repeatedly pushing boards that were too high to kick.

A commotion stirred in the direction of the shacks. We looked through the cracks to see fifteen of them gathered, forming a circle. Something in the center of the circle had their attention. Those to our side of the circle separated, and a round object skipped between them. The object was a man's head that had been kicked until it was almost unrecognizable. It skidded to a stop twenty feet from where we stood. A child, no more than three, emerged running from the center of the group racing after it. As he neared his toy, he became aware of us. The toddler picked up the head by its hair and walked to our cell wall.

If I live to be one hundred, I'll never forget the creature that stood a foot from me. The head hung down in its hand as another child might hold a doll. As it approached the boards, my feet caught its attention through cracks in the planks. I looked down, seeing only the top of its head, when it unexpectedly turned, looking up into my face. The unholy countenance, with its cold eyes and evil, adult-like demeanor, caused my knees to grow weak. I fell back onto the dirt floor, instinctively drawing away. My head was still spinning when I spotted the creature staring at me eye level through a crack in the boards.

Two adults took the creature by its hands and led it back to the crowd. I saw the gleam of joy it derived from my fear. It released a horrific screech like something out of a Tarzan movie.

"Easy does it there, buddy," Daggett said, as he helped me to my feet. "You okay?"

The sun had set an hour before on the overcast,

moonless night, veiling the woods in black. A campfire's flickering light shimmered across the clearing in front of us. Only darkness was visible through the cracks in the wall on the other side.

We heard them approaching from the campfire's direction. With nothing better to use as a weapon, our plan was to attack with the heels of our hiking boots. Daggett stood to the side of the cell door, and I stood on the other. The door creaked open, and three men, all taller than either of us and many pounds heavier, entered. The first one took the keys from the hook while the other two stood to each side of the cell door. Our plan was doomed to fail, but if nothing else, we were going to give them a fight.

The man with the keys entered the cell holding an eighteen inch tie-wrap. I stepped back holding a hiking boot by the toe behind me and hid my shoeless foot behind the booted one. As he reached out with the tie-wrap for Daggett's hands, I stepped forward and cracked the heel against the back of the man's head with everything I had. The loud crack it made against his skull brought me relief that the large man would be incapable of retaliation. My relief was short lived. He whirled to face me, and Daggett punched him in the ear with a roundhouse that would have dropped most men. Without the tiniest reaction to Daggett's punch, he drew back a meaty fist and caught me squarely on the jaw. I fought for consciousness but lost that battle on the way to the floor.

When I awoke, Carmen was holding my head in her lap. As my head cleared, I could hear Daggett's agonized screams. "How long was I out?"

"About an hour," Carmen said. Tears streamed

down her cheeks. "They've been doing those things to him for forty-five minutes." Then her face lit up. Without a word, she stood to look through the cracks at the group around the campfire, then turned toward the cell door. She swung it open then carefully closed it.

"How did you manage that?" I asked. My pulse was racing.

"While they were fighting to get him out the door, Daggett head butted one in the nose. Blood was pouring from both his nostrils." She stopped to look at the drips of blood on the dirt floor outside the bars. "They all began to attack Daggett, savagely. When he quit fighting, they started to walk him to the door with Bloody Nose leading the way. Daggett head-butted him again—this time to the back of his head. During the scuffle, he was able to pull away to face the keys with them punching him from behind. He knocked the keys off the hook and kicked them to the cell. I grabbed them and hid them behind me before they saw. After they left, I opened the cell and put them back on the wall."

"We've got to get out of here and help Daggett," I said.

"It's too late to do him any good," she said, with a sob. "I saw them take his hands and were working on his feet with a hand saw when I looked away." She lifted her hands to her face. "They're dragging it out as long as they can."

I looked through the cracks for any sign that Daggett was alive. He was slumped forward on his knees, hanging by a rope under his arms. The toddler creature approached him holding something. In the poor lighting, I could only see the creature's arms working back and forth. It turned facing the group holding something I couldn't see. I looked back to see Daggett's headless body slumped forward. "You're right, we've got to escape and tell the police."

We checked through the cracks so they wouldn't see, then cautiously stepped through the doors and into the dark forest. We crept carefully with each footstep, fearing we'd snap a dry twig, until the flickering light was far behind us then ran as fast as the darkness would allow.

The stench was first noticeable in the breeze fifty yards into the woods. It was the smell of a dead animal that was growing stronger. The odor overwhelmed my senses. Attempting to hold my breath while I ran proved useless. We ran as fast as we dared between the trees in the darkness. I spotted a gap in the tree tops where they met the sky and slowed, otherwise I would have fallen into the pit. I twisted backward and dropped facedown to stop my momentum, leaving my feet hanging over its edge. Carmen fell to the ground behind me extending her arms to help stop my slide and helped me pull myself up.

The pit was a pitch black rectangle the size of a basketball court. Nothing was visible within the black rectangle except the bodies stacked five feet below the edge where we stood. The mound of corpses sloped downward to the center of the pit, disappearing into darkness. About a hundred bodies rose high enough in the pit to be visible, but most of the pit's contents were hidden in darkness. This had been the fate of those on Jim Elliott's disappearances list plus many, many more.

Carmen and I ran through the night hoping we wouldn't be missed until morning. We ran for two days before finding a clearing in the tall trees with a house and a beat up pickup truck parked in front of it. We waited in the trees to see who lived there before approaching, fearing they were more of our captors. An elderly woman left the shack to get into the truck. We hobbled from the woods to ask for her help. We were in Apache County, in eastern Arizona.

***

We weren't sure the New Mexico State Police would believe our story. Working out of the Silver City Star's office, we contacted the State Police Chief, and with Jennifer Milam's help, convinced him to check out our story. More than fifty officers were organized within a day and set out to locate the camp. The group backtracked through the forest on ATVs from the elderly woman's home. We ran in darkness the first several hours of our escape, so we had only a notional idea of the direction. After a few mistakes, we retraced the route to the camp. The site was deserted with nothing but campfire ashes to show anyone had been there. Their shacks and the shack that held us were gone. The police didn't doubt we witnessed Daggett's murder, but they didn't fully understand the magnitude of the horrors there until we showed them the pit with bodies.

Troopers lifted the bodies out of the pit for six days. They counted four-hundred and sixty-three. They accepted the rest of our story without question. TEC was investigated and shut down in spite of their attempts to hide evidence. Killings all over the world were traced to Las Maquinas' cells with more than three-hundred members identified, but none were ever caught.

Carmen and I traveled afterward, hiding the first few months. A year passed with no trace of them. We figured they were no longer interested in us, since everyone now knew as much about them as we did. Soon, they were forgotten by everyone; everyone except Carmen and me. We knew they were gathering in some isolated area, multiplying and planning their attacks, the likes of which the world had never seen.

Perrollo's Ladder

JOHN PALISANO

Blood rained down onto the leaves of the trees and brush. A thousand *criaturas* were let loose from Hell and rose to Heaven. Instead of meeting embraces, they met the angels' swords in the sky. Many perished, their limbs and bodies tumbling and burning. Globes of fire lit the night. Ashes and embers settled to the ground, mixing with the mountain's topsoil, which was already saturated with their blood. This was how Ojo Mountain got its dark color, unique to those surrounding it. This is where those surviving *criaturas* remained and hid, unable to show their defeated faces in the underworld, and unable to move freely during daylight. In the darkness, if you look carefully, you might glimpse *criaturas* scurrying about the high, thin ledges, watching and wishing someone might summon them down.

***

Antonio visited Perrollo every Thursday. He'd walk from his small apartment on Huevo Road, leaving behind the strip malls, electronic billboards, and the never-ending noise of his life with the computer firm. He eagerly turned off his phone. Near the bottom of Ojo Mountain, Antonio always stopped for an ear of corn bathed in lime at his favorite pushcart vendors. No matter how many times he'd ask, Perrollo would always gently decline. "Next time I'm bringing one for you, too. They're delicious, satisfying, and cheap."

"Thank you, but no," Perrollo said. "There are only certain things that I can eat."

"Like what?" Antonio asked. "Mountain goats? Birds? It's so cold and there's nothing up here."

"I get by. Do you want to see the ladder?" Perrollo said.

"I do," Antonio said.

They walked through Perrollo's mountain cottage where he'd lived since school. Perrollo's occult projects filled every shelf, windowsill, and tabletop. Antonio glimpsed lanterns detailed with golden beads his friend claimed only shined in alien worlds, complex dioramas of Heaven's streets, and handmade books scored with symphonies Perrollo heard while he meditated.

Antonio spotted a picture of Perrollo and himself from high school. Perrollo had decorated the frame with castings of their school ring, each painted with bronze or silver shades. Antonio recalled Perrollo's voice from that era.

"The time has come for me to move from my parents' house in this valley, now that we're graduating," he'd said.

"I'll miss you," Antonio had said. "I'm sure you'll do wonderful at college."

"There's nothing for me there," Perrollo had said.

"I'm only moving a mile away. On Ojo Mountain. I can be closer to the sky."

"There's no houses. No streets," Antonio had said.

Perrollo had smiled. "I'm going to build them."

***

Antonio peered over Perrollo's shoulder. "How long have we been coming back here and watching your ladder come together?"

"More years than a tree has rings." Perrollo grinned. He lifted a leg of his oversized white cotton pants upward in order to climb onto a rock ledge.

Antonio nodded. "We've always had that push to find out what made things work, didn't we? I embraced technology and betted everything it'd change the world. I get a hundred messages an hour and I've never felt more alone. You walked away from all that. You seem happier."

"Your answers are in the sky," Perrollo said and pointed up. "But you've always known that, haven't you."

***

Barola's claws curled around the lip of Claudia's dresser. He watched her sleep. If Claudia woke she would not have believed there was a *criatura* such as Barola perched in her room. Five wiggling tendrils slithered out from Barola's mouth. They crawled along his bumpy face, eager with anticipation.

He remembered the night her parents conceived Claudia. How her parents had prayed! They'd wanted a baby so badly, and he'd answered. Countless attempts didn't take. Barola followed their prayers, crawling down the mountainside. What else could he do? Barola lived to grant wishes.

As Fernando and Maria slept, Barola had perched on their dresser. Barola curled up next to Fernando and used the tendrils, prying within Fernando's belly. Their tips were coated with an anesthetic not unlike a mosquito's proboscis. Barola pushed downward inside Fernando's hanging pear-shaped sacks, where he'd suck the nectar. There were more direct routes, but Barola liked exploring, and wanted to take his time. On the end of one tongue, a small bulb inflated as Fernando's juice flowed inside. He'd keep it safe within his mouth.

Used to eating the small, bitter black snakes he found on the mountainside, Barola also chewed green leaves to stave his hunger when there were no snakes. Fernando ate heavy foods and marinated himself with beer and mescal until he fell asleep. The infused fats and fluids made a sweet, luxurious meal for Barola.

Fernando wouldn't notice the scars once Barola finished. Not only was Fernando's belly covered in hair, but the entry points were small and would cover over quickly. At worst, the man would feel itchy and might have a small stomachache for a day.

Once he'd had the man's magic nectar, Barola moved on to the best part: squeezing the juice inside Maria from the bulb. Fernando would sleep soundly beside them while Barola burrowed his head between Maria's legs, opened his mouth and his five tendrils made their way between her folds. The other tongues squeezed the bulb, oozing the essence deep within Maria.

They would have their child, and they wouldn't have the slightest idea, he knew, and that was the best part. They could go on living just as they had, and he could do the same. They'd just be missing a few precious ounces of Claudia. Barola liked cradling the swollen bulb using his other tongues as they swept across the inner walls of his cheeks. He blinked several times to freshen his sore, sand-swept eyes. Barola tried his best to remember the sleeping girl in the bed; he probably would never see her again. If their paths crossed later, Claudia would be grown, and she would likely need something from him. At the moment, though, she was blissfully unaware.

***

Ojo Mountain towered above them at the furthest part of Perrollo's backyard. The view always made Antonio dizzy. There were small trees and ledges and he wondered what sort of wildlife made such an inhospitable place home. Then he looked at Perrollo and knew they'd at least have to be just as stubborn, smart, and tireless as him. "You didn't ask me to help you build the ladder."

"These things," Perrollo said, "have to be started and ended with one set of hands, otherwise they won't work."

Antonio scurried up and over another small plateau. He found it challenging keeping pace with Perrollo. "What do you mean, it won't work?" Antonio asked. "It's just a ladder."

Perrollo shook his head. "Do you believe your old friend would spend all this time building something as simple and ordinary as a ladder? Why couldn't I just buy one?"

"I don't know. I just thought it was a challenge. A fun project for you to keep busy."

Perrollo shrugged, turned and hurried toward the

ladder. He stepped closer and Antonio made out more details; Antonio could see its outline in the shadow. It looked higher. Finger holds were sanded into each rung. The ladder glistened from thousands of gems.

"I've always preferred night. The sun's gone down and the evening breeze arrives." Perrollo bent down and eyeballed the lower rungs. "I could really use a good glass," Perrollo said, "filled with red wine."

"Sounds like a great plan." Antonio tried to catch Perrollo's eye, but couldn't.

"Yes," Perrollo said. "I've got the perfect bottle."

Perrollo rose, hurried past Antonio, and stumbled toward his hand made cottage. After Perrollo ducked safely inside, Antonio reached out and touched a rung.

***

Barola writhed onto Claudia's bed without waking her. His five skinny tongues slithered toward Claudia and penetrated her. *They make it so easy*, Barola thought. *Their ears are wide-open holes with no coverings. Their noses have two equally open holes. Their mouth might be shut, but their soft lips open with the slightest touch.* He imagined what it might be like to kiss with such plump things on his face. His own mouth was thin, hard, and callous. Did theirs contain sensitive nerves, like he'd heard?

The girl's mouth parted as his tendril touched her lips, just as he'd expected. Electric sensations stretched from inside his mouth all the way to the tips of his claws. Barola tasted Claudia's exquisite, intoxicating flavor.

Barola felt his inner organs drink her essence, expanding like dry, brittle sponges dipped in a warm tub. His eyes glistened and his blood flowed smoothly for the first time in what felt like forever. Her vigor would be enough to last him several months.

He looked over her smooth face. The finest of wrinkles inched from the corner of her eye. Barola wondered how one so young could even have wrinkles.

Wrinkles?

Have I gone too far? Have I taken too much? Would she now be prematurely aged because of his greed and selfishness? Barola remembered what Vecelio would do to him. Barola could not suffer another eternity inside Vecelio's dark prison box. He twitched at the idea of being alone with his own thoughts and stench.

Barola pulled his tendrils from inside Claudia.

Because he hadn't slipped his probing tongues from her smoothly, Claudia stirred. Her eyelids fluttered and she sighed. Barola wanted to shush her but his lips could not form the right way to make the sound. Instead, he exhaled slightly so that he made what he thought would be a similar noise. It came out much more like a cat coughing up a hairball.

Claudia stretched; the back of her hand grazed Barola's scaly chest. He stiffened, frightened she'd open her eyes. Instead, she rolled on her side, her back to Barola. He stared at Claudia's scalp through the tiny slivers in her pitch-black hair. He wondered what her dreams were. Had he somehow changed her thoughts? Would she know? Would she be forever changed? He would never find out.

No wonder they wanted her, he thought. *So new. So fresh. So interesting.* His bottom claw twitched as Claudia's juices burned inside his veins. He couldn't stay, and so, Barola left her to her dreams and her life.

Claudia's essence would enable the ladder, and both he and Perrollo would benefit. He recalled Perrollo's recipe. "Essence drawn from an heir of the one who builds the ladder. One who is innocent and does not know the meanness of the world."

Barola understood as Perrollo had pointed to a passage inside the large book. "We need Claudia. Do this and the ladder will bring us rightfully home."

***

"Don't touch it," Perrollo said. "You're going to ruin everything."

Antonio stepped back, taking his hand with him. "I didn't mean . . ."

Perrollo made it over to him. "I should have told you." He lifted an uncorked, black-labeled bottle of wine and swigged. Perrollo handed Antonio the bottle.

"Okay," Antonio said. "Can you please tell me why this is a big deal?"

"I can use the ladder to fix my cottage's roof. I can use it to lie against the mountain and pick pears and oranges. Tonight? I can use it to call people from the sky."

Antonio squinted.

Perrollo said, "They talk to me. I hear them. They need me to invite them. Otherwise they're trapped."

"You sure it's not just the sunlight baking your brain inside your skull like an egg?" Antonio thought his friend might have been putting him on, or talking in some kind of intricate metaphor, which was not uncommon.

Perrollo said, "You know the story about this mountain? The blood of the underworld stains the dirt. The angels above sealed the gates. Tonight I'm going to open the doorway."

"So the demons can get inside Heaven?" Antonio said.

"I don't believe in such primitive mythologies," Perrollo said. "Only what I've seen."

"Which is?"

"Lost souls live on this mountain," Perrollo said. "Many of them. They appear primitive and scared. They just need a helping hand."

Antonio said, "Shouldn't we call some organization or the government if that's the case? It could be scary. There could be diseases. They could be cannibals. Anything."

"They're none of those," Perrollo said. "They're the Enlightened Ones. There will soon be a whole new level of understanding and illumination. They've been waiting, just as we've been waiting. They are the missing ones in our history. When we feel spiritual voids it is because they have not been there to guide us." Perrollo shut his eyes.

***

In the evening the mountain appeared different. The scraggly brush gave the area character during the day. Darkness camouflaged the brush, which slowed movement. The sharp sunbaked branch tips cut bluntly and quickly, and took much too long to heal. Barola still kept hurrying. It didn't matter to him. Someone called. How could he be so lucky? He'd just filled himself and finished his vampiric relationship with the family. A new one was about to begin, and how perfect that he had renewed energy and strength. Barola would be able to grant any kind of wish, even one of his own.

Barola peered up at the moon. *Maybe that's where*

I came from. When he was younger, the other *criaturas* told him their story. Barola couldn't remember a time when he didn't live on the mountain. The older *criaturas* told him their race once fell from the sky. There was an older life they'd come from. One day they'd be called back to the sky. Until then, Barola was to remain hidden and listen for the prayers of the desperate. He'd only hear them if he was quiet and alone, and not too well fed. He would answer the humans' prayers. In return he'd gain nourishment from their golden sanguinity. Nothing more.

As he got older, many *criaturas* disappeared. He'd discovered several of their remains at different times. They'd all died the same way, their bodies shriveled and stiff. It'd looked like they'd tried digging themselves into the ground.

Just thinking of it frightened Barola. What else could he have done? They never came to him for help. They'd split up, afraid ganging might make them easier for the wrathful humans to spot.

Barola heard the call, much stronger than any before. Somehow the voice was coming not from the village, but impossibly, from the mountain itself. He recognized the voice.

***

Perrollo pointed toward the ladder, which had grown taller. Antonio had missed it. He didn't understand. He'd only looked away for a moment. "What is it doing?" he asked.

Perrollo said, "Reaching for the sky. Like I always said it would."

"I always thought you were exaggerating," Antonio said. "You weren't joking?"

"You didn't believe me when I told you things. Aren't you my friend?" Perrollo said.

"Of course. You have to admit that you do exaggerate things. They're like Bible stories. Like angels fighting in the clouds," Antonio said.

Perrollo wasn't smiling.

"You will find nothing I told you all these years was false. If anything I've left things out. These worlds are more fantastic than I can describe to you." Perrollo shook his head. "You'll see."

Just then, something large rustled behind the ladder. Antonio hopped backward. His arm shook. He had no weapons. Not even a stick. He thought it had to be a mountain lion; one so close could certainly gash them fatally. Perrollo was closest and Antonio raced through a thousand thoughts. How could he scare the mountain lion away? He reviewed conversations, websites, images hovered within blurry edges of his memory. *What should I do?*

Two big eyes caught the light and blinked.

The *criatura* stood only a few feet from them. Antonio tried to say something to warn Perrollo but couldn't find his voice.

Perrollo looked right at the *criatura*, seemingly unafraid.

He reached out a hand. "Come out from there," Perrollo said.

The *criatura* was certainly not a mountain lion.

"Have you been here long, Barola?"

Antonio realized Barola was not human. The creature looked to him like a lizard standing on its hind legs. Barola spoke. "You have called for me." His mouth moved, although the words didn't seem to match the movements. "I am here to offer what little I can." His voice sounded hollow, as though he spoke through the inside sound hole of a flamenco guitar.

Antonio remained still, even though he wanted to run away from the *criatura*.

"Three things make the ladder work. You need to hear the call. That's why I've built my home as close to the sky as I could. Then there's the building of the ladder, of course. Last, we're sprinkling the ladder with Claudia's essence. Barola helped us."

The *criatura* opened his mouth and slid out his tongues, four of which cradled the fifth's bulb.

Perrollo finished the last of his wine with a sigh and offered the glass to Barola. The *criatura's* tongues squeezed the bulb. Clear fluid dripped from its bulb and filled Perrollo's glass.

The tongues squeezed one last drop and slid back inside Barola's mouth. "I only took just enough. She'll never feel it."

"Perfect." Perrollo took the wine glass filled with Claudia's essence to the ladder and dipped his fingers in the fluid. He painted the sides and rungs of the ladder with the essence. As his fingers grazed past, the coated areas glistened as though backlit from fireflies.

Antonio could not be sure, but he swore the ladder twitched from Perrollo's touch.

Antonio knew Perrollo's promises were real. The ladder would work.

"I've finished the ladder." Perrollo gestured to the still-growing structure. "You can go home."

Barola inched forward; he touched the ladder with one of his talons. "You have led the way."

"What am I supposed to do?" Antonio asked.

"You were invited to my home, and so, you are invited to come along with us," Perrollo said.

Antonio shook his head. "I don't know. Where would we go? Are we coming back?"

"All these questions! Life's too short to second-guess everything. You just need to trust that I would never steer you wrong."

"So there's no choice?"

"You can stay here and dream of what you see. Maybe one day your prayers will be answered and you'll be able to join us then. If there is anyone left to hear you, that is." Perrollo put a foot on the bottom rung and his hands on the sides. "You can simply stay here and watch. I bid you my best desire either way."

"I don't know," Antonio said. "This is all so sudden."

"You haven't been listening to me all these years." Both Perrollo's feet were on the ladder now.

Barola stood behind Perrollo. His mouth opened and Antonio could see things moving around within. *My friend is going to die*, he thought. *That creature might kill him and there's nothing I can do to stop it.*

Antonio knew he was wrong. Barola was not going to kill Perrollo. He realized this because, during that moment, the sky opened. Rolling cloud planes hovered a few hundred feet beyond. The air smelled of the sweet mountain flowers mixed with the storm's broken electric ozone. The insects on the mountainside harmonized.

All manner of *criatura* gathered near Antonio. His face flushed as they crowded nearby. One being hunched in such a way that Antonio could only place it as some kind of upright dog. It shared the same sort of mottled, grayish fur, bare in patches, and dried to the root, as a coyote. Its black eyes glistened. Antonio saw his reflection on their curvature. The *criatura* matched his stare and opened its mouth, licking its skinny, grey lips with an even thinner, drier tongue. Its nib-like teeth chattered. Black stains dotted its otherwise pale, pink throat.

A scent not dissimilar to bleach overtook Antonio as another of the hidden beings slithered behind him. Feeling the weight of something peering over his shoulder, Antonio moved his head. A thin scaly face looked back, its eyes only inches away, hovering over his right shoulder. The head lingered and a hollow ticking sounded from the chamber of its mouth. A long neck stretched nearly to the ground, colored in rings of light browns and greens. If it'd coiled up, or leaned against a tree, Antonio imagined no one would give it a second thought, because it may have been a large piece from a dried old desert tree. As it moved, he was reminded of the coral snakes he'd seen on a television program as a child. One moment they were still, the next, they'd strike and deliver a deadly bite. This thing could end his life on a whim, he knew.

Others circled Perrollo. One looked very much like Barola, only taller and had missing one arm from below its left elbow.

In back of them, a large white entity gracefully climbed down the mountain. Each leg was only the thickness of a pencil, it seemed. Even so, the overall size rivaled the others. A slightly segmented body dangled between the dozen legs, and eye tipped stems kept tabs on the goings on. This pale insect was followed by two more, each smaller than the one before.

"Now that we are all here," Perrollo said, "let's hurry."

***

Perrollo climbed the ladder and Barola followed.

Nothing inside Antonio made him want to join them. Everything inside him made him want to watch.

Something brushed past him. Other beings similar to Barola went to the ladder and climbed.

Thunder rumbled. The clouds darkened and rolled.

Perrollo arrived near the middle of the ladder. Barola stood underneath him. The other *criaturas* caught up.

Perrollo turned backward and his eyes met Antonio's. He didn't smile or nod. He just climbed another step. The ladder stretched higher than Antonio realized.

The clouds ahead of Perrollo parted. He hesitated before he climbed inside. The storm turned magnificent colors as he disappeared. Pinks turned into deep reds. Blacks turned into oranges. Veins of lightning danced through the thunderheads.

Maybe I should have gone, Antonio thought. *Maybe it's not too late.* He stepped forward and hurried toward the ladder. Above him the others had nearly vanished inside the clouds. He watched their feet disappear.

As each step brought him higher Antonio remembered the warnings Perrollo had uttered.

And as Antonio put his first foot on the ladder he felt anything but brave. *Why am I doing this? Doesn't this go against everything I thought I wouldn't do? I always said I wouldn't follow Perrollo on his weird occult adventures.*

This was different. This was a ladder that reached inside Heaven. How could that be frightening?

His entire body was on the ladder and he looked up, despite his thinking he shouldn't. The ladder stretched impossibly high until it touched the clouds. Antonio saw no sign of what might be keeping it upright. What? Was he supposed to have faith that it would hold him and stay upright?

This thing is as high as airplanes. Even higher. How the hell am I supposed to climb so high so quickly? How did Perrollo manage? It just physically doesn't seem possible that quickly.

A thought blanketed his mind.

The ladder helps. The ladder takes you and raises you toward the sky, if you are one of the chosen.

Perrollo's words.

Am I one? He thought for a moment while he climbed. He must have been. Not only had Perrollo invited him along, but Antonio had never settled down, either. He'd taken his jobs and cycled through his relationships. Commitments broke, if he even agreed to them in the first place. But he found himself, finally and absolutely, called to a higher place. Called by Perrollo. Called by the ladder.

Antonio looked up. *Doesn't seem too high yet.* The bottom of the clouds seemed a lifetime away.

Don't look down.

He did, despite himself. He was sorry he did because Antonio found himself much higher than he'd anticipated. He grabbed the sides of the ladder; the height made him dizzy. His hands were sweating and he very much wanted to rush back down the ladder. He could see the cottage and the town below.

Don't look down. Look up. Keep climbing. There's no turning back. He steeled himself, took a breath, and stretched his fingers for the next rung.

After Antonio reached halfway to the top, the heavy air made breathing difficult. He hung his head on a step. The world around him spun as though he'd drunk half a bottle of tequila. He clutched the sides. *Make it stop. Please don't let this happen. I'm too high on the ladder to fall without breaking something.*

Then the ladder shook. It was small at first, but he still felt it. He couldn't lift his head. The dizziness had bloomed into a horrid migraine. His eyes watered and fingers of bright acidic pain burrowed through his sinuses and behind his eyes.

Don't fall, whatever you do. Hang on.

He could only pray.

The ladder jostled. He felt like a plastic soldier on the end of a toy fire truck ladder. He crouched against it as hard as he could, but he was weakening by the second. The pain was too intense.

Then the ladder's movements became violent. He wished there were wind and rain so that that might explain why the ladder was moving, but there was nothing. He still heard the chorus of insects and still smelled the broken nighttime air.

His stomach hurt. To add to his misery, Antonio sensed what little strength remained sift away from his muscles. *I'm too high off the ground!*

Switching quickly to the right and the left, the ladder's feet came loose, spraying small bombs of dirt. He imagined a toddler twisting the ladder like a straw in a bottle of warm milk and laughing at him. Then he pictured Perrollo doing so.

He heard something snapping. The ride intensified. The edges of the ladder spread apart. The ladder cracked and he felt the split coming from above. He still couldn't look up. There was too much movement. Antonio felt too weak and sick to fight.

Maybe if he just hung on long enough it would stop and he'd be able to calmly lower himself safely—

The rungs broke free. One smacked his nose and chin. The ones he held onto lost their weight and he felt air and gravity pull him.

He fell from the ladder as it exploded into pieces around him. *How will Perrollo get back?*

Antonio dropped. Hundreds of shredded pieces of the ladder fell around him. For a brief moment he felt nothing at all. His headache was gone. His stomach was not sour. His body felt just fine. Then pain flowed into every nook. He tried to raise his head to see how he'd fallen and found he was straight on his back. *Please don't let me be paralyzed*, he thought and wiggled his toes and back to make sure. Doing so nearly blinded him from pain.

The pieces of Perrollo's ladder continued to drop from the sky. Tiny splinters and half-pieces crashed everywhere throughout Perrollo's backyard.

Antonio felt the first rain drop on the middle of his left cheek. Quickly, there was more. The drizzle felt oily and warm as though infused with pollutants and acids. Then the rain pelted Antonio. Only it was not truly rain.

Antonio turned his hands over and found them coated with reddish, runny blood. *It has to be blood,* he thought. *What else could it be?*

He did his best to struggle to his side. The pain was

excruciating. He'd had to have broken something, he was sure. A rib or three. His legs did work. He kicked and pushed his way through the dirt.

The blood rained down.

Antonio was coated and dripping, the fluid warm and fresh. The dirt muddied every bit of him. Blood showered him. He smelled hot, recently spilled organic minerals; he gagged.

Please let it stop, he thought. *Please. So much blood. Everywhere on everything. The mud soaked with blood.*

Antonio's eyes stung. He couldn't keep it from his mouth or nose. He wondered if Perrollo was dead.

Not dead. Just his body's gone. Changed. Distilled.

***

The downpour of blood lightened.

Perrollo's stories came back to him. The creatures from the underworld tried to rise, but were cut down at the gateways.

Cut down.

Perrollo.

The earth turned dark red, soaked with blood. The plants looked painted. The small furniture, the rocks, the steps, the wine bottle: every bit oozed with sanguine color. Perrollo's blood nourished the land where he'd worked and lived. His essence covered Antonio.

They had to have been killed, Antonio believed. How else could he explain the deluge of blood? How else to define the gruesome explosion? How else, unless there was another reason Antonio could not readily grasp? Had they actually been slaughtered, or had they crossed over, the Angels lowering their swords?

Antonio could not know for sure. Perrollo had been right about that, after all. He could only ask and hope for an answer.

He turned on his back. His body ached and stunk, his skin sticky from the quickly drying gore.

The clouds parted, showing the same clear sky as before they'd arrived. There was no trace of Perrollo, Barola, or the *criaturas*.

Antonio wondered what he would do next. Would he heal? How would he explain his condition? Where would he go to wash the blood from his body and clothes? He didn't know.

Ahead of him, though, when he blinked, he could still see Perrollo's ladder in his mind's eye. In that moment Antonio knew . . . knew exactly what he would have to do.

Game On

CHARLES DAY

Johnny pulled into the driveway to his apartment and shut the engine to his old Mustang. The sounds of the pistons slowing to a stop reminded him of a bad cough. But he made it home without stalling again. That was a good thing. The second good thing (and even better): he was done with another week of working pools, a job he had with a few friends who had joined him on some business venture they started right out of high school. It was okay, he guessed. Paid the bills and left some money in his pocket for beers.

Eager to get inside and begin his weekend, Johnny took his key out of the ignition and opened the car door, slamming it shut once his dirty old sneakers hit the black tarred driveway of his landlord's house. He went around back and up the stairs that led to his rusty old door.

Once inside his small abode, he planned to unwind immediately. He kicked his sneakers off on his way to the fridge, grabbed a few beers and a half eaten chicken cutlet sandwich from last night—which he never finished due to an upset stomach—and shuffled toward his favorite spot, the recliner.

Johnny sat his overweight body down, wiggled his ass between the nice and comfy padding, and reached for his next favorite thing, the controller to his Xbox 360. He quickly turned on the console and placed his new headset over his shaven skull, ready to join his virtual buddies online for a night of blowing up aliens with all that green slime tossed around in different directions. It reminded him of the times he used to ram a few firecrackers in the mouth and ass of some unlucky frogs who were hopping around in the wrong place on the fourth of July.

The game started. The action, intense. It filled his time, satisfied with where he was at in play, yearning for more, more. Johnny's fingers moved furiously though, hitting the right buttons to execute his deadly maneuvers. One-by-one, alien scum were terminated. "Gotcha, you dirty rat bastards." He spoke into his headset, sent commands to others online in the midst of the action there by his side, displayed in all its glory on the large HDTV screen that sat on his new entertainment center.

"Move forward, I've got yer back," Johnny yelled.

"We're on it," some voice replied.

"I'm taking out the aliens behind the large rock, I think there's two of 'em," Johnny blurted out. "Keep me covered."

"Hey, fat Johnny!" a crackling voice echoed among the other chatter in his head set. Remember me? I'm coming for you, you . . . fucking . . . bastard. You're going to rot in Hell for what you did."

Johnny stopped pressing the buttons when he

heard this voice, a familiar voice. It couldn't be, this voice among the other continuous chatter and the commands and shouts to strategically kill alien scum, a voice that shouldn't be included in this game. *It can't be. It just can't.*

"Take 'em out," another voice spoke from the headset. Johnny witnessed the man he controlled so very well, now killed off. He didn't see the large alien, the creature who came up from behind his elite military person, didn't have the time to counter his attack because he'd been lost in thought.

And then that strange, familiar voice again. "Wait till I get you, fat Johnny. I'm going to do more than shoot you in the head like that alien just did, you low-life piece—" Johnny pulled the headset off, tossed it to the floor.

"What the fuck?" he spoke out loud. That voice again, not part of the game, not part of anything. That voice, his friend, his dead friend. It couldn't be.

Johnny pushed off his recliner, took his beer and went to the bathroom. He gazed at the reflection in the mirror, an unshaven face and a bald head, a large round head with a shiny red glow like a freaking cherry tootsie pop. *How the hell can this be? Mike is dead, been dead since last week. In my head . . . it's just in my fucking head. I'm imagining it, that's all.*

The door bell rang. The jingle of keys and a soft voice followed. "Hey, Johnny! Where are you, you hunk of a man?" His girlfriend, Nina. Sexy, Nina. She'd arrived earlier than expected.

"I'm in the bathroom. Be right out," he yelled from behind the closed door.

Yes, his girl for the last two months. And she was

okay in Johnny's book, the special book titled, "Girls Gone Bad." Much better in bed though, but certainly not a keeper, or at least not for now. He wasn't sure actually.

Nina had that personality and good looks, certain to bring him back to reality. Exactly what he needed right about now, to ease his mind, make the craziness go away. The fucking voice in his head, *mind tricks is all. Need to ease back on the drugs.*

Johnny threw cold water on his face and then guzzled down the rest of his beer before opening the bathroom door. Nina had already made it to the kitchen, leaning down for something in the fridge. Her ass cheeks peeked out of her low cut miniskirt, a pair of sweet melons ready for squeezing. It gave him a rise in his tight blue jeans. He was ready to play. "And what brings you here so early, woman?"

She turned and looked up at him with her wide tinted green eyes, her black eyeliner racing across them, like the tire burns he'd left on the street with his car, except much thinner.

He admired those lips she'd painted black. They reached out for him from her pale face. She did a good job with her short black hair, too. Well, except for the strand of pink she had dyed down the left side. And that nose ring, it had an unusual shine to it as she spoke. She may have given it a good polish. "Got off work early, figured we could start our night. You in the mood for—"

"I'm always in the mood for you, babe." Johnny smiled as he came toward her and held her hips with his huge hands.

"I'm talking about in the mood to go to Levels . . .

for some drinks, horny toad. It's two-for-one tonight. I hear that cover band, Hell's Fury, is playing. They sound just like Metallica. Let's check it out." She shot Johnny a seductive smile and moved in closer to embrace him. He pulled her closer and rubbed her crotch with his throbbing dick.

"I'd rather check you out . . . bitch." He grasped some of her hair as if he were ready to ride her like a horse. She showed some pearly white teeth and quickly bit his shoulder like a vampire would a pulsating neck. Fast, painful.

Johnny lifted Nina off the ground as she swung her legs in knee-high black leather boots around his waist like a clamp. He carried her to the bed and tossed her on it so that she bounced as if thrown on a trampoline. On her way up Johnny pulled his pants down to engage in some rough sex. She grabbed hold of his pants which were mid-way toward his knees and used her free hand to scratch his back with her long black fingernails. He liked that.

For the next twenty minutes they were like two sexually aroused bunnies, and it didn't take long after they were finished and smoking cigarettes, for the room to fill up with a cloud of tar and chemicals.

Johnny leaned over and took his time staring at this naked woman. "You know, the strangest thing happened to me earlier."

She turned and blew some smoke in his face. "And what's that?" She didn't even look at him when she said it. Her eyes were fixated on his lower appendages.

"I was playing my game with my new headset, right? And then I hear this voice . . . like it was my friend, my buddy Mike."

"Maybe he's okay? You know . . . there is a distinct possibility, Johnny. A chance he ran away from home, from family problems. Maybe he was doing the same thing you were doing, getting your video game fix on. Some people keep secrets. I bet you have a few skeletons in that there closet of yours, too."

Johnny raised his brows and sat up in bed. "What you getting at, Nina?"

"Nothing! Just saying that Mike may have disappeared for a reason."

"Yeah, sure. That's it. Let's just drop it."

Nina climbed out of bed, still naked as she traversed toward the bathroom. "Maybe he's with some girl. Probably some slut at Levels he picked up." Her ass wiggled, and he wanted to go at it again with her, but figured he'd wait, give her a rest.

"Couldn't be, Nina. He wouldn't go missing and not call me. Something's not right?" And he couldn't be further from the truth.

Fact was, Johnny knew Mike wouldn't be getting in touch anytime soon . . . because he'd killed him. Stuffed a bunch of small rocks down the prick's throat while he held him to the ground in the woods behind Levels bar and club, late last Friday night.

They'd become good and drunk before the argument. Mike had threatened to physically hurt him for stealing some money out of his desk drawer in his apartment. Mike wanted his cash. He knew it was Johnny, because he was the only one in the apartment the night before he found him in the bar. He didn't give a shit what Johnny had to say. "I want my money, you bastard. I know it was you," he said, poking his finger against Johnny's chest.

Well, Mike was right. He was always right, or at least that's what he aimed to be. Sure Johnny took the cash, and he snorted most of it up his nostrils with the cocaine he bought, and even had some money left to get the new Xbox headset.

If Mike would have let it go, accepted the fact that Johnny was jumped by a few thugs before coming to the bar, it would have been over. But Mike persisted, followed him out of the bar to the parking lot, past the cars and into the woods where Johnny stopped to take a piss, even swung at him. That's when Johnny went into a rage. He managed to get on top of Mike, holding his arms with the God-given weight Johnny had, using his legs so that when he sat on top of Mike, there was no way the kid was getting up. But he wouldn't stop screaming for help. That's when the rocks around Johnny's immediate area came in handy.

One after the other, as Mike's eyes bulged from both the fear and the gagging, Johnny continued to stuff them down his friend's esophagus until he stopped breathing. His eyes swelled, and the prick must have taken a shit in his trousers because Johnny could smell an awful, putrid smell, like he was sitting on a dead corpse.

His thoughts about this dreadful night had taken awhile to suppress, but it seemed to show up for the first time and haunt the shit out of him today, thanks to the voice.

Johnny quickly jumped when he heard a loud noise in his living room. The sounds of guns going off, aliens screaming, and the military calling out commands. The Xbox, the fucking Xbox was on, and at full volume no less.

"Why the hell you playing your games so loud? You want the tenants upstairs to complain." Nina's voice screamed from behind the bathroom door. "Jesus, you're going to blow out your eardrums, ass-wipe."

Johnny didn't answer. He came out of the bedroom and walked toward the TV. Mike was staring straight at him from within the game, and it looked like his lifeless body was trapped underwater for a good month and he came out looking like a shriveled up, large raisin. The face on the screen was pale, bloated, and wrinkled, and his mouth seemed wider than normal, much wider. His eyes were dead but his puffy lips moved. "I'm coming for you, fat Johnny. You're going to get yours for what you did. I. Want. My. Cash!"

Johnny grabbed the controller and used the features to shut the Xbox off. It worked. "What the—" He felt like he jumped out of his skin when Nina came up from behind, placing her cold hands on his neck.

"What's with all the noise, sexy?" Nina asked?

"Nothing. We should go to Levels. Seriously, I need to get out of here." Johnny admitted to himself he was nervous. Mike had been on that screen. The Xbox. His ghost. Was he going crazy? Was Mike's ghost coming back for revenge?

Hell, Johnny had always been an atheist. Ghosts aren't real. There has never been any concrete proof they exist. And even if Mike was out to fuck with him, why the Xbox? Made no sense. Hell, his friend wasn't an avid gamer. He still owned the PS2.

"Alright, sure," Nina replied. "Let me just fix myself up some more. You should do the same. Take a shower. You're all sweaty and you look like you just saw a ghost. You okay?"

"Yeah, fine." He raised one of his grapefruit sized hands, made a fist and slammed it down on the Xbox. The top cracked open like an eggshell and a few pieces fell onto the wooden coffee table. "Prick! You want to go at it, fucker, bring it, Mike, bring it."

Nina turned and looked toward Johnny. "What the hell, Johnny? What are you talking about?" Her face turned bright red. She looked frightened.

"Nothing, Nina, leave it. Go. Get ready."

"But you just smashed your—"

"I said . . . let's go."

Johnny went back into the bathroom to take a piss, his mind returning to thoughts about that night. He lifted the lid and began to relieve himself when he heard a loud sound again. The TV was on. The noise sounded familiar, the yells and screams. Of course, it was him, they were yelling at each other.

Johnny didn't bother to zipper his pants as he ran out of the bathroom and into the living room where he found Nina staring at the image on the TV, tears flowing from her eyes. "Holy Jeez, Johnny! What did you do to Mike? What's happening?"

Johnny ran toward the TV, witnessing himself murdering his friend in real time, his last gasp for air and then silence. With that, he took the TV off the top of the entertainment center and smashed it to the floor. Yellow streaks of light and bright red sparks went everywhere like a bunch of fireworks. He looked over at her, breathing heavily. "Let's go."

"No. No. You did something to Mike, what did you do?" she screamed looking directly at him with a face of rage, which actually had him worried about their relationship, but Johnny didn't answer. Instead, he grabbed his car keys off his kitchen table and stepped into his sneakers before running out the door. He climbed into his car, slammed the door, started the ignition and drove to the Levels bar parking lot. It was a short trip, but to Johnny, whose mind was now racing, it felt like forever.

He's dead. I know it. I took his lifeless body and placed it deep in the river. Stuffed his body under a bunch of large boulders and placed another on top to keep him secure so no one would ever find him. Ever!

When he pulled into the parking lot, the gravel under his tires crunched. He came to a halt and got out of the car after shutting the ignition. The engine coughed to a stop. He ran into the woods and down the trail until he came to the spot by the river, the final resting place for his friend. "Son-of-a-bitch, Mike. You won't let it go, will ya? You just have to mess with me." He spoke out loud under his heavy breathing. "You always had to have the last word, even now, you fucker."

Johnny stepped into the water and waded toward the spot where the boulders were. He was sure Mike was still down at the bottom, wedged between some rocks. As he came closer, he went under to check. He had to check. He didn't know why. It wasn't like Mike could be alive and cursing at him for what he did.

Johnny swam over to the spot about six or seven feet deep. The river was strong tonight. Its currents were doing their best to grab hold of him and send him further down to the large waterfall, the one which lead into a bigger body of water. And it was damn cold in the water tonight. He could feel his joints slow, his bones chill, making it harder to control his movements.

As he swam closer, he went to see if maybe a leg with a sneaker attached to it were sticking out from under the boulders, something to reassure him, confirm that Mike hadn't somehow woke up and got away. But how? The rocks lodged in his throat had suffocated him. He remembered that he'd felt Mike's pulse that night . . . there was none. And even if God had somehow intervened and brought Mike back to life, the almighty God, sure as shit wasn't coming down to move the boulders out of the way to release him.

Johnny came up to the spot. An arm was floating out between the rocks. He had to come up to the surface for air. He swam up fast and popped his head out above the water, just enough so that small waves slapped at his ears and tried to make its way into his nostrils.

After trying to remain calm about this whole situation, he took a deep breath, ready to go back down for one last look, one more visual of Mike there, rotting away, eaten by fish and whatever else floated around in these waters. He quickly swam down toward the waving arm. He was just above the big boulder and the smaller one he'd used to keep Mike secure, and he tried his best to peek down the small gap amongst all the green weeds. Mike's face was now in view. His friend's eyes were wide open, staring back just like on the TV. His eyeballs moved back and forth before they locked onto Johnny's. Why, why haven't they been eaten by fish or other underwater creatures? His bloated lips flapped in the water as if he were talking, pearly white teeth clearly visible.

Mike's eyes rolled and his furry brows moved to create the letter V.

Johnny let out a scream and took in some water. Fearful he'd drown for sure, he started his retreat back up, but something grabbed hold of his leg. He looked down, terrified that he knew what it was, Mike's hand, the same one he saw attached to the arm flapping around in the water. It had a tight grip and wouldn't let go.

Johnny forced himself to look up at the surface not far away, but he became more frightened and let way too much water into his lungs.

And he could hear it in his head, Mike's voice, but his lips didn't move.

Only the eyes.

The eyes followed his every move as he struggled to get away. "Told you I would get you! Now die!"

The Lady of Lost Lake

BEV VINCENT

Sitting beside Lost Lake on a Friday afternoon with a cold beer in your hand, a few more cooling in the lake, and nothing but time on your hands is like no other experience on earth. It was our secret hideaway, a Utopia miles from civilization. The place to go when everyday life has taken its toll.

The serenity my three friends and I achieved on arrival was worth every bit of the seventy-five mile drive from the havoc of the city, the six-mile walk through the woods with our canoe and gear, and the waist-deep river we had to wade across to get to Paradise. We had plenty of beer—you can never have too much beer—food in case the fish didn't bite, and all the right lures to ensure they would. The best part was we had Saturday, Sunday and a holiday Monday before we had to return to Bedlam.

All I could see of Bill in the canoe in the middle of the lake were his feet, his hat—pulled down low over his eyes to block out the hot summer sun—and his fishing rod poking over the side, trailing a fiber of temptation to the residents of Lost Lake, the plumpest lake trout I've ever seen. Freddy relaxed on the large flat stone that jutted into the water from the shore near camp. He sat yoga-style, contemplating the placid lake rippling gently around him. I could hear Alf lumbering through the woods, rounding up enough firewood to cook the fish we'd already vanquished that afternoon. Content to sit on the shore with a cold one, I dangled my line in the water and basked in the sun. I didn't care if I caught anything else that day.

Out here we were four of a kind. Rugged outdoorsmen, like you see on beer commercials. In real life we were as different as men get. Bill was a research professor in Philadelphia, Freddy an accountant in Toronto, Alf an architect in California and I a writer living in rural eastern Canada. We had all gone to school together in the same small town, but the others had spread out as they moved up in their respective fields. Even now that I've become moderately successful, I'm content to stay close to where I grew up.

We got together at least once most years since graduation. Sometimes we went skiing out west. A couple of times we chartered a boat to dive off the Florida Keys. The blissful shore of Lost Lake, though, was our favorite place. Here we could spend days with nothing but nothing on our minds.

I drained the last of the beer and tossed the can onto an already impressive heap of empties. Pulling the brim of my Blue Jays cap around my eyes, I let the peaceful surroundings usher all the worries from my head. This weekend I intended to studiously avoid thinking about the mortgage, car payments and the likelihood that our son would be spending another year in seventh grade. No thoughts of writer's block. I wouldn't dwell more than a few seconds on the fact that Terri and I were at odds more often than not these days. The judicious application of beer would take care of what the serenity couldn't handle.

The whistle-singing of the birds lulled me to another place even sweeter than this. For a while I dreamt of a beautiful lady with long blonde flowing hair. She sat near me smiling, her eyes sparkling. Her milk-white dress clung to her body like it was held in place by magnetism. She tossed her head and laughed at the least little thing. She urged me to go with her, but I couldn't figure out where she wanted to take me. Away from my strained marriage, perhaps.

The smell of fish frying in the heavy cast-iron frying pan Alf had lugged along with him brought me out of my reverie. I rescued another beer from our reservoir in the lake, broke open a fresh case and replenished the stock. Our load was going to be a lot lighter on the way out.

Soon only a pile of well-picked bones remained of the trout. Even the heads were gone. Bill had tried to persuade the rest of us to try them, but we weren't convinced. He'd spent way too much time in Japan, we decided, threatening to serve him trout sashimi for breakfast.

While my supper settled, I decided to take the canoe out and work—but not too hard—at catching tomorrow's lunch. Freddy volunteered to go, too, and I didn't mind the company. Though we were all close, Freddy was my best friend. We were the first of the gang to meet, but I think it would have ended up that way anyway. We knew each other well enough to know when to keep our mouths shut. That's part of being friends, I guess.

The dark water beneath us promised depth and a rich supply of fish. We let the canoe drift, guided by the slightest of July afternoon breezes. Lake water ticked softly against the hull.

Selecting my current favorite lure, I set up my rod, slipped it through the loop on the gunwale, and locked it into place. Now I could relax, letting my body settle into the bottom of the canoe. I dangled my bare feet over the side, welcoming the cool touch of the lake. At the other end, Freddy positioned himself similarly so we balanced each other out. We were ready for the trout to come if they wanted. Things were peaceful, as peaceful as I'd ever seen them. The flies weren't biting and it didn't really matter that the fish weren't either.

A cold, slimy hand grabbed my left ankle, tightening its grip like a vise. I struggled briefly against the relentless downward pressure and freed myself from its grasp. I sat up abruptly and swung my feet back into the boat. The clammy sensation on my lower leg persisted.

Dazed and disoriented, I hesitantly leaned over the side of the canoe, expecting to see Alf with a sheepish grin on his face. Only my distorted, darkened faced stared back at me from the placid waters.

Had something tried to drag me overboard?

Freddy roused himself and asked groggily, "Get a bite?" He squinted at me to clear his eyes.

"Suh-something grabbed my foot," I blathered. "Something in the water. It was cold and—ugh—clammy. It tried to pull me in."

He squinted at me a moment longer, then burst into laughter. When he realized I wasn't joining him, he stopped. "Come on, Steve, quit shitting me. If you get me all paranoid, you'll have to sit up with me to keep away the night creatures!"

"No shit, Freddy. It grabbed me by the leg . . . " I stopped at what I saw. Wrapped around the leg I was indicating, the very leg I had been certain a moment earlier had been fondled by the creature from the Black Lagoon, was a soggy piece of brown wrapping paper. Gingerly I peeled it off my calf and dropped it into the bottom of the boat. I grinned at Freddy shamefacedly. "It *felt* like a hand."

Of course, Freddy couldn't wait to tell the other guys the whole story when we beached the canoe. With wide eyes and dramatic arm gestures he made it seem like I'd been frantic, climbing the mast of the ship to get away from whatever lurked below. We didn't even have a mast fercrisesakes.

I was the butt of their jokes for the rest of the evening. While I doused the campfire we'd been sitting around for the past couple of hours, swapping old fish tales, Bill quipped, "You better be careful. Your friend in the lake might come back for you later tonight!"

Freddy drew a stick monster with fangs and barbed-wire hair on the shred of brown paper and nailed it to a tree outside the tent. Alf made some half-witted comment about the dangers of an over-active imagination. I took the whole thing with good cheer. Everyone was still chuckling as we crawled into our sleeping bags.

By then, an unseasonable chill tinged the night air and a dense fog cloaked the half-moon. Freddy closed the flaps on the four-man tent to ward off the dampness and we all settled down to sleep shortly before midnight.

When I awoke later, it took a while to orient myself. The surroundings were totally unfamiliar. Terri wasn't sleeping at my side, her back turned to me as it so often was of late. To add to the confusion, I could hear something above the constant background wilderness noises: a high, thin, ill-defined melody. It tugged ever so slightly at me, fueling urges deep within me that I couldn't understand.

Beside me, Alf tossed and turned in his sleep, as if troubled by nightmares. Suddenly he sat erect, mumbled something totally incomprehensible, then climbed out of his sleeping bag. The ties at the door of the tent gave him some trouble and he tugged at them impatiently. After he solved their puzzle, he stumbled outside. Going to relieve himself, I assumed.

A few moments later, I heard him dragging the canoe from the shore into the lake. This unexpected sound helped me clear my head. Crawling to the open doorway, I poked my head out into the fog-bound night just in time to see Alf paddle into the mist. The moonlight reflected around him, giving the whole scene an ethereal, transcendental look.

"Alf? Alf! What the hell are you doing?" I stage-whispered at him, trying not to wake the others. He didn't seem to hear me, although I was sure he should have been able to. The night had grown so calm I could hear the soft swishes of his oars in the water. Gradually I became aware of the high, melodious sound I'd heard earlier.

Behind me, someone else started moving around

inside the tent. Bill poked his head out beside mine a moment later.

"What are you doing? Is there something out here? A bear?"

"Just him," I replied, pointing at Alf. He was barely visible, paddling toward the center of the lake.

"Christ! What on earth is he doing out there at this time of night?"

"I have no idea," I said. "He just got out of his sleeping bag and climbed into the canoe."

Bill was silent for a moment. "You don't suppose he's still asleep, do you?"

I shrugged.

"What should we do?" Bill asked.

I no longer heard the paddles, but I could still hear that mysterious, unsettling, thin wail. Alf sat absolutely motionless, letting the canoe drift.

"Maybe he just wants to be alone," I said.

"I think we should try to get his attention, in case something's wrong."

I crawled outside the tent and was about to call to Alf when he stood up. I looked at Bill, perplexed. Alf knew better than to stand up in a canoe. What was going on?

A hand reached up from below the lake's surface and grasped the side of the boat. Something on the pale, thin hand—a ring perhaps—glinted in the moonlight. A weak groan escaped from Bill's mouth. I might have moaned, too, if my lips hadn't been pursed together so tightly.

I would like to say the boat lurched suddenly and Alf fell overboard. That might have made things easier to accept. We could have dismissed the hand as an optical illusion. But the way Alf just stepped over the side without hesitation can't be explained away. He disappeared beneath the surface of the lake with barely a splash.

Bill started toward the edge of the lake, ready to dive in to Alf's rescue, but I restrained him. As we watched, the hand swished twice in the air, then seemed to beckon us. Then it disappeared below the surface. Simultaneously, the thin, disturbing music stopped, leaving only silence.

The canoe, guided by some unseen force, propelled itself back to the shore, grinding to a halt in the gravel at our feet.

We stared blankly for what seemed like minutes. Crickets came back to life in the woods around the lake, breaking the preternatural silence.

Bill was halfway back to the tent by the time I caught up to him. "Where are you going?" I hollered.

"To wake up Freddy and get the hell out of here. Do you want to stick around?" My own panic reflected in his eyes.

He stuck his head inside the tent flap and started to say Freddy's name but his voice cut off in mid-syllable. I pushed him aside and entered the tent to find myself alone. Freddy's sleeping bag was empty.

Bill and I called Freddy's name as we searched the area around the camp, but he didn't respond. If Freddy had gone wandering into the forest, we had no hope of finding him in the darkness.

I stared at the lake for a long time before approaching it just long enough to grab a case of beer. We returned to the tent, tied down the flaps and zipped the door tight. The beer tasted bitter in my mouth, but drinking it was something to do to keep me awake. I sat in my sleeping bag and tried to wrap my mind around what had happened. I thought of Terri, her hands planted firmly on her hips, sending me off on this weekend outing with the biting words of an old argument. I contemplated the manuscript that lay half-finished on my desktop and the irritating roadblock that had kept me from adding pages to the stack for over a month. I weighed the merits of chucking everything and moving somewhere far away to start a new life.

I snapped awake some time later. Guilt and fear gripped me, knowing that I shouldn't have gone to sleep. It was nearly two a.m. I'd been out for almost an hour.

I felt wetness in my crotch and discovered that my nearly full can of beer had spilled. The spreading puddle should have been enough to wake me up. I became aware of the thin wailing sound again, and then heard the sound of the canoe being pushed into the lake. Three crushed beer cans surrounded Bill's empty sleeping bag. Apparently he had fended off sleep more successfully than I had.

I leapt up and tore my way out of the tent, running headlong down the slope to the lake. I gashed my bare foot on something and yelled in anger and frustration. Bill was already nearing the center of the lake when I reached the shore. The feminine hand beckoned him. For a brief instant I felt jealous that it was not calling to me. I remembered how the woman in my reverie looked in her form-fitting white gown, how she had laughed.

I yelled at him but I couldn't distract him from

whatever had him in its power. I was ready to dive into the water, but I felt something lurking just beneath the surface, waiting for me. I was safe as long as I was on the shore. I could do nothing but watch as Bill stood up and stepped overboard to join Alf, and presumably Freddy, at the bottom of the lake. I cursed my inability to help. The hand waved three times and once again beckoned to me. Then it vanished beneath the surface, taking the wailing with it.

I watched, mesmerized, as the canoe propelled itself back toward me. When it got within throwing distance, I pelted the largest stones I could find at it. My first shots missed, raising geysers near the boat. The third stone hit the prow, knocking the canoe temporarily off course, but it soon re-oriented on me. I lofted the fourth rock high into the air. It landed dead center, breaking through the fiberglass bottom. I watched in quiet satisfaction as water slowly filled the passenger compartment. The foam-filled seats kept the canoe from sinking completely but it no longer advanced toward the shore.

A solitary oar floated over the gunwales and drifted away.

I headed back up the slope to our camp, found the first aid kit and bandaged the gash in my foot. I stuffed two wads of cotton batting in my ears, then I grabbed my knapsack, threw a few necessities in it and climbed toward the top of the rise.

The further from the lake I got, the slower I moved. Something tugged at me, beseeching me to turn around. I finally surrendered.

Hovering above the water's surface in the center of the lake was the most beautiful woman I'd ever seen, the woman from my reverie. She had long flowing blonde hair and a white gown barely contained her supple, beckoning body. The only thing missing was the sword Excalibur.

I stared, motionless, for the longest time and suddenly I knew how much happier I would be if I went to her. Everything would be peaceful. All my problems would be washed away. We would be together always and there would be no harsh words of recrimination, no nights on the couch, no days of silence.

I started down the slope and it seems now that I had no thoughts but absolute peace. I stopped at the bottom and looked at her again. I ached to be with her. She laughed and teased her hair with a slight toss of her head. Her body moved under the gown as if gravity held no reign here.

I moved toward the lake again. Near the shore, mesmerized, I tripped on a large rock and sprawled in the dirt. My outstretched hand barely dipped into the water.

The spell broke. When I looked at the Lady again, she was slowly sinking into the lake. Her bones grew visible through her fair skin. A disappointed grimace melted with her face. Her arms spread as if she were delivering a benediction.

It was almost six-thirty in the morning by the time I reached the car that had brought us to Lost Lake just the morning before. After three hours of hiking through the woods in a stupor, I realized I didn't have the keys.

Another ten miles to the highway. I was wet, dirty, hungry, tired and confused. I sat on the ground by the roadside and cried.

At least thirty cars passed before I got a ride. I can't say I blame the other drivers. I wouldn't pick up a hitchhiker that looked like I did that Saturday morning.

I convinced the police there had been a boating accident, and the sunken canoe helped sell the story, though I could tell they had questions—and no bodies. The vivid, waking nightmares lasted for months after the investigation ended.

At night, the Lady still comes to visit me, looking as she did before she vanished out of sight beneath the surface. Rotting and decomposing. Beckoning me to come back and join her. Disappointed when I can't.

I live alone now, but I still get to visit my son on occasion. We have become quite close—maybe the separation has enhanced our relationship. He's been trying to convince me to take a weekend off from writing and go fishing with him.

I'm trying to get him to settle for a baseball game.

Junksick

G.N. BRAUN

"**W**here the fuck is he?" Joel turned to me as though the connection's absence was my fault.

"Fucked if I know, dude." I turned to look out the window, as if that simple act would result in the miraculous appearance of 'The Man'. "He should be here by now."

I tried to act like I wished the fucker would hurry up. I *did* feel like crap. Junk-sickness was setting in: achy legs, and the twitches and cramps were starting.

Joel wrapped his arms around himself, sweating and shivering despite the temperature being in the high thirties. He had it bad. Worse than I did. That didn't mean I was going to tell him about the secret emergency stash hidden in my sock. Junkies always looked after *numero uno*. That's just what we did. We kept our secrets. Junkies loved secrets: secret stashes, secret dealers, secrets kept purely for the sake of secrets. It gave us a sense of power to think we knew something no-one else did. And if there's one thing junkies both crave and lack, it's power.

"Fuck man, where the hell is he?" Joel shuffled over to stand above me, arms akimbo. "He ain't coming, is he?" He glared down at me, blaming me for his pain and discomfort. It wasn't my fault. I didn't get him hooked on the shit. Well, actually I did, but it still wasn't my fault he was sick today.

Joel had burnt his dealer, giving him up to the pigs when they held him overnight on some trumped-up charge. The pigs loved doing that to junkies. Grab them, hold them, watch them sweat and degenerate into a mess of pain and misery. Then they would get some gear out of the evidence locker to tease them with. They'd lay it out on a table just outside the cell, spoon and syringe sitting next to it.

You have to understand, the sickness of a junk-less junkie is part physical, part mental. The mental side is the hard one to beat. If you can take your mind off scoring with some other activity, like sex or drinking yourself stupid, the physical withdrawals are much less severe. However, if all you can do is think about the next hit, then the suffering is so intense there's nothing you can compare it to. Maybe being set on fire while a million electric fleas gnaw away at you from the inside. No. On second thought, that doesn't even come close to the feeling. And there is nothing worse than being in withdrawal while staring at a fix not five feet away from you. It takes real strength to not give in to the temptation. And not many junkies retain any real mental fortitude. You know what they say: never trust a junkie, and ninety-nine times out of a hundred, they're right.

"*Fuck!*" Joel turned away from me and slammed his fist into the plasterboard, smashing a hole through it.

"Dude, relax. He's here now."

Joel almost leapt into the air in his hurry to turn towards the door.

As soon as he turned his back, I stabbed him.

I stabbed him hard, and I stabbed him deep. The blade glanced off bone, then I heard the breath rush from his lungs as the shock and impact sent him staggering toward the door. I pulled a mobile phone from my pocket, and hit the speed dial for the only number that was programmed.

"Yes?" The androgynous voice that answered still creeped me out after all these years.

"I've got another one for you. Three forty-seven Cummings Street. Ground floor. Male. Mid-twenties. Addict." I had the spiel down to a fine art.

I didn't know what they did with the bodies, and I didn't want to know. My conscience already ate at me, but I'd do it all again in a second. After all, you can never trust a junkie. I fetched my sock stash and fixed up a taste of heroin. That would hold me until the real thing got here.

After a long, sweaty, and stoned twenty minutes, the door opened, and the collectors came in. They would remove the body, and then one would return and pay me. That was the routine. A grand for every adult corpse I sent their way, plus the bonus—the real reason I had chosen to kill. I also got five hundred milligrams of Apocalypse each time.

No one really knew where 'lypse had come from. It had started in Melbourne, appearing on the streets around December of '09. It began in the clubs, a party drug for the ravers and the trance-heads, although it didn't take long for the junkies to try injecting it.

Word got around fast. *Inject this shit, it's the bomb.* After that, demand went through the roof, as did the price. The level of addiction was 100%. That's how I started trading in the business of death. The 'lypse owned me.

I slumped in the corner as the two men in white collected the body, strapped it to the gurney and took it out to what appeared to be a normal ambulance. I knew better. I had seen these two attendants numerous times, and I'd bet my life they weren't real paramedics.

Paramedics didn't wear runners to work. And they didn't retrieve murder victims on the side. It was always the same two guys. One was tall and solid, like a weightlifter gone to seed. The other was smaller, and had a face like a hatchet, all sharp lines and angles, with one hell of an overbite. Axe-face was the one who doled out the gear and the cash.

Their routine never changed: grab the body, then Axe-face would come back to pay me. This time they both returned. Bulk-boy gestured in my direction and grunted something to his partner. I tried to focus on their words, but the heroin had well kicked in. Everything had dulled: faces, words, the world. They came over and picked me up, shaking their heads and avoiding my gaze.

"You're looking a little worse for wear, old son." Bulk-boy had breath that stank of onion and salami, and as I tried to slide further into the corner to get away from the foul odor, I found I couldn't move, held as I was by both men. With no strength to argue, and too off my head on smack to do anything else, I let them lead me out to the ambulance.

The second gurney was mine.

I lay there, wondering what the fuck was going on. But mostly I wondered if I was going to get my fix. The heroin held me okay, but I needed a taste of the real stuff. I needed some 'lypse.

The engine growled to life as I looked over at Joel's body. There was no guilt, no fear, just the desperate need for a taste of Apocalypse. The ambulance took the corners fast, siren blaring. The axe-faced attendant rode in back with me, a small leather case cradled in his hands.

Thank fuck. It's the 'lypse bag.

I relaxed as he removed a small green vial and syringe. My gut loosened and my head swum at the thought of a taste.

Axe-face inserted the needle into the ampoule, drawing up half a syringe full of the dull green liquid. My skin crawled and my hair stood on end in anticipation of the rush. There was no other drug like Apocalypse. Believe me, I've tried 'em all. I willed my veins to pop as he applied a tourniquet and tapped my elbow joint. I pumped my hand as best I could. The needle slipped into my skin, and blood blossomed as it hit a vein. I watched him push down the plunger and felt the rush immediately.

Apocalypse is like no other drug on Earth. You can drink it to get a brilliant high; one perfectly suited for dancing and partying all night. But you can also inject it. It's like being hit by lightning. There's a rush of energy and clarity of thought. Of *power*.

It's what God must have felt like the day he finished the universe. All powerful, all knowing, all God. Lord and master of all he surveyed. Your whole body just tingles. It's sorta like cocaine, but a thousand times more intense: the rush, the feeling of perfection, the feeling of pure pleasure. Super-coke.

On 'lypse, you *know* you can do anything you want, but you don't really want to do much at all except sit back and enjoy the fuckin' high. I sank into the gurney, euphoric and suddenly not giving a fuck where I was being taken.

By the time the ambulance ground to a halt, the initial rush had worn off. I just felt numb, like a strong heroin-high. The double-doors of the ambulance swung open to reveal an underground parking garage, empty of all other vehicles. I tried to stand, but the gurney straps were fastened tight.

"Hey guys, what gives?"

Silence.

The two attendants lowered the gurney to the ground and rolled me towards a bank of elevator doors.

"Any chance of another taste?"

No answer.

I tested the ties that held me down, but there was no give.

"What the *fuck* is going on?" I demanded.

My anger swelled. I tensed my upper body and strained against the restraints. It was futile. There was nothing to do except see where this was leading.

The elevator pinged.

Sweat trickled down my temples, pooled beneath my armpits as the doors closed behind us.

I tried to see which button Axe-face pushed, but the strap across my forehead did its job well. All I could do was watch the indicator above the doors to see what floor I was being taken to.

The lift started to drop, but there were no numbers to indicate the floors below ground. As we lurched to a stop, the doors opened to reveal a hospital-type corridor. I saw white walls, and I assume floors of the same colour. We turned right into a new corridor, and I tried to keep track of the path we were taking. I would find my way back to the lift when . . . if . . . I could escape from these goons.

A harsh chemical smell pervaded the halls, assaulting my nostrils and causing my eyes to water. I blinked to clear them as I was pulled to a stop before double doors. Only the top three feet of the doors was visible. I heard one of the attendants tap something into what could only be a keyboard. It had to be an entry code. The doors slid open silently. Bright artificial light, harsher than that in the outside corridor, slammed into my already irritated eyes, taking away my vision.

I heard plenty, though.

Someone said, "Move him to that table and strap him down securely. The extraction process can be quite painful, and I don't want him moving about."

I recognised the voice from the phone. Fear raced through my body, faster than the rush of a taste of 'lypse, as I thought about the words *extraction* and *painful*.

"The process is irreversible and fatal. I need you to stick around and remove the body for me. But first, you can take the hormones I extract to the refining and distribution centre."

More words. *Irreversible* and *fatal* resonated in my mind most of all, but I retained the overall concept this time. I was being killed, and something from my body, the body of a junkie, was being farmed and sold as Apocalypse.

Like all the bodies I had supplied them with in the past, I would soon become nothing more than a product. Somehow, in the drugged-up recesses of my guilt-ridden psyche, this seemed fitting.

Soon, I wouldn't just *feel* like a god. Soon, I would *make* gods.

Witch-Compass

GRAHAM MASTERTON

On his last night in Libreville, Paul went for a long aimless walk through the market. A heavy rainstorm had just passed over and the air was almost intolerably humid. He felt as if he had a hot Turkish towel wrapped around his head, and his shirt clung to his back. There were many things he would miss about Gabon, but the climate wasn't one of them, and neither was the musty smell of tropical mold.

All along the Marché Rouge there were stalls heaped with bananas and plantains and cassava; as well as food-stands selling curried goat and thick maize porridge and spicy fish. The stalls were lit by an elaborate spider's-web of electric cables, with naked bulbs dangling from them. Each stall was like a small, brightly colored theater, with the sweaty black faces of its actors wreathed in theatrical steam and smoke.

Paul passed them by, a tall rangy white man with short-cropped hair and round Oliver Goldsmith glasses, and already he was beginning to feel like a spectator, like somebody who no longer belonged here.

A thin young girl with one milky eye tugged at Paul's shirt and offered him a selection of copper bracelets. He was about to shoo her away when he suddenly thought: what does it matter anymore? I won't be here tomorrow, I'll be on my way back to the States, and what good will a wallet full of CFA francs be in New Milford, Connecticut?

He gave the girl five francs, which was more than she probably made in a week, and took one of the bracelets.

"*Merci beaucoup, monsieur, vous êtes très gentil,*" she said, with a strong Fang accent. She gave him a gappy grin and twirled off into the crowds.

Paul looked down at his wallet. He had hardly any money left now. Three hundred francs, an American Express card which he didn't dare to use, and a damp-rippled air ticket. He was almost as poor as the rest of the population of Gabon.

He had come here three and a half years ago to set up his own metals-trading business. Gradually he had built up a network of contacts amongst the foreign mining companies and established a reputation for achieving the highest prices for the least administration costs. After two years, he was able to rent a grand white house near the presidential palace and import a new silver Mercedes. But his increasing success brought him to the attention of governments officials, and before long he had been summoned to the offices of the department of trade. A highly amused official in a snowy short-sleeved shirt had informed him that, in future, all of his dealings would attract a 'brokerage tax' of eighty-five per cent.

"Eighty-five per cent! Do you want me to starve?"

"You exaggerate, Mr. Dennison. The average Gabonese makes less in a year than you spend on one pair of shoes. Yet he eats, he has clothes on his back. What more do you need than that?"

Paul refused to pay. But the next week, when he had tried to call LaSalle Zinc, he had been told with a great deal of apologetic French clucking that they could no longer do business with him, because of 'internal rationalization'. He had received a similar response from DuFreyne Lead and Pan-African Manganese. The following week his phones had been cut off altogether.

He had lived off his savings for a few months, trying to take legal action to have the 'brokerage tax' rescinded or at least reduced. But the Gabonese legal system owed more to Franz Kafka than it did to commercial justice. In the end his lawyer had withdrawn his services, too, and he knew there was no point in fighting his case any further.

He walked right down to the western end of the Marché Rouge. Beneath his feet, the lights from the market stalls were reflected like a drowned world. The air was filled with repetitive, plangent music, and the clamor of so many insects that it sounded as if somebody were scraping a rake over a corrugated iron roof.

At the very end of the market, in the shadows, an old woman was sitting cross-legged on the wet tarmac with an upturned fruit box in front of her. She had a smooth, round face and her hair was twisted into hundreds of tiny silver beads. She wore a dark brown dress with black-printed patterns on it, zigzags and circles and twig-like figures. She kept nodding her head in Paul's direction, as if he were talking to her and she was agreeing with him, and as she nodded her huge silver earrings swung and caught the light from the fish stall next to her.

On the fruit box several off items were arranged. At the back, a small ebony carving of a woman with enormous breasts and protruding buttocks, her lips fastened together with silver wire. Next to her feet lay something that looked like a rattle made out of a dried bone and a shrunken monkey's head, with matted ginger hair. There were six or seven Pond's Cold Cream jars, refilled with brown and yellowish paste. There was a selection of necklaces, decorated with teeth and beads and birds' bones. And there was an object which looked like a black gourd, only three or four inches long and completely plain.

Paul was about to turn back to his hotel when the woman said, *"Attendez, monsieur! Ne voulez-vous acheter mes jouets?"*

She said it in surprise, as if she couldn't understand why he hadn't come up to her and asked her how much they cost.

"I'm sorry, I'm just taking a walk."

She passed her hands over the disparate collection on top of her fruit box. "I think that is why you come here. To buy from me something."

"No, I'm sorry."

"Then what is bringing your feet this way?"

"I'm leaving Libreville tomorrow morning. I was taking a last look around the market, that's all."

"You come this way for a reason. No man comes looking for Jonquil Mekambo by accident."

"Listen," said Paul. "I really have to go. And to tell

you the truth, I don't think you have anything here I could possibly want."

The woman lifted up the ebony figure. "Silence those who do you bad, *peut-être*?"

"Oh, I get it. This is ju-ju stuff. Thanks but no thanks. Really."

The woman picked up the bone with the monkey's head and tapped it on the side of the box. "Call up demons to strangle your enemy? I teach you how to knock."

"Listen, forget it. I got enough demons in my life right now without conjuring up any more."

"Jonquil knows that. Jonquil knows why you have to go from Libreville. No money, no work."

Paul stared at her. She stared back, her face like a black expressionless moon. "How did you know that?" he demanded.

"Jonquil knows all thing. Jonquil is waiting for you here *ce soir*."

"Well, Jonquil, however you found out, there's nothing you can do to help me. It's going to take more than black magic to sort my life out. I'll have to start over again, right from scratch."

"Then you need witch-compass."

"Oh, yes? And what's a witch-compass going to do for me, whatever that is?"

Jonquil pointed with a red-painted fingernail to the gourd. "Witch-compass, genuine from Makokou."

"So what does a witch-compass do?"

"Brings your feet to what you want. Money, woman, house. Work all time."

"I see. Never fails. So what are *you* doing, sitting in the street here, if you could use the witch-compass to guide you to whatever you want?"

"Jonquil has what she wants. All thing."

Paul shook his head. "It's a great idea, Jonquil. But I think I'll pass."

"Pick it up," Jonquil urged him.

Paul hesitated for a moment. For some reason, the pattering of drums sounded louder than usual, more insistent, and the insects scraped even more aggressively. He picked up the black gourd and weighed it in his hand. It was quite light, and obviously hollow, because he could hear something rattling around inside it. Beads, maybe; or seeds.

"See in your head the thing you want," said Jonquil. "The witch-compass makes its song. Quiet when you want is far off distance. Louder—louder when close."

"Kind of a Geiger counter, then," smiled Paul. "Except it looks for luck instead of radiation."

"Money, woman, house. Work all time."

Paul rolled the witch-compass over and over in his hand. There was something very smooth and attractive about it, like a giant worry-bead. "I don't know . . . " he said. "It depends how much it is."

"*Il y a deux prix,*" said Jonquil.

"Two prices? What do you mean?"

"*En termes d'argent, le prix est quatorze francs. Mais il y a également un prix moral à payer, chaque fois la boussole pointe sur ce que vous désirez.*"

"I have to make a moral choice? Is that what you said?"

Jonquil nodded again. "No thing you truly desire come free."

Paul gently shook the witch-compass and heard its soft, seductive shaking sound.

"All right," he said. "Fourteen francs. If it works, I'll come back and thank you in person. If it doesn't, I won't be able to afford to come back."

"You will come back," Jonquil assured him, as he counted out the money. "Your feet will bring you back."

***

It was dry and breezy when he arrived back in New Milford. The sky was startlingly blue and red-and-yellow leaves were whirling and dancing on the green. He drove his rental car slowly through the town, feeling just as much of a ghost as he had on his last night in Gabon. He saw people he knew. Old Mr. Dawson, with a new Labrador puppy. Gremlin, his previous dog, must have died. Jim Salzberger, leaning against a red pick-up truck, talking to Annie Nilsen.

The same white-painted buildings, dazzling in the sunlight. The same town clock, with its bright blue dial. Paul drove slowly through but he didn't stop. He didn't want anybody to know he was back, not just yet. He had been crackling with ambition when he left this town, and his parents had been so proud of him when he made his first hundred thousand dollars in Libreville. But here he was, back and bankrupt, more or less, without even the will to start over.

He drove out along the deserted highway to Allen's Corners, past Don Humphrey's general store. The sunlight flickered through the car windows, so that he felt he was watching an old home movie of his previous life.

At last he took the steep turn up through the woods that led to his parents' house. It wasn't much of a place: a single-story building on the side of a hill, with an awkwardly angled driveway and a small triangular yard. His father was out back, sawing logs with his old circular saw, and there was a tangy smell of wood smoke in the air.

He parked behind his father's Oldsmobile and climbed out. His father immediately called out, "Jeannie! Jeannie! Look who's here!" and came hurrying down the steps. He was a tall man, although he wasn't as tall as Paul, with cropped grey hair and the slight stoop of somebody who has worked hard in an office all his life, and never quite managed to fulfill himself. Paul's mother came out of the kitchen still carrying a saucepan. She was tall, for a woman, and although her hair was grey she looked ten years younger than she really was. She was wearing a pink checkered blouse with the sleeves rolled up, and jeans.

"Why didn't you say you were coming to see us?" asked his mother, with tears in her eyes. "I don't have a thing in!"

His father slapped him on the back and ushered him up the steps into the house. "I guess he wanted to surprise us, didn't you, son?"

"That's right," said Paul. "I didn't know I was coming back until the day before yesterday."

"It's great to see you," smiled his father. "You've lost some weight, haven't you? Hope you've been eating properly. All work and no lunch makes Jack a skinny-looking runt."

"I should have gone to the market," said his mother. "I could have made your favorite pot roast."

"Don't worry about that," his father said. "We can eat out tonight. Remember Randolph's Restaurant? That was taken over, about a year ago, and you should see it now! They do a lobster chowder to die for!"

"Oh Dan, that's far too expensive," said his mother.

"What do you mean, our son here's used to the best, aren't you, son? How's that Mercedes-Benz of yours running? Or have you traded it in for something new?"

"Oh . . . I'm maybe thinking about a Porsche."

"A Porsche! Isn't that something! A Dennison driving a Porsche! Listen, how about a beer and you can tell us how things are going."

"Well, to tell you the truth, I'm kind of pooped."

"Sure you are, I'm sorry. Why don't you go to your room and wash up? You can fill us in when you're good and ready."

His mother said, "How long are you staying for?"

He gave her a quick, tight smile. "I don't know . . . it depends on a couple of business deals."

She held his eye for a moment and there was something in the way she looked at him that made him: she suspects I'm not entirely telling the truth. His mother had always known when he was lying. Either that, or he always felt guilty when he lied to her, and it showed.

He hefted his bag out of the car and carried it through to the small room at the back. It was depressingly familiar, although it had a new green carpet and new curtains with green-and-white convolvulus flowers on them. His high school football trophies were still arranged on top of the bureau, and there was a large photograph of him at the age of eleven, clutching a shaggy red dog. He sat down on the bed and covered his face with his hands. Eleven years of work. Eleven years of talking and travelling and staying up till two or three in the morning. All of it gone, all of it—and nothing to show for it but a single suitcase and twenty-three CFA francs—not convertible into dollars, and not worth anything even if they were.

His father came in with a can of Coors. "Here—I'll bet you can't get this in Libreville."

"No, we get French beer mainly. Or there's the local brew. Okay for cleaning drains."

He opened up the suitcase. Two pairs of pants, one crumpled linen coat, a pair of brown leather sandals, socks and shorts. His father said, "You're travelling extra-light. The last time you came, you had so many cases I thought Madonna was visiting."

"Well . . . I wasn't given too much notice."

He took the witch-compass out of the side pocket in his suitcase and put it next to his football cups.

"What the two-toned tonkert is that?" asked his father.

"It's kind of a good-luck charm."

"Oh, yeah?" His father picked it up and shook it. "Looks like a giant sheep dropping to me."

Paul hung his clothes up in the closet.

"You're quiet," said his father. "Everything's okay, isn't it?"

"Sure, sure. Everything's okay."

His father laid a hand on his shoulder. I'll tell you who else is around. You remember Katie Sayward you used to like so much? Her marriage broke up, so she's back here with her aunt, to get over it."

Paul said, "What? I didn't even know she was married."

"Yeah. She married some actor she met in New York. Real good-looking guy. *Too* good looking, if you know what I mean. I met him once when she came up to Sherman to see her aunt. So far as I know, he had an affair with some girl in the chorus-line and Katie was totally devastated. If you do see her, I wouldn't mention it if I were you. Not unless she brings it up first."

Paul went to the window and pressed his forehead against the cold glass. Outside, the yard sloped steeply uphill towards a thicket of dry brown bracken. Katie Sayward. He had always adored Katie Sayward, even when he was in grade school. Katie Sayward, with her skinny ankles and her skinny wrists and her shining brown hair that swung whenever she turned her head. Even when she was younger, her lips always looked as if she had just finished kissing someone. She had grown into a beautiful young woman, with a head-turning figure. Paul had only plucked up the courage once to ask her for a date. He could remember it even today—walking into the home room in front of all the other girls, and saying, "Katie, how about you and me going out for a burger tonight?" Katie had clamped her hand over her mouth, and widened her eyes, and then she had burst out laughing. The memory of it still made him feel hot and uncomfortable.

So Katie Sayward has married. Well, of course she had married, a lovely girl like that. It was just that he hadn't wanted to hear about it. And worse than that, her husband had cheated on her. How could he have cheated on Katie Sayward, when she was the perfect, perfect girl?

His mother came into the room. "You're sure you don't want anything to eat? I could make you a bologna sandwich. I don't suppose you get much bologna, in Gabon."

"I'm fine, Mom. Honestly. Let me grab a few zees, that's all."

"Okay," said his father, giving him another affectionate clap on the shoulder. "I'll wake you up in time for dinner."

***

Randolph's Restaurant was decorated in the style of an old Colonial inn, with wheelback chairs and softly shaded lamps on the tables and antique warming-pans hanging on the walls. They sat right in the middle of the restaurant, and Paul's father kept turning around in his chair and calling out to people he knew.

"Dick! Janice! Paul's back from darkest Africa! Sure, doing real good, aren't you, Paul? Business is booming! Counting on buying himself a new Porsche, top-of-the-range!"

Paul glanced at his mother. She was still smiling, but he definitely had the feeling she knew something wasn't quite right.

His father ordered two large martinis to start, and a mimosa for his mother. Then he opened up the oversized leather bound menu and said, "Okay! Let's push the boat out!"

He ordered oysters and caviar with sour cream and blinis. He ordered steak and lobster and fresh chargrilled tuna. They drank Roederer champagne with the hors D'oeuvres and Pauillac with the entrées, $97.50 a bottle.

Paul's father did most of the talking. Paul sat with his head lowered, chewing his way unenthusiastically through his meal. He couldn't even taste the difference between the steak and the lobster, and he left his beans and broccoli untouched.

"You must be feeling jetlagged," said his mother, laying her hand on top of his.

"Yes . . . kind of. I'll be okay tomorrow."

The pianist on the opposite side of the room was playing a slow bluesy version of 'Buddy, Can You Spare A Dime?' and he almost felt like standing up and walking out.

"You know something?" said his father, with his mouth full, and a shred of lobster dangling from his lip, "I'm so proud of you, Paul, I could stand right up in this restaurant and shout it out loud. My only son, started from humble beginnings, but had the guts to go to Africa all on his own and make himself a hundred million."

"Well, I'm not so sure about the hundred million," said Paul.

"You mark my words . . . if you haven't made a hundred million yet, you sure will soon! That's what you're made of! That's why I'm so proud of you!"

They finished the meal with Irish coffees in the cocktail lounge. Paul's father grew more and more talkative and when he started to tell stories about his high school days, losing his shorts in the swimming-pool and falling into the rhododendron bushes, Paul asked for the check.

"That's real generous of you, Paul," his father beamed. Then he turned to his mother and said, "How many people have a wealthy young son who can take his folks out for a night like this?"

Paul opened the leather folder with the check inside. It was $378.69, gratuity at your discretion. Suddenly he couldn't hear the piano music any more.

"How is it?" asked his father. "National debt of Gabon, I'll bet."

"Something like that," said Paul, numbly, and reached into his coat with fingers that felt as if they were frostbitten. He took out his wallet and opened it, while his mother watched him silently and his father chatted with the cocktail waitress.

"In Gabon, you understand, they respect Americans. They trust them. Wouldn't surprise me at all if Paul ends up running a big mining corporation over there."

Paul said, "Shit."

"What? What is it?"

"All the money I changed . . . I left it back in my suitcase."

"You can use your card, can't you?"

"No, no, I can't. It's only for use in Africa."

"But that's an American Express card. That's good anywhere."

"Not this one, no. I have a special deal. They bill me in CFA francs, so that I save myself twelve-and-a-half per cent handling charges."

Paul's father pulled a face. "Don't you have Visa, or MasterCard?"

"Left them back in my suitcase, too. Stupid of me. Mom's right. I must be jetlagged."

"Looks like we're going to have to wash the dishes," said his father.

"I'll tell you what I can do," Paul volunteered. "I can come back early tomorrow, soon as you open, and pay you then. How's that? I can leave my watch if you like."

"Oh, that's okay," smiled the waitress. "I think we can trust you, don't you? And what is it they say in those gangster movies? We know where you live."

They all laughed and Paul tucked his wallet back in his coat and said, "Thanks." Shit. Where was he going to raise more than four hundred dollars by lunchtime tomorrow? He could pawn his watch, he supposed. It was a nine hundred dollar Baume & Mercier that had been given to him by the sales director of a French copper company. His ten thousand dollar Rolex had long gone, in legal fees. He just hoped Robard's jewelers was still in business.

His mother took his arm as they left the restaurant and walked across the parking lot. It was a cold, dry night.

"Winter's coming early this year," said his mother. His father was weaving ahead of them, singing erratic lines from 'Buddy Can You Spare A Dime?' "Once I was a bigshot . . . now I'm broke."

"Well, we don't get much of a winter in Libreville."

"Is everything all right, Paul?"

"Sure. What do you mean? Everything's great."

"I don't know. You look—I'm not quite sure what the word is. *Haunted*, I guess."

"Haunted?" he laughed. "You make me sound like Hill House."

"But everything's okay? The business? You're not sick, are you?"

"I got over the dengue months ago."

"You will tell me, though, if anything's wrong?"

He gave her a kiss and nodded, and then hurried her along a little faster, so they would catch up with his father. "Dad! Dad! Come on, Dad, there's no way that I'm going to let you drive!"

***

That night he lay in bed listening to the leaves

whispering in the yard outside. He felt infinitely tired, but he couldn't even close his eyes. The moonlight fell across the wall as white as a bone.

He ought to tell his parents he was bankrupt. He ought to tell them he was never going back to Gabon, couldn't go back. He knew his father would be crushed, but how much longer could he keep up this pretense? Yet he felt if he told his parents, he would reduce himself to the level of a hopeless alcoholic, finally admitting that he couldn't summon up the willpower to quit on his own.

His parents' admiration was all he had left.

The digital clock beside the bed told him it was 3:57. It clicked on to 3:58—and it was then that he heard a soft shaking noise, like dry rice in a colander.

He raised his head from the pillow. It must have been the leaves, skittering in the wind. But as he lowered his head he heard it again, much sharper this time. *Shikk—shikk—shikk!* And again, even louder. *Shikk—shikk—shikk!*

He swung his legs out of bed and walked across to the bureau. There, amongst his football trophies, lay the black smooth shape of the witch-compass. It was shivering, very slightly, and as it shivered the beads or seeds inside it set up that *shikk—shikk—shikk!* sound.

Cautiously he picked it up. It felt as pleasant to hold as it always did; yet tonight it seemed to have life in it. It vibrated, and shook again. He pointed it towards the window. It stopped vibrating, and the *shikk* sound stopped, too. He pointed it towards the closet. It vibrated again, but only softly. Next he pointed it towards the door. It gave a brisk shiver and almost jumped out of his hand.

It's guiding me, Paul thought. *It's guiding me to what I want.*

He tested it again, pointing it back at the window, back at the closet, back at the door. As soon as he pointed it towards the door, it became more and more excited.

Supposing it's showing me how to find some money. That's what I need more than anything.

Hurriedly, he pulled on his shirt and his pants and his shoes. Then, breathing hard, he eased open his bedroom door and stepped into the darkened hallway. He could hear his father snoring like a beached whale, and the clock ticking loudly on the wall. He pointed the witch-compass north, south, east, and west. It shook most vigorously when he pointed it towards the front door. It was guiding him out of the house.

He walked as quietly as he could across the polished oak floor. He lifted a nylon windbreaker down from the pegs by the door. Then he eased open the chains, drew back the bolts and went out into the cold, windy night.

The witch-compass led him down the front steps and down the narrow, winding road that led to the main highway between New Milford and New Preston. Although it was only four in the morning, the sky was strangely light, as if a UFO had landed behind the trees. Paul's footsteps scrunched through the leaves at the side of the road and his father's windbreaker made a loud rustling noise. It smelled of his father's pipe smoke, and there was a plastic lighter in the pocket.

And all the time, the witch-compass rattled in his hand with ever-increasing eagerness.

He had just reached the hairpin that would take

him down to the highway when he heard a car coming, from quite a long way off, but coming fast. He hurried around the bend and down the steeply sloping road, and as he did so he glimpsed headlights from the direction of New Milford. It looked as if it were travelling at more than seventy miles an hour.

He hadn't even reached the highway when he heard a sickening bang and a shrieking of tyres, and then a sound like an entire junkyard dropping out of the sky. Wheels, fenders, mufflers, windows, crunching and screeching and smashing. Then complete silence, which was worse.

Paul came running around the corner and saw the bloodied body of a dead deer lying in the scrub on the far side of the highway, its legs twisted at extraordinary angles, as if it were trying to ballet-dance. Almost a hundred feet further up, a battered, dented Chevrolet was resting on its roof. Shattered glass glittered all over the blacktop.

"Jesus." Paul ran towards the wreck. As he came closer her saw that the driver was still in his seat, suspended upside-down in his seatbelt. His deflated airbag hung in front of him, and it had obviously saved his life. He was groaning loudly and trying to wrestle himself free.

"Hold on!" Paul called out. He crunched through the glass and then he realized he was splashing through a quickly widening pool of gasoline.

"Get me out of here," the driver begged him. He was a heavily built, fiftyish man. His grey hair was matted with blood. "I think my goddam legs are crushed."

"Okay, okay, just hold on," Paul reassured him. He

was about to put the witch-compass into his pocket when it gave a high-pitched *shikkashikkashikka!* that sounded like a snake hissing. Paul looked down and saw the driver's pigskin billfold lying on the road, right in front of him. Even without picking it up, he could see it was stuffed with money.

"Oh, God, please get me out of here," moaned the driver. "This is hurting so much."

Paul reluctantly took his eyes away from the billfold. He took hold of the Chevrolet's door-handle and tried to drag it open, but it was wedged solid. He went around to the other side of the car and tried the passenger door, but that wouldn't budge either.

He came back to the driver's side and reached into the broken window. He managed to locate the man's seatbelt buckle. But the crash had jammed it and the man's bulging stomach was straining against it. His shirt was soaked in warm, sticky blood.

"Please, I'm dying here. Please."

Paul said, "Okay . . . but I can't get you out by myself. I'm going to have to call the fire department."

"Hurry, please."

Paul took hold of his hand and squeezed it. "Just hold on. I'll be as quick as I can."

But in his pocket the witch-compass went *shikkashikkashikka!*

Paul slowly stepped away from the wreck. He looked down and there was the pigskin billfold. He could see fifties and twenties. More than enough to settle his restaurant bill. More than enough to buy him a new coat and a new pair of jeans and see him through the next few days. He hesitated for a second and turned back to the man hanging in the car, and the man was looking up at him, bleeding and broken and pleading with him, get me out of here, for chrissakes. But the worst possible idea came into his head—an idea so terrible he could hardly believe he had thought of it. And inside his pocket, the witch-compass rattled and shook as if it were a living thing.

He stooped down and picked up the billfold. The man in the car watched him, unable to comprehend what he was seeing. Paul took all of the cash out of the billfold except for $50. He didn't want to make it obvious that the man had been robbed. He held up the billfold for a moment and then he dropped it back onto the road.

Shikkashikkashikka.

"What are you going to do?" the driver asked him. "Look, take the fucking money. I don't care. Just call the fire department, get me out of here."

But Paul knew it would be different once the man was released, I was trapped, I was dying, and he stole my money, right in front of me.

He walked a few paces back down the road. *"No!"* the driver screamed at him. *"Don't leave me here! Don't!"*

Paul stopped. He lowered his head. In his pocket he felt the witch-compass, warm and thrilling. The witch-compass was guiding him away from the wreck, back to his parents' house. Leave him, what does he mean to you? He was driving too fast anyhow. Everybody knows there are deer on these highways. Supposing you hadn't woken up? Supposing the witch-compass hadn't brought you here. The stupid bastard would have died anyhow, alone.

"Don't leave me!" the driver screamed at him. *"I'm dying here, for chrissake! Don't leave me!"*

In one pocket, Paul felt the witch-compass. In the other, he felt his father's cigarette lighter. He turned around. There are two prices, Jonquil had told him. Fourteen francs, and a moral choice, every time the witch-compass finds you what you want.

The driver was suddenly silent. He had seen Paul flick the cigarette lighter, and stand in the road with the flame dipping in the early-morning breeze. The flame was reflected in the gasoline which was running across the road into the ditch.

Paul genuflected, and lit it.

The fire raced back towards the upturned car. The driver twisted and struggled in one last desperate effort to pull himself free.

"*You could have had the money!*" he screamed at Paul. "*I would have given you the fucking money!*"

Then the whole car exploded like a Viking fire ship and furiously burned. Paul gradually backed away, feeling the heat on his face and the cold wind blowing on his back. He saw the driver's arm wagging from side to side, and then it kind of hooked up and bent as the heat of the fire shriveled his tendons. As he walked up the winding road towards his parents' house he could still see it burning behind the trees.

Afterwards, he sat down on his bed and counted his money. Six hundred and fifty-five dollars, still reeking of gasoline. On top of the bureau, the witch-compass lay silent.

***

He drove into New Milford the next morning to pay off Randolph's Restaurant. "Glad you didn't try to leave the county," smiled the owner, counting his money. "I'd have had to set my old dog out looking for you."

The dog lay in the corner of the restaurant, an ancient basset-hound, snoring as loudly as Paul's father.

On his way home, he took a different route, the road that led up to Gaylordsville and then meandered through the woods to South Kent. He didn't want to go past the scene of last night's auto wreck again. This morning, when he had driven by, the rusty and blackened Chevrolet was still lying on its roof in the road, surrounded by fire trucks and police cars with their lights flashing.

It was another pin-sharp day. All around him, the woods were ablaze with yellows and crimsons and dazzling scarlets. Every now and then he checked his eyes in the rearview mirror to see if he could detect any guilt, or any emotion at all. But all he felt was reasonably satisfied. Not over-satisfied, but the edge had been taken off his anxiety.

He slowed as he reached the intersection where the road led back towards New Preston. About a quarter of a mile beyond it, screened by trees, stood the yellow-painted house where Katie Sayward's aunt lived, and where Katie was staying after the break-up of her marriage. The times he had driven past here when he was younger, hoping to see her. Maybe he should pay her a visit now. But what would he say? "You thought I was an idiot when we were at school together, sorry about your marriage"?

He drove past slowly, no more than ten miles an hour, ducking his head so he could peer beneath the branches of the trees. Nobody was in sight. But as he pressed the accelerator to move away, he heard a crisp *shikk! shikk! shikk!*

He slowed down again. The witch-compass was inside the glove-box. It started a series of quick, rhythmic rattles. As he drove further away from Katie's house, however, the rattles became less and less frequent. When he reached the next bend, they stopped altogether.

He pulled the car in by the side of the road. The witch-compass remained silent. *It's trying to tell me something about Katie. It's guiding me back.*

He turned the car around and drove slowly back towards the yellow-painted house. Inside the glove-box, the witch-compass started to rattle again *shikkaSHIKKAshikkaSHIKKA* like a Gabonese drumbeat.

Katie's marriage has broken up. Maybe the witch-compass is trying to tell me she needs somebody. Maybe it's trying to tell me that Katie needs me.

Cautiously he drove in through the gates and up the driveway to the house. Nobody came out to greet him and the place looked as if it were deserted. No vehicles around, and no smoke pouring from chimneys. Paul climbed out of the car and went up to the front porch and knocked. There was no answer, so he knocked again. He didn't like the knocker. It was bronze, cast into the face of a sly, blind old man. He waited, whistling between his teeth.

No, nobody in. The witch-compass must have made a mistake. He walked back to the car and opened the door. The rattling inside the glove-box was practically hysterical, and he could hear the compass knocking from side to side, as if it were trying to break out.

"All right, already," he said. He took the witch-compass out of the glove-box and held it in his hand. Then he walked back to the house, and knocked again—so loudly this time that he could hear the knocks echo in the hall. Still no reply.

"There, what did I tell you? There's nobody home."

Shikkashikkashikka rattled the witch-compass.

Paul pointed it towards the front door of the house, and its rattling died away. He swept it slowly backwards and forwards, and the witch-compass rattled most excitedly when he pointed it to the side of the house.

"Okay, let's check this out."

He walked around the house, past a trailing wisteria, until he found the kitchen door at the back. He knocked with his knuckle on the window, just in case there was somebody inside, and then he turned the handle. It was unlocked, so he opened it and stepped inside.

"Hello!" he called. "Anybody home?"

Shikkashikkashikka.

"Look, it's no good shaking like that. There's nobody home."

Shikkashikkashikka.

The witch-compass guided him into the hall, towards the foot of the staircase. At the top of the staircase there was a landing with an amber stained-glass window, so that the inside of the house looked like a sepia photograph.

Shikkashikkashikka.

"Upstairs? All right then. I just hope you know what you're doing."

Paul climbed the stairs and the witch-compass led him along the landing to the very last door. He knocked again, but there was no reply, and so he carefully opened it. The witch-compass was shaking wildly in his hand and he had to grip it tight so he wouldn't drop it.

He found himself in a large bedroom, with an old-fashioned dark-oak bed, and a huge walnut armoire. The windows were covered in heavy lace curtains with peacock patterns on them, so the light inside the bedroom was very dim. The bed was covered with an antique patchwork quilt; on top of the quilt lay Katie Sayward, naked.

Now the witch-compass was silent. Paul took a breath and held it, and didn't know if he ought to leave immediately, or stay where he was, watching her. She was older, of course, and she had cut her long hair short, but she was still just as beautiful as he remembered. She was lying on her back with her eyes closed, her arms spread wide as if she were floating, like Ophelia. She was full-breasted, with a flat stomach and long legs. *My perfect woman*, thought Paul. *The kind of woman I've always wanted.*

He took two or three steps into the room. The floorboards creaked and he hesitated, but she didn't show any signs of waking. Now he could see between her legs, and he stood transfixed, breathing softly through his mouth.

He took another step closer. He wanted to touch her so much that it was a physical ache; but he knew what would happen if he tried. The same ridicule he had suffered when he asked her for a date at high school. Shame and embarrassment, and trouble with the law.

It was then, however, that he saw the empty bottle

of Temazipan tablets on her nightstand and the tipped-over bottle of vodka on the quilt and the letter she was holding in her right hand.

He took another step closer, then another. Then he sat on the bed beside her and said, "Katie . . . Katie, can you hear me? It's Paul."

Katie didn't stir. Paul gently patted her cheek. She was still breathing. She was still warm. But she was deathly pale. He peeled back one of her eyelids with his thumb. Her blue eye stared up at him sightlessly, its pupil widely dilated.

He lifted her right wrist so he could read the note. "Dearest Aunt Jessie. I know this is a selfish and horrible thing to do to you. But a life without James just isn't any kind of life at all."

Paul felt her pulse. It was thready, but her heart was still beating. If he called the paramedics now, there was a strong possibility they could save her. She would be grateful to him, wouldn't she, for the rest of her life? There might even be a chance that—

His arm brushed against her bare breast and it gave a heavy, complicated sway. There might be a chance in the future that he and Katie could get together. But if they got together *now*, then he could be sure of having her. Maybe just once. But even once was better than never.

He stood up and very deliberately took off his clothes, staring down at Katie all the time. He had never dared to dream this could ever happen; and now it was: and he could do whatever he wanted to her, anything, and she wouldn't resist.

He climbed onto the quilt. His body was thin and wiry and his skin was very white, except for his face and his forearms and his knees, which had been tanned dark by the equatorial sun. He kissed Katie on the lips, and then her eyelids, and then her cheeks, and he whispered in her ear that he loved her, and that she was the most desirable woman he had ever known. He squeezed her breasts and sucked at her nipples. Then he ran his tongue all the way down her stomach and buried his face between her thighs.

He stayed in her bedroom for over an hour, and he used her body in every way he had ever fantasized about. He couldn't believe it was real, and he wanted it never to end. He turned her over, face down in the pillow, and forced himself into her, but it was then that she gave a shudder that he could feel all the way through him, right to the soles of his feet.

He leaned forward, his cheek close to hers. "Katie? Speak to me, Katie! Just let me hear you breathing, Katie, come on!"

She was silent and her body was completely lifeless. He took himself out of her and stood up, wiping the back of his hand across his forehead. *Shikk!* went the witch-compass.

Paul dressed, feeling numb; and then he rearranged Katie as he had found her. He cleaned between her thighs with tissues, wiped her face. He had bruised her a little: there were fingermarks over her buttocks and breasts, and a love bite on her neck. But who would ever think *he* had inflicted them? So far as anybody was aware, they hardly even knew each other.

He left the house by the kitchen door, taking care to wipe the door handle with the tail of his shirt. He drove back the way he had come, through

Gaylordsville, crossing the Housatonic at Fort Hill so that he could deny having driven back towards his parents' house on the South Kent Road. He even made a point of tooting his horn and waving to Charlie Sheagus, the realtor.

And how do you feel? he asked his eyes, in the rearview mirror.

Satisfied, his eyes replied. Not *fully* satisfied, but it's taken the edge off.

***

His father was waiting for him in the living-room when he returned. He was wearing a checkered red shirt and oversized jeans and he looked crumple-faced and serious. His mother was sitting in the corner, sitting in the shadows, her hands clasped on her lap.

"Where've you been?" his father wanted to know.

"Hey, why the long face? I went down to Randolph's to settle the check."

"It's a pity you haven't been settling all of your checks the same way."

Paul said, "What? What are you talking about?"

"I'm talking about Budget Rental Cars, who just called up to say that your credit rating hadn't checked out. And Marriott Hotels, who said you bounced a personal check for two hundred dollars. And then I called Dennison Minerals, your own company, in Gabon, and all I got was a message saying that your number was discontinued."

Paul sat down in one of the old-fashioned wooden-backed armchairs. "I've been having some cash flow difficulty, okay?"

"So why didn't you say so?"

"Because you didn't want to hear it, did you? All you wanted to hear was success."

His father jabbed his finger at him. "What kind of person do you take me for? You're my son. If you're successful, I exult in it. If you fail, I commiserate. I'm your father, for chrissakes."

"Commiserate? Those Gabonese bastards took my business, my house, they took everything. I don't want commiseration. I want revenge."

His father came up to him and laid both of his hands on his shoulder and looked him straight in the face. "Forget about revenge. You can always start over."

"Oh, like you started over when you lost your job at Linke Overmeyer? With a little house, and a millionth-of-an-acre of ground, and a row of beans? I had a mansion, in Libreville! Seven bedrooms, four bathrooms, a swimming-pool, a circular hallway you could have ice skated on, if you'd had any ice, and if you'd had any skates."

"So what?" his father asked him. "That's what life is all about. Winning and losing. Why did you have to lie about it?"

"Because of you," said Paul.

"Because of *me*? What the hell are you talking about?"

"Because you always expected me to do better than you. That was all I ever got from you, from the time I was old enough to understand anything. 'You'll do better than me. One day, you'll be rich and you'll buy a house for your mother and me. With a lake, and swans.' Jesus Christ! I was nine years old, and you wanted me to give you fucking *swans*!"

His father closed his eyes for a moment, trying to summon up enough patience not to shout back. His mother said nothing, but sat in the shadows, a silhouette, only the curved reflection from her glasses gleaming. In the distance, Paul heard the dyspeptic rumbling of thunder. It had been a dry day, and the air had been charged with static electricity. Lightning was crossing Litchfield Hills, walking on stilts.

Paul's father opened his eyes. "Are you going back to Africa?"

"There's nothing to go back to. I'm all washed up in Gabon. I still owe my lawyer seven thousand francs."

"So what are you going to do?"

"I don't know. Right now, I don't want to do anything."

"You're going to have to find yourself a job, Paul, even if it's waiting tables. Your mother and I can't support you.

"I see. So much for my fucking four-hundred-dollar dinner then? 'Who has a son who takes his parents out for a meal like this?' You didn't even offer to pay half."

"I'm sorry. If I'd known you were busted I wouldn't have suggested going to Randolph's at all. We could have eaten at home. And don't use language like that, not in this house."

"Oh, I beg your pardon. First of all you won't support me, and now you take away my rights under the First Amendment."

"The First Amendment doesn't give you the right to use profanity in front of your mother."

Paul was about to say something else, but he took a deep breath and stopped himself. He felt angrier than he had ever felt in his life. But what was the point in shouting? He knew he wouldn't be able to change his father's mind. His father had almost made a religion out of self-sufficiency. Even when Paul was young, he had never given him an allowance. Every cent of pocket-money had been earned with dishwashing or raking leaves or painting fences. He would rather have burned his money than given anything to Paul for nothing.

"All right," said Paul. "If that's the way you feel."

He walked around his father and went to his room. He slung his suitcase on the bed and started to bundle his clothes into it. His mother came to the door and said, "Paul . . . don't be angry. You don't have to leave."

"Oh, but I do. I might accidentally breathe some of Dad's air or flush some of his water down the toilet."

"Sweetheart, he doesn't mean you can't stay with us, just till you can get yourself back on your feet."

"You don't get it, do you? I don't want to get back on my feet. I've spent eleven years working my rear end off, and look what I've ended up with. One tropical suit, two shirts, and a rental car I can't even pay for. I just want to lie down and do nothing. That's all."

"Do you want to see Dr. Williams?"

Paul pushed his way past her. "I don't want to see anybody. I'm not sick. I'm not disturbed. I'm just exhausted, that's all. Is it a crime to be exhausted?"

"Paul—" his father began, but Paul opened the front door and went down the steps. "Paul—we can talk about this. I'm sure we can work something out."

"Sure," Paul retorted. I can clean out your gutters and mend your roof and you'll pay me in hamburgers. Forget it, Dad. I'd rather go to the Y."

With that, he climbed into his rental car and

backed out of the drive with a scream of tires. His father sadly watched him go.

***

By nine o'clock that night the rain was lashing all the way across Litchfield County and the hills were a battlefield of thunder and lightning.

Paul had driven into New Milford, where he spent his last $138 on a steak and fries and a bottle of wine at the Old Colonial Inn. Now he didn't even have enough money for a room. It looked like he was going to have to spend the night in the car, parked on a side road.

He left the inn, his coat collar turned up against the rain, but by the time he reached the car his shoulders were soaked. He wiped the rain from his face and looked at himself in the rearview mirror. If only he had someplace to sleep. A warm bed, and enough money to last him for six or seven months, so he wouldn't have to do anything but sit back and drink beer and think of nothing at all.

He started the engine, and the windshield wipers flapped furiously from side to side. It was then that he heard the softest of rattles. *Shikk—shikk—shikk.*

A prickling sensation went up the back of his neck. The witch-compass was telling him he could have just what he wanted. A bed for the night, and money. But the question was, how was he going to get it, and what kind of moral decision would he have to make?

*Shikka—shikka—shikka—*rattled the witch-compass, and Paul took it out of his pocket.

For one second, Paul was tempted to throw it out into the rain. But it felt so smooth and reassuring in his hand, and he knew it would guide him to a place where he could sleep, and where he wouldn't have to worry for a while.

He nudged his car out of the green onto the main road to New Preston. He turned the wheel to the right, and the witch-compass was silent. He turned it to the left, and the witch-compass went *shikkashikkashikka.*

He was almost blinded for a second by a crackling burst of lightning. But then he was driving so slowly through the rain, hunched forward in his seat so he could see more clearly, heading northwards.

After twenty minutes of silence, the witch-compass stirred again. *Shikk—shikk—shikk.* He had reached the intersection where the Chevrolet had collided with the deer—the intersection that would take him up the winding road towards his parents' house.

"Oh, no," he said. But the witch-compass rattled even more loudly, guiding him up the hill. Another fork of lightning crackled to the ground, striking a large oak only a hundred feet away. Paul saw it burst apart and burn. Thunder exploded right above his head, as if the sky were splitting apart.

He drove around the hairpin bend towards his parents' house. Now the witch-compass was shaking wildly, and Paul knew without any doubt at all where it was taking him. He saw the roof of his parents' house silhouetted against the trees, and as he did so another charge of lightning hit the chimney, so that bricks flew in all directions and blazing wooden shingles were hurled into the night like catherine-wheels.

The noise was explosive, and it was followed only a second later by a deep, almost sensual sigh, as the air rushed in to fill the vacuum that the lightning had created. Then there was a deafening collision of thunder.

Paul stopped in front of the house, stunned. The rain drummed on the roof of his car like the juju drummers in Marché Rouge. He climbed out, shaking, and was immediately drenched. He walked up the steps with rain dripping from his nose and pouring from his chin. He pushed open the front door and the house was filled with the smell of burned electricity, and smoke.

"Oh, Jesus," he said.

He walked into the kitchen and the walls were blackened with bizarre scorch-marks, like the silhouettes of hopping demons. Every metal saucepan and colander and cheese-grater had been flung into the opposite corner of the room and fused together in an extraordinary sculpture, a mediaeval knight who had fallen higgledy-piggledy off his charger.

And right in the center of the floor lay his mother and father, all of their clothes blown off, their bodies raw and charred, their eyes as black as cinders, and smoke slowly leaking out of their mouths.

Shikk—shikk—shikk rattled the witch-compass.

So this was how he was going to find himself a warm bed for the night. However stern he had been, his father had always told him that he was going to inherit the house, and all of his savings, as well as being the sole beneficiary to their joint-insurance policies. No more problems. No more money worries. Now he could rest, and do nothing.

He slowly sank to his knees on the kitchen floor and took hold of his mother's hand, even though the skin on her fingers was crisp and her fingernails had all been blown off. He pressed her hand against his forehead and he sobbed and sobbed until he felt he was going to suffocate.

"Dad, Mom, I didn't want *this*," he wept. "I didn't want this, I swear to God. I'd give my right arm for this never to have happened. I'd give anything."

He cried until his ribs hurt. Outside, the electric storm grumbled and complained and eventually disappeared, *perpendosi*, into the distance.

Silence, except for the continuing rain. Then Paul heard the witch-compass go *shikk—shikk—shikk.*

He raised his head. The witch-compass was lying on the floor next to him, softly rattling and turning on its axis.

"What are you offering me now, you bastard?" said Paul.

Shikkashikkashikka.

"This doesn't have to have happened? Dad and Mom—they needn't have died?"

Shikk—shikk—shikk

"What are you trying to tell me, you fuck? I can turn back the clock? Is that what you mean?"

Shikk—shikk—shikk

He let his mother's hand drop to the floor. He picked up the witch-compass and pointed it all around the room, 360 degrees. "Come on then, show me. Show me how I can turn the clock back."

Shikkashikkashikka

The witch-compass led him to the kitchen door. He opened it and the wind and the rain came gusting in, sending his mother's blackened fingernails scurrying across the vinyl like cockroaches. He stepped outside, shielding his face against the rain with his arm upraised, holding the witch-compass in his left hand, close to his heart. He wanted to feel where it was taking him. He wanted to know, this time, what it was going to ask him to do.

But of course it didn't. He stumbled on the wet stone step coming out of the kitchen and fell heavily forward, with his right arm still upraised. It struck the unprotected blade of his father's circular saw and the rusty teeth bit right through the muscle, severing his tendon and his axillary artery. For a terrible moment he hung beside the saw-table, unable to lift himself up, while blood sprayed onto his face and all over his hair. The rain fell on him like whips, and his blood streamed across the patio in a scarlet fan-pattern and flooded into grass.

***

Jonquil was waiting for him at the very end of the Marché Rouge. On the upturned fruit-box in front of her stood the carved figure of a woman with her lips bound together with wire; and a rattle with a monkey's head on top of it; and several jars of poisonous-looking unguents.

He walked along the row of brightly lit stalls until he reached the shadowy corner where she sat. He stood in front of her for a while, saying nothing.

"Your feet brought you back," she said.

"That's right," he told her. "My feet brought me back."

"How is Papa and Mama?" she asked, with a broad, tobacco-bronzed smile.

"They're good, thanks."

"Not dead, then? Bad thing, being dead."

"You think so? Sometimes I'm not so sure."

"You'll survive. Everybody has to survive. Didn't you learn that?"

"Oh, sure. Even if I didn't learn anything else."

He reached into the pocket of his crumpled linen

coat and produced a smooth black object that looked like a gourd. He laid it down on the fruit-box, next to the carving.

"I don't give refunds," said Jonquil, and gave a little cackle.

"I don't want a refund, thanks."

"How about a new arm?"

He looked down at his empty sleeve, pinned across his chest. He shook his head. "I can't afford it. Not at your prices."

She watched him walk away through the equatorial night. She picked up the witch-compass and put her ear to it and shook it.

Shikk—shikk—shikk—it whispered. Jonquil smiled, and set it back down on the upturned fruit-box, ready for the next customer.

Biographies

Before 2002, **John Paul Allen** didn't dream of becoming a writer. He taught at an alternative high school near Houston, Texas and loved his job. He never read horror. That year he took a college creative writing course and shocked his classmates with a five-page short story. The reaction to it led him to consider expanding it into a longer piece—he did. By the end of the next school year he was questioned by local detectives for his writing, lost his teaching position, received death threats and published his first novel, *Gifted Trust*.

Fourteen years later he's released a revised edition of *Gifted Trust*, two novellas including *Monkey Love*, several short stories and a collection of shorts titled, *Dark Blessings*. He calls himself a semi-complete unknown who is constantly inspired by events around him. That said, his popularity grows. "It's all material," Allen says. "Life is the best source, and nothing is off limits."

Originally from Michigan, he served 14 years in the US navy, traveled to over 30 countries, resided in Cuba, Florida, Virginia, South Carolina, Texas and now Tennessee. He now lives near Nashville where he spends time with his girlfriend enjoying his new title of grandfather, while he balances being called Paw Paw with his life as a writer of very bad things.

John Paul Allen can be reached on Facebook at www.facebook.com/absoluteallen and much can be discovered about him through a Google/Bing search.

G.N. Braun is an Australian writer raised in Melbourne's gritty Western Suburbs. He is a trained nurse, and holds a Cert. IV in Professional Writing and Editing, as well as a Dip. Arts (Professional Writing and Editing). He writes fiction across various genres, and is the author of many published short stories. He has had numerous articles published in newspapers, both regional and metropolitan. He is the past president of the Australian Horror Writers Association (2011-2013), as well as the past director of the Australian Shadows Awards. He is an editor and columnist for UK site *This is Horror*, and the guest editor for *Midnight Echo #9*. His memoir, *Hammered*, was released in early 2012 by Legumeman Books and has been extensively reviewed. He is the owner of Cohesion Editing and Proofreading, and has now opened a publishing house, Cohesion Press.

Tim Curran is the author of the novels *Skin Medicine, Hive, Dead Sea, Resurrection, Hag Night, Skull Moon, The Devil Next Door, Hive 2, Long Black Coffin, House of Skin,* and *Biohazard*. His short stories have been collected in *Bone Marrow Stew* and *Zombie Pulp*. His novellas include *The Underdwelling, The Corpse King, Leviathan, Worm* and *Sow*. His short stories have appeared in such magazines as *City*

Slab, Flesh&Blood, Book of Dark Wisdom, and *Inhuman,* as well as anthologies such as *Eldritch Chrome, Shivers IV, High Seas Cthulhu,* and, *Vile Things.* His fiction has been translated into German, Japanese, and Italian. Find him on Facebook at: https://www.facebook.com/tim.curran.77

Charles Day is the Horror Writer Association's Mentor Program Chairperson, Co-Chair for the NY/LI Chapter, and a member of the HWA Library committee. He is also a member of the New England Horror Writers Association, the American Library Association and the Young Adult Library Services Association.

He is also the Bram Stoker Award® nominated author of *The Legend of the Pumpkin Thief.* His 2013 published books are the recent release of *Deep Within* and the first book in his Adventures of Kyle McGerrt trilogy, a YA western heroic fantasy, *The Hunt for the Ghoulish Bartender.*

His forthcoming publications and projects in development for 2014 include his first co-authored novel with Mark Taylor, *Redemption* (April, 2014) a comic book series based on the *Adventures of Kyle McGerrt* trilogy, *The Legend of the Pumpkin Thief* comics series, and his first middle-grade series, *The Underdwellers,* and his third YA novel, *Immortal Family.*

On the publishing business side of things, Charles is the co-owner with Taylor Grant at Grant-Day Media Inc. with corporate offices in Hollywood and New York, which houses the successful imprints Evil Jester Press, Evil Jester Comics, and Hidden Thoughts Press (Non-Fiction).

He's also an artist and illustrator who is passionate about creating the many characters he's brought to life in his published or soon to be published works. You can find out more about his upcoming writing projects, check out his illustrations and art, or find out what he's cooking up next with that evil dude-in-the-box, the evil Jester, by visiting his Facebook page or blog:

http://charlesdayfictionwriter.blogspot.com/ or https://www.facebook.com/charles.day.92

Joan De La Haye writes horror and some very twisted thrillers. She invariably wakes up in the middle of the night, because she's figured out yet another freaky way to mess with her already screwed up characters.

Joan is interested in some seriously weird stuff. That's probably also one of the reasons she writes horror.

Her novels, *Shadows* and *Requiem in E Sharp*, as well as her novella, *Oasis*, are published by Fox Spirit.

You can find Joan on her website (http://joandelahaye.com/) and follow her on Twitter.

Taylor Grant is a professional screenwriter, author, actor, award-winning filmmaker and copywriter. His work has been seen on network television, the big screen, the stage, newspapers, comic books, national magazines, anthologies, the web, and heard on the radio.

He is co-author of the critically acclaimed, bestselling horror comic *Evil Jester Presents*, along with horror luminaries Jack Ketchum, Jonathan Maberry, Joe McKinney, and William F. Nolan. His dark fiction has been published in two Bram Stoker Award nominated anthologies: *Horror Library Vol. 5* and *Horror For Good,* as well as *Cemetery Dance Magazine, Fear the Reaper, Of Devils and Deviants, Blood Type: An Anthology of Vampire SF, Nightscapes Vol. 1, Box of Delights, Night Terrors III,* and *A Feast of Frights from the Horror Zine.*

Taylor is the Co-Founder and Editor in Chief of publishing company *Evil Jester Comics,* and is an Active Member of the Horror Writers Association.

Learn more about Taylor's dark imaginings at: http://www.taylorgrant.com

Jennifer Loring's short fiction has appeared in numerous magazines, webzines, and anthologies including *Tales of Obscenity, Cold Flesh, PULP!,* and *Of Devils and Deviants.* Her novella *Conduits* will be published by DarkFuse in September 2014. Jenn holds an MFA in Writing Popular Fiction from Seton Hill University and is a member of the Horror Writers Association. She is also an editor for Red Adept Publishing. Jenn lives in Philadelphia, PA, with her husband and their turtle named—what else? —Ninja. Connect with her online at http://jenniferloring.wordpress.com.

Elizabeth Massie is a Bram Stoker Award- and Scribe Award-winning author of horror novels, short horror fiction, media tie-ins, mainstream fiction, historical novels, and nonfiction. More recent works include stories in, *Mammoth Book of Ghost Stories by Women, Dark Discoveries #25,* and *Shadow Masters,* zombie novel *Desper Hollow* (Apex Books), and historical horror novel, *Hell Gate* (DarkFuse). Massie the creator of the Skeeryvilletown slew of cartoon zombies, monsters, and other bizarre misfits. In her spare time she manages Hand to Hand Vision, a Facebook-based fundraising project she founded to help others during these tough economic times. Massie lives in the Shenandoah Valley of Virginia and shares life and abode with the talented illustrator/artist Cortney Skinner. She can be reached through her website: www.elizabethmassie.com or through Facebook.

Graham Masterton was born in Edinburgh in 1946, the grandson of John Masterton, the chief inspector of mines for Scotland, and Thomas Thorne Baker, a world-renowned scientist who was the first man to send news pictures by radio.

After joining his local newspaper at the age of 17 as a junior reporter, Graham was appointed deputy editor of Mayfair the men's magazine at the age of 21. At 24 he became executive editor of Penthouse.

His career at Penthouse led him to write a series of best-selling sexual advice books, including *How To Drive Your Man Wild In Bed*, which solid 2 million copies worldwide and 250,000 in Poland alone, where it has recently been reprinted.

After leaving Penthouse he wrote *The Manitou*, a horror novel about the vengeful reincarnation of a Native American spirit, which was filmed with Tony Curtis in the lead role, and also starred Susan Strasberg, Burgess Meredith and Stella Stevens. Three of Graham's horror stories were adapted by the late Tony Scott for his TV series *The Hunger*. Over the years he has published five collections of short stories, several of which have won awards.

Graham has also written historical sagas like *Rich, Maiden Voyage* and *Solitaire*, as well as thrillers and disaster novels such as *Plague* and *Famine*. The newest disaster novel *Drought* will be published in May, 2014.

In 1989 Graham's Polish wife Wiescka was instrumental in his becoming the first Western horror novelist to be published in Poland since World War Two, and his sex books have not only won popular success in Poland but acclaim from the medical profession.

He was a regular contributor of humorous articles to the satire magazine Punch, as well as scores of articles on sexual happiness to American women's magazines.

He has encouraged younger writers in several countries, including France, Germany and the Baltic States. For the past 13 years, he has given his name to the prestigious Prix Masterton, which is awarded annually for best French-language horror novel. He was the only non-French winner of Le Prix Julia Verlanger for best-selling horror novel and he has also been given recognition by Mystery Writers of America, the British Fantasy Society and many others.

He edited an anthology of short stories by leading horror writers, Scare Care, in aid of children's charities, and has been honoured by the Irish Society for the Prevention of Cruelty to Children for his fund-raising.

Recently he has very successfully turned his hand to crime writing, although his murder scenes are as stirring as anything he has written in the horror genre.

Drawing on the five years in which he and his late wife Wiescka lived in Cork, in southern Ireland, he has created a series of novels featuring Katie Maguire, the first woman detective superintendent in An Garda Siochána, the Irish police force – *White Bones*, *Broken Angels* and *Red Light*.

He currently lives in Surrey, England. www.Grahammasterton.co.uk

Blaze McRob has penned many titles under different names. It is time for him to come out and play as Blaze.

In addition to inclusions in numerous anthologies, he has written many novels, short stories, flash fiction pieces, and even poetry. Most of his offerings are Dark. However dark they might be, there is always an underlying message contained within.

Join him as he explores the Dark side. You know you want to: http://www.blazemcrob.com/

Joe Mynhardt is a South African horror writer, publisher, editor and teacher with over fifty short story publications. He has appeared in dozens of publications and collections, among them *For the Night is Dark*, *Dark Minds*, *Dark Moon Books*, *Silver Blade Magazine*, and *The Bestiarum Vocabulum*.

Joe is also the owner and operator of Crystal Lake Publishing. He has published and edited Paul Kane' *Sleeper(s)*; Daniel I. Russell's *Tricks, Mischief and Mayhem*; *Fear the Reaper*; Kevin Lucia's *Things Slip Through*; Gary McMahon's *Where You Live*; *Tale From the Lake Vol. 1*; William Meikle's *Samurai and Other Stories*; *Horror 101: The Way Forward*; and Jasper Bark's *Stuck On You*.

Upcoming collections Joe have edited include *The Outsiders* (Simon Bestwick, Gary McMahon etc.) and *Children of the Grave* (Joe McKinney, Armand Rosamilia etc.).

Crystal Lake Publishing also won the Publisher of the Year Award in the This Is Horror Awards 2013.

Joe's collection of short stories, *Lost in the Dark*, is available through Amazon. He is currently working on his first series *Painted Black*, and his next short story collection, *Lake of Fire*.

Read more about Joe and his creations at www.Joemynhardt.com and www.crystallakepub.com or find him on Facebook at "Joe Mynhardt's Short Stories."

Joe is also an Associate member of the HWA.

John Palisano is a two-time Bram Stoker nominated author. His short fiction has appeared in venues such as the Lovecraft eZine, Horror Library, Terror Tales, and many more. His novel *Nerves* was released by Bad Moon Books. He is also a contributor to FANGORIA magazine. Check him out at:
www.johnpalisano.wordpress.com

William Ritchey was born and raised in Atlanta. He is a lifelong Horror and Science Fiction fan who began writing short stories in elementary school. He wrote his first horror story in sixth grade, modeled after the stories he enjoyed in Creepy and Eeriemagazines. When he left for college, the plan was to get a degree in journalism, but the opportunity for travel and adventure lured him from school. After three years in the US Navy, spent mostly in Maine, he returned to school with GI Educational Benefits and a new major. He stuck with it this time, earning a degree in Electrical Engineering from the University of Central Florida. He has started many stories since, but until recently, had not gotten around to finishing any. Still, the thrill of dreaming up a good scare never left, manifesting itself in campfire stories to put a scare into his five kids.

After more than twenty years, he is back at it. He recommitted to writing a few months into 2013 and has written several short stories since. The plots he enjoys are similar to the ones he read as a kid: dark speculative fiction with a Twilight Zone like, twist ending. "To Serve Man . . . It's . . . It's a Cook Book," she said as Lurch wrestled him onto the Spaceship. His passion continues to be short stories with an eye on beginning something longer.

William did manage to travel after graduating from college. He lived for many years with his family on a tiny, two mile long by a half mile wide island in an atoll of the Marshall Islands. He now lives in Huntsville, "The Rocket City", Alabama, with his wife, two sons, and two dogs.

J. Daniel Stone is a twenty-six-year-old writer who was born and raised in New York City. His stories appear in Grey Matter Press, Prime Books, Icarus: The Magazine of Gay Speculative Fiction and more. His debut novel *The Absence of Light* was published by Villipede Publications. Currently, he is hard at work on his second novel and is putting together stories for his first short story collection. Come find him on twitter @solitaryspiral.

Bev Vincent is the author of three books, the most recent being *The Dark Tower Companion*. His first book, *The Road to the Dark Tower*, was nominated for a Bram Stoker Award and his second, *The Stephen King Illustrated Companion*, was nominated for both a Stoker and an Edgar.

He has published over 70 short stories, including appearances in two MWA anthologies, Ellery Queen's Mystery Magazine, Cemetery Dance, Doctor Who: Destination Prague, Legends of the Mountain State, The Mothman Files and five of the SHIVERS anthologies. For more details, see www.bevvincent.com.

Shirley Jackson Award-nominated author **Tim Waggoner** has published over thirty novels and three short story collections of dark fiction. He teaches creative writing at Sinclair Community College and in Seton Hill University's Master of Fine Arts in Writing Popular Fiction program. Visit him on the web at www.timwaggoner.com.

Rocky Wood is the Bram Stoker Award winning author of *Stephen King: The Literary Companion*, *Stephen King: Uncollected, Unpublished* and the graphic novels *Witch Hunts: A Graphic History of the Burning Times and Horrors! Great Stories of Fear and Their Creators*. He has been President of the Horror Writers Association since 2010.

Connect with Crystal Lake Publishing:

Website:
www.crystallakepub.com
Facebook:
www.facebook.com/Crystallakepublishing
Twitter:
https://twitter.com/crystallakepub

I hope you enjoyed this title. If so, I would be grateful if you could leave a review on your blog or any of the other websites and outlets open to book reviews. Reviews are like gold to writers and publishers, since word-of-mouth is and will always be the best way to market a great book. And remember to keep an eye out for more of our books, especially future Tales From the Lake volumes.

Crystal Lake Publishing also publishes short story collections and novellas.

THANK YOU FOR PURCHASING THIS BOOK

Other Crystal Lake Publishing Anthologies:

FEAR THE REAPER—Edited by Joe Mynhardt

A horror anthology about Death and the Grim Reaper.

Includes stories by Rick Hautala, Taylor Grant, Joe McKinney, Gary Fry, Ross Warren, Marty Young, Stephen Bacon, Dean M Drinkel, Richard Thomas, Sam Stone, Eric S Brown, Mark Sheldon, Steve Lockley, Robert S. Wilson, Jeremy C Shipp, Jeff Strand, Lawrence Santoro, E.C. McMullen Jr., Rena Mason, John Kenny and Gary A. Braunbeck.
Includes a poem by Adam Lowe, an introduction by Gary McMahon and a cover by Ben Baldwin.
Interior artwork by Will Jacques.

Crystal Lake Publishing (Kindle):
http://www.crystallakepub.com/fear-the-reaper.php
Amazon (Kindle and paperback):
http://myBook.to/fearthereaper
Smashwords:
https://www.smashwords.com/books/view/390994
Barnes & Noble:
http://www.barnesandnoble.com/w/fear-the-reaper-joe-mynhardt/1117908315?ean=2940045539968

FOR THE NIGHT IS DARK—Edited by Ross Warren

A horror anthology about the fear of the dark, and that which hides within.

Stories by Gary McMahon, William Meikle, Jasper Bark, Jeremy C Shipp, Robert W. Walker, Stephen Bacon, Mark West, Scott Nicholson, Tonia Brown, G. N. Braun, Blaze McRob, Benedict J. Jones, Daniel I Russell, Kevin Lucia, Tracie McBride, Armand Rosamilia, John Claude Smith, Ray Cluley, Carole Johnstone and Joe Mynhardt.
Cover by Ben Baldwin.

Crystal Lake Publishing (Kindle):
http://www.crystallakepub.com/for-the-night-is-dark.php
Amazon (Kindle and paperback):
http://mybook.to/ForTheNightIsDark
Smashwords:
https://www.smashwords.com/books/view/388969
Barnes & Noble:
http://www.barnesandnoble.com/w/for-the-night-is-dark-joe-mynhardt/1114995155?ean=9780992170721